Bolan felt a boot plunge into his gut

With a stubborn effort, he let the momentum of the kick flip him onto his side.

There was a terrible ringing in Bolan's ears, a sound that pierced his throbbing brain as if an icepick had been lanced through his eardrums. Through a gray fog, he saw Kam Chek loom over him, resting clenched fists on his hips. Bolan knew he could take Kam Chek, tensed his muscles to spring.... Then he thought about Grimaldi and relaxed, wondering if his friend had survived. If he hadn't, the Executioner vowed there would be hell to pay.

Kam Chek smiled. To Bolan the expression looked like a vision from his worst nightmare. The Oriental barbarian spoke in a gloating voice that stirred Bolan's rage.

"Ferang."

That word again, Bolan thought, that voice... It echoed through his head, a swirling, swollen heat.

Dimly, Bolan saw Kam Chek's smile disappear. Before he lapsed into blackness, he heard the final words.

"Welcome to hell."

D0962950

MACK BOLAN

The Executioner

DON PENDLETON's EXECUTIONER

MACK BOLAN

Devil's Horn

A GOLD EAGLE BOOK FROM

W🌐RLDWIDE

TORONTO · NEW YORK · LONDON · PARIS
AMSTERDAM · STOCKHOLM · HAMBURG
ATHENS · MILAN · TOKYO · SYDNEY

First edition August 1987

ISBN 0-373-61104-8

Special thanks and acknowledgment to
Dan Schmidt for his contribution to this work.

Printed in Canada

"Our duty is to be useful, not according to our desires but according to our powers."
        —Henri Frederic Amiel

"What then is your duty? What the day demands."
        —Goethe

"Duty lies in standing firm against the enemy, whomever or wherever he may be. I have no options in the game at this point. I must do my duty, take each day as it demands."
        —Mack Bolan

PROLOGUE

A black fury stoked the fire spreading in Mack Bolan's guts. A virulent cancer was eating away at the vitals of American society, festering right before the eyes of the night's denizens. Drugs were being bought and sold on every corner of Houston Street. And no one seemed to be paying the least bit of attention to that malignant disease. No one seemed to give the first goddamn. It was business as usual, Bolan thought, as a streak of sadness sliced through his mounting rage.

The night hitter sensed the deadliness of the environment, an insidious concrete jungle made even worse by the indifference of the inhabitants to human suffering and to the monsters that suffering spawned. The big guy was just another deadly player on that ugly ground. The Bowery. The Lower East Side of Manhattan Island.

The big warrior was togged in combat blacksuit, the silenced Beretta 93-R snugged in its holster beneath a black leather bomber-style jacket. He knew he was just seconds away from turning this stone-and-brick labyrinth into a battle zone. In the black duffel bag he had just taken from the trunk of his rental car—which had been stowed in a nearby garage during the two weeks he had spent in the neighborhood—the instruments he needed to wage the fight here in a new but very old and very familiar hellground. He was heading back into the fire.

Into the devil's grip.

Give me your tired, your poor...

Into hell on earth.

Your huddled masses yearning to breathe free...

Into another blazing doorway of the War Everlasting.

The wretched refuse of your teeming shore, send those, the homeless, tempest-tossed to me: I lift my lamp beside the golden door....

And Mack Bolan, briefly thinking of those immortal words inscribed on the pedestal of the Statue of Liberty, was counting down the numbers in his head. Zero hour had dawned.

"Hey, Lonnie! Where ya been hidin', ol' boy? L-long time...no see, baby cakes. Ya gotta come 'round more often, eh? Got some good Night Train here. Wanna sip?"

Combat senses on full alert, Bolan turned his head, the chilly night air feeling like a whiplash against his face for an instant. The voice that had beckoned him came from the shadowy niche of a tenement building. In the darkness, the Executioner could just make out the filthy, tattered bundle of cloth that held together something that appeared less than human. Something that had once been human, yeah, but now hovered on the edge of the abyss, having finished that terminal walk down the road to nowhere. Bolan passed that testament to living death without another look.

The drunk babbled on, as if the man in black were some long-lost friend, and Bolan heard a strangled wail of grief, like the cry of a wounded animal. But the shadow that was Bolan forged ahead, his ice-blue eyes glittering as they stayed fixed on the corner of Houston and Bowery. His sights were set on two men, one white, one black. Two pieces of scum cut from the same tub of shit. Pushers. And the scum didn't notice the boot that was about to step on them. Good, Bolan thought. He wanted to launch this blitzkrieg with a good and sudden peal of thunder.

Even at this early-morning hour, the streets were alive with the teeming refuse of failure; disappointment and shattered dreams. A dark inferno of zombies. An open wound of frustration and despair. For two weeks Bolan had done his damnedest to look like just another dead-end loser in the Bowery, but his face and manner now suggested a grim determination, a predatory wariness that was hard to ignore. He was a man with a mission, and the pretense was over.

Having holed up in a flophouse, camouflaged as a down-and-out vagrant, he had done a thorough reconnaissance on the streets and the people of the Bowery and the Lower East Side. He had hung around the pool halls and saloons, canvased the streets, watching the drug trade and sizing up the action. He had some names, and he knew some faces. He had seen something else, too, something that surprised him very little but still made him wonder about the chunk of wall around the heart of man.

Life here was dirt cheap because anything alive was just another number, another cog in the clunking machinery, another human obstacle in the way, filling space and draining the machine. This was a breeding ground for savages. But, he concluded, like just about any other part of New York City, a swirling bowl of humanity that was home to the best and the worst of some eight million people, the cannibals were always sharpening their claws. Always the weak got weaker, while the strong got stronger. And it was the blood of the weak and the innocent that fed the beast called Animal Man.

The black guy in the purple two-hundred-dollar sweat suit suddenly spotted the shadow stepping straight toward him. There was a steely determination in the grim eyes of the shadow that alerted the drug runner that Bolan wasn't just another buyer. Nor a cop. The runner froze, the crisp wad of hundred- and twenty-dollar bills in his hand crinkling from the sudden tension in his arms. The ounce man in the BMW poked his head out into the night. His fat, bulbous nose wrinkling, his nostrils twitching as if he smelled shit in the air, the ounce man stared at Bolan for a second.

Then curiosity gave way to suspicion, which turned to realization born from a sixth sense that could only develop after years of hard-earned experience among the savage animals. Panic struck, then terror, and the ounce man in the Armani suit turned into a slab of quaking fat when the silenced muzzle of Bolan's Beretta snaked out of nowhere.

"Get in," Bolan growled at the runner. "Open the door and let me see that right hand."

"Hey, man, what the fuck's this shit? I thought you said you wasn't tagged, man. I thought you said this act was clean. What's this bullshit? I thought..."

"Shuddup! That's the trouble with you fuckin' punks—you think too much," the ounce man snarled. The Beretta had confirmed what his instinct had told him as soon as he saw the big man in the black jacket—the dude was not someone to cross swords with. Carefully, showing his free hand, he opened the door, then grunted sharply as Bolan shoved the runner onto his lap like a sack of garbage.

"Move over," Bolan ordered the runner in the fancy running suit. "Crawl. Now!"

"Get the hell off me!" the ounce man rasped, pushing the punk in the ass. Before the runner, cursing, had wiggled off his lap, the shadow moved off the sidewalk and into the back seat of the BMW in less time than it takes to blink an eye.

Bolan locked all the doors. Roughly, he frisked the ounce man.

"Hey, pal, those are three-hundred-dollar threads you're rubbing your stinking hands over. Easy, huh. I'm clean, pal, awright? Jesus Christ!"

Finding no weapons on the ounce man, Bolan settled back into the seat. "Like a bull's ass. You're about as clean as the East River...pal. And you're going on a one-way ride to the bottom of that river unless you start talking."

"About what?"

The guy was starting to sweat, Bolan noticed, the first beads popping up on his bald dome. Both pushers knew instinctively that he wasn't the long arm of the law. They feared he was something worse.

"We'll talk on the way there," Bolan said in a graveyard voice, his face a dark death's-head in the rearview mirror as the ounce man met his gaze.

"On the way where, goddammit!"

"To the top. I'm taking you boys all the way to the top. Where you want to be. Where you belong."

The ounce man and the runner exchanged bewildered looks. Then it dawned on the dealers just where it was they were headed.

"You're crazy, pal."

"And you're dead unless you get these wheels rolling. And one more thing," the Executioner said, pressing the silencer against the base of the dealer's skull.

"Y-yeah . . . wh-what?"

"I'm not your pal. Let's get that straight. To me, you and your buddy here are nothing but parasites. You're maggots that feed off the hell of other people's lives. And I'm here to wipe you off the face of the earth. You can go slow. You can go fast. If I get who I want, you may get lucky and not go at all. It's up to you."

Bolan waited a second for the ice to settle in. Then he reached over the seat, plucked up the large black briefcase between the two dealers. As Bolan eased back in his seat, the ounce man steered the BMW away from the curb, his lips twisted as if he was amused by some private joke. The Executioner could see his threat had had very little effect on either drug-pushing piece of trash. They believed they were taking their invader into the lion's den. They believed their position was invulnerable, and that they were untouchable.

Bolan opened his satchel. He pulled out his hip holster, then filled it with the .44 AutoMag. There was a mini-Uzi in the satchel, also. Ten fragmentation grenades. A garrote. Spare clips for all hardware.

The Executioner was all set to change some viewpoints.

The war was on.

The city was about to become a battlefield.

A human hurricane of violence and fury had blown into town.

1

He was long overdue to jump back into this war with blazing hellfire. The Pandora's box was wide-open, he knew, and drugs were invading the U.S.A. with the strength and ominous swiftness of a Waffen SS black march, with the destructiveness of a typhoon pounding at the economic and spiritual heart of America. It didn't matter if the user addict was an executive in a three-piece suit in some major corporation, a so-called sports hero or the easy prey of ghetto zombies. The cancer was eating away at every cell of society, spreading like a goddamned raging fire storm. Okay, Bolan thought, with no small amount of cynicism, there was a lot of lip service being paid to this twentieth-century Black Plague by politicians up for reelection. Their efforts might get a few more people up off their butts in this war on drugs. But the streets were still chock-full of those breeding maggots, the pushers, and lip service didn't do one damn bit of good to the men and women being devoured by the scourge, or to their families. As far as the Executioner was concerned, there was only one cure for this disease.

Bolan looked at the two men in front of him, the stone-and-glass canyons of Midtown dwarfing the BMW as the car slid on through the night. Bolan had given the guy behind the wheel orders to head uptown. Into the dead zone. Where the drug houses were churning out their poison. Where the big boys played their losing game.

Bolan knew his two marks were nothing more than middlemen, lackeys looking to claw their way up through the pecking order. As far as the Executioner was concerned, though, they were all on the bottom rung of the ladder up the Superfly hierarchy. They had hitched their fortunes to an evil star. And Bolan was going to blow that star out of the sky. He had already decided to make an example of the garbage these two lackeys squirreled for. He would show these two scumbags what waited for them at the end of the line if they didn't haul themselves out of the cesspool. Fast. With no looking back.

Bolan caught the nervous glances the ounce man kept throwing toward his runner. Through hooded eyelids, the Executioner saw the gaze that flickered toward the glove compartment. The stink of fear and sweat poured into Bolan's nostrils. It was their fear, though, and their sweat. Mack Bolan knew he was holding all the cards. Someone up front was about to deal out a losing hand.

"It's suicide," Bolan quietly growled.

The black dude pretended he didn't hear the warning.

His senses on full alert, eyes boring into the heads of the two punks, Bolan took a moment to reflect on his briefing with Hal Brognola.

It had been a grim talk with pessimistic, almost fatalistic overtones—at least on the part of Brognola. The big, grizzled Fed was in this war, with fists and fire all the way, and he was glad Bolan had been brought in out of the cold. The Bolan blitz had again been given government sanction, and for that the Executioner was grateful. They were all soldiers on the same side, and Bolan didn't need to waste time and energy dodging the bullets of the good guys as well as thwarting the potential deathstrikes of the cannibals.

Brognola's top priority now was to take a chunk out of the rampant drug trade. A big chunk.

"It's worse now than it ever was, Striker. It seems like we're waging a losing war. The whole goddamn thing is making me sick."

"Tell me about it."

Brognola snorted. What could he possibly tell this hellfire warrior about the arena that he didn't already know. Maybe he'd just go ahead and blow off some steam anyway, he thought. All that bottled-up frustration. All that . . . Hell . . . Brognola had popped an antacid tablet into his mouth, washed it down with water. It was a new habit for the old warrior, and Bolan knew that the strain of duty, when it looked like good men were doomed to bash their brains out in futility while all hell kept breaking loose, threatened to chew up Brognola's guts.

"It's full-scale war out there, Mack, and the Justice Department and the DEA are losing this one hard and fast. The pushers, the Mafia, the growers in foreign countries seem to be multiplying like flies on shit. Hell, you know how it goes, dammit. Ten go down, and ten times ten rise up to take their place. Crack, heroin, pot. The country's degenerating, trying to cut its own throat. If you stop and really think about it, it's frightening. And, yeah, it makes me *sick*."

Brognola shook his head, a dark scowl etching his face like the inscription on a headstone. "What we've got now looks worse than this lousy crack. A new

batch of heroin has hit the streets. By the tons. The
number of heroin addicts has doubled in the past eight
months alone, and it's estimated there are at this moment more than one million users. The dope is purer
now, it seems, either because there's more of it coming into the country and the pushers can afford to
bring down the street price, or they're being ordered
by the head cocks to step up the grade—or both. More
smack, stronger grade, means more addicts and bigger bucks for the scum peddling the garbage, and that
means somebody is producing a better grade of heroin in larger quantities. The pushers are cutting a lot
of the heroin with crack, and they're reeling in the
users like one giant catch of fish. Guys are willing to
kill and die for this heroin, and that's exactly what
they're doing. In every major city, all over the country. In New York, burglaries and armed robberies have
tripled in the past month alone, the cops are stacking
prisoners on top of prisoners, and the courts are turning the punks right back out onto the streets because
the caseloads are overwhelming them.''

Then, Bolan recalled, Brognola had mentioned
something that pricked icy needles at the base of his
neck. The drug trade had become more organized,
more efficient, more deadly than ever in the past year.
This ''revamping,'' according to Brognola, had begun about the time the new heroin had hit the streets.
The Mafia was involved, yeah, but arrested pushers
claimed there was somebody else, another organization pulling the strings on the Mob.

The Devil's Horn, they called it.

The Devil's Horn was Bolan's mission. That raging
human virus, those poisoners of mind and body, who
thought they were safe somewhere behind the for-

tressed walls of their drug empire, were the main targets of the Bolan blitz. But just who were they? And where were they? The best place to start, he had figured, was at the bottom of the pecking order. But he wanted to go to the top in a hurry, a lightning flash. He wanted to lop off the Hydra's head. He wanted the top dog's blood, and he wanted them to eat their own poison, choke on their own evil vomit. He wanted to blow the cancer right out through their goddamn guts. He was every bit as sick and tired of this drug crisis as Hal Brognola, and he intended to do something about it.

This was his mission alone, and in his mind it could be no other way. He had asked Brognola to sit tight on this one, and the big Fed had complied, offering all intelligence, any assistance the warrior needed for free movement in the field. Even though he was in from the cold, Bolan still liked free rein, with no strings. He didn't need stumbling blocks, human obstacles, on this one.

There was one exception. One very important exception.

Jack Grimaldi, he knew, was on standby at an airstrip in New Jersey. There, the ace pilot waited with his new, heavily armed, armored Lear jet, and Bolan carried a miniature radio transmitter that could reach Grimaldi in a heartbeat and have that warbird ready for action. The mission, Bolan knew, would go hard quickly and with little warning, and the Hydra's head was somewhere overseas. But where? Somewhere in South Asia, most likely, he knew. Yeah, it was time for an assault on the Golden Triangle. But first Bolan needed hard intel on who and what he was up against. He had already gotten the ominous rumblings out of

Washington on this one, and warning bells were sounding in his mind. Louder by the minute. The black siren of doomsday was wailing for somebody unlucky enough to be on the wrong side of the Bolan fury.

And the Grim One came like a crackle of lightning for the black punk in front of Bolan.

The Executioner had known it was coming, but the runner acted with surprising speed. Bolan had hoped to give him a chance to wise up, but the punk blew his one chance of saving grace in a frenzied moment of glory-seeking and ass-saving.

The would-be Superfly committed suicide.

The runner spun around in one smooth motion, a .357 Colt Python filling his fist. His dark eyes glittered for a split second, betraying his arrogance in the face of certain triumph over the lone dude in the back seat.

Bolan looked the punk dead in the eye and blew his brains out.

The Beretta 93-R sneezed once. Muzzling at 375 mps, the 9 mm parabellum slug punched a gory hole in the black guy's forehead. Shock became the runner's shattered death mask, as the back of his skull blasted open in a spray of blood and gray brain matter. There was a dull crack, the parabellum round drilling through the BMW's windshield, spiderwebbing the glass, which was dappled with thick crimson rivulets.

The dead punk crunched against the dashboard and slid to the floor.

The ounce man glanced at the corpse, forcing indifference into eyes that a split second ago had held naked fear when he saw his ace-in-the-hole burned out of the picture.

"He was dumb," Bolan said, his voice sounding as if it came from the bottom of a tomb. "How much smarter are you?"

"Hey, look," the dealer said, a nervous smile dancing over his lips, "that nigger was nothin' to me. You just did this city a small favor. He's a dime a dozen."

"So are you. And I'm not out of favors yet."

"Look, p-mister, I'm a family man, for Chrissakes. I got a legitimate business in Jersey. I got a wife and three kids, awright? I'm a citizen, I pay taxes. I ain't some scumbucket out of Harlem."

"You should've thought a little harder before crossing the battles lines...citizen."

"Hey, look, we all got problems, okay. Mine happens to be money. Look, goddammit, I don't enjoy this kinda life, I ain't no Superfly. And I sure as hell ain't no hero. You go charging into that main cuthouse, mister, you'll get us both fried."

"I hear you," Bolan quietly replied. He noticed the garbage was sweating hard now. Good. The guy wasn't about to try anything. He was along for the ride. It was up to the garbage whether or not this was a one-way ticket to the incinerator.

With a few quick folds and tucks, Bolan turned the duffel bag into a rucksack. He slapped a 32-round clip into the mini-Uzi, "Little Lightning."

The ounce man watched Bolan in the rearview mirror. As the Executioner strapped on the holster with the stainless-steel hand cannon, dropped the frag grenades, spare clips and mini-Uzi into the rucksack, the dealer shook his head and sighed. "You crazy..."

"The Devil's Horn."

The dealer went as rigid as a board. "What did you say?"

"It's no secret in my circle, guy. What is it, who is it, and where is it?"

The dealer chuckled, as if Bolan had said something absurd, then he laughed out loud. His throaty laughter ended just as abruptly when Bolan jammed the silenced Beretta muzzle against his neck.

"I don't remember telling you to laugh."

"Y-yeah, sure, mister, sure." There was a moment of tense silence as the guy worked on his composure. "So you're after the Horn, huh. Well, there's nothing I can really tell you about it."

"Then you'd better make up something fast," Bolan growled, pressing the muzzle into the guy's neck, knowing the dealer was trying to bullshit him.

"Awright, awright. Like I said, I'm only small potatoes in this organization."

"What organization? The Mafia?"

"Hell, buddy, from what I've heard on the streets and among the other ounce men, these guys *own* those Sicilian creeps, lock, stock and barrel."

"Who are they?" the Executioner prodded. He already knew the answer, but hoped to dig more information about the Devil's Horn out of his handle by playing dumb.

"I dunno," the dealer answered gruffly, glancing sardonically in the mirror at Bolan as if he'd been asked a stupid question. "How the hell should I know?"

Bolan's jawline flexed, and he pinned the guy in the mirror with graveyard eyes.

The dealer got the message. "Look, I'm sure you know as much as I do. I ain't the guy to talk to. You want Ronny Brennan, the pretty boy uptown. He's the big gun, the guy in bed with the Families here. I hear he's the one who got the Horn in on the action in the first place."

Bolan knew exactly who the dealer was talking about. Ronny Brennan was the sweetheart of the New York jet set, a playboy with big tastes and big ambitions. He was strictly a Mob puppet, but he was a front-runner in heroin and crack. And Ronny Brennan owned a big chunk of the city's drug traffic. He was dirty, and Bolan was grimly intent on rubbing the maggot's face in his own shit. But first, that pretty boy would squawk.

"I'll get to him. He's next in line. Tell me more about the Horn."

"Hell, buddy, I told you all I know. The stuff comes from overseas, y'know, Southeast Asia, the big Golden Triangle. The heroin anyway. And that's what the Horn is working. The Horn is here, it's there, it's friggin' everywhere, buddy. They've muscled in on some pretty tough turf and kicked some butt, Mafia butt. I gather that these guys in the Horn must be controlling the operation on the other end. Hell, who knows? Maybe they threatened to cut the pipeline if the Sicilians don't dance to their tune. What do you think?"

Bolan glanced at the guy, knew the dealer didn't give a damn what he thought. The only thing Armani Suit was interested in was getting out of this alive, in one piece, and with his reputation intact so he could carry on being a "citizen."

Bolan flicked up the latches on the briefcase. Opening the case, he saw the dealer's stash. He counted twelve large plastic packets of heroin, maybe fifty vials of crack, and a thick wad of hundreds, twenties and tens.

"Looks like business is good."

The dealer cracked a smile. "Better than usual. And growing," he said, but the smile died when he realized what he'd confessed and who was in the back seat.

"I thought you said you were a smart guy?"

"I may not be brilliant, pal, but I'm smart enough to know you ain't gonna make it through the night."

Bolan looked into the mirror, met the dealer's gaze and showed the guy another graveyard smile.

"Yeah, you keep grinnin'."

The dealer muttered a curse, turned off Park Avenue. Dirty tenement dwellings loomed above the narrow streets that were like slits in the black curtain above the city. Cats and mangy dogs roamed the gutters and alleyways. Beneath the fractured maze of streetlight, cars became dark hulks. Shadowy figures were hunched in niches and alleyways or scuffling down the sidewalks.

"Nothin' but niggers and spics here," the dealer grumbled in an acid voice, as Bolan gestured for him to pull over and park in the next alley. "I'll be lucky if they don't walk away with my car, for Chrissakes."

"Your luck should hold out," the Executioner said, slipping his arms into the rucksack, fisting the briefcase and opening the door. "Get out. Look casual. Play it cool."

The Executioner fixed his gaze on the dark maw of the alley, the shadow-dark abyss that opened up before him. He saw no sign of life. Then a door at the far end of the alley squeaked open on rusty hinges. A hulk showed in the pale yellow light, then moved out into the alleyway. Bolan figured they'd been spotted by a lookout on the roof. This was it, the Executioner thought, the main drug house where his mark did business, bought and distributed the poison.

The first tentacle of the Devil's Horn octopus.

His blood racing hot, Bolan nudged the dealer ahead.

The shadow closed the door to the drug house and stepped into the stygian gloom.

"Stop right there, both of you!" the hulk snarled.

And Bolan saw the guy reach inside his jacket.

Yeah, this was it.

Paydirt!

2

Bolan had intended the hit on the crack house to be search and destroy, take no prisoners. Still, he at least wanted to get inside the door to size up the action, separate the wheat from the chaff. Then again, he reasoned, anyone inside this house of poison was dirty. They were all chaff, and Bolan had come to reap this filthy harvest.

The black hulk who guarded the doorway to the house of poison decided for Bolan how the opening round would go. The stiletto that slid from inside his denim jacket glinted in a shaft of fractured light from a nearby window.

"Whatsa hassle down there, Skeebo?"

Bolan pinponted the voice from the rooftop, directly overhead at nine o'clock. Damn! He had played this one without recon, opting to go for the long odds instead. But he knew the anatomy of a crack house, and had resolved to blaze into the wolves' lair and burn the goddamn house down. In and out. Hit and run.

Bolan threw the dice.

The black hulk crapped out.

With a front snapkick, the Executioner drilled the steel-capped toe of his black rubber-soled wingtips into wristbone. There was a sickening crack as the giant guard's wrist bones shattered. A howl of pain ripped from Skeebo's mouth, but Bolan silenced that cry with a piledriving roundhouse right that slammed off jawbone like a thunderclap.

"Shit!" the rooftop lookout snarled.

The ounce man from Jersey decided to play it cute, and bolted as the hulk hit the alley. Bolan finished off the guard with a stomp kick that snapped his neck like a brittle twig. In his panicked flight into the shadows, the dealer tripped over a cardboard box. Bolan was all over him, snatching him off the alley floor like a hawk swooping up a hare.

Bolan shoved the briefcase against the dealer's chest. "Take it," he rapsed. The ounce man didn't have to be told twice.

The .44 AutoMag filled Bolan's fist, a four-pound stainless steel hand cannon searching for the head of the first cannibal there. Scanning the rooftop, he saw no sign of the lookout. Bolan was certain the guy had rabbited to alert that den of wolves.

Time to dig in and let it rip.

The numbers had sent Bolan tumbling into the eleventh hour.

The dealer, jacked up by the nightscorcher and hauled toward the doorway, began whimpering and shaking like a pissed-on leaf. He, too, sensed the icy specter of doom.

And Bolan became the vanguard of death and destruction.

The door to the drug house flew open. Bolan saw the muzzle of a shotgun stab through the pale yellow light, glimpsed a grim black face intent on slaughter. It was all the Executioner needed to see.

Big Thunder cannoned, split the night asunder. At the sight of the head in the doorway exploding like some rotten tomato the ounce man in Bolan's grasp nearly fainted.

Bolan shoved the thug through the doorway. In less than a heartbeat the Executioner took in the contents of the viral caldron: six viruses, five of whom were clawing for iron, and one long wooden table in the far corner of the room. The table was covered with vials, white packets, a scale and pools of dirty cash.

The five blacks around the table leaped to their feet, their faces twisted by fear and feral rage.

"Don't shoot!" the ounce man shrieked, and fell to his knees. He dropped the stash case and spread his arms as if imploring some almighty force he had never believed in until then to spare him, because all hell was breaking loose and he was the lone, the only, sonofabitching dogface in that shell-plastered foxhole. "Noo-o-o-o, you fucking black bastards!"

Big Thunder roared, bucking out peals of cleansing death that shook the flimsy, dirty room. Five slugs sizzled the air at 1640 fps, and the hollowpoint 240-grain screamers exploded faces and blasted open skulls, as they hammered through the table and drilled into the wall. Gore spattered the wall as headless human bowling pins toppled.

The kneeling ounce man, who had suddenly found God, sputtered, then puked, tears rolling down cheeks drained of color.

Bolan clubbed the guy over the head and dropped him in his own vomit. From above he heard shouts, feet pounding out of the rooms and down the hallway. Soldiers, zombies or punks? He'd find out.

Then the Executioner turned his attention to the sixth occupant, who was sitting in a chair hugging the far wall and looking as if he wished he was part of that wall. Bolan took two big steps toward him. On the seated dude's lap was an open case, in which fat white packets and dozens of vials trembled as the pusher's knees knocked. The guy's right hand was frozen in midair, his fingers just inches from the butt of a large-caliber handgun in a shoulder holster. The blitzkrieg had taken the pusher by complete surprise, and Bolan could tell he wasn't ready to cashier out.

Tough. Too bad for him, Bolan thought.

"Hey, man, gimme a break," the dealer whined. "I didn't do nothin'."

The pusher wore skintight black leather pants, white snakeskin boots with spurs, and a black leather vest. In his ear a diamond stud glittered, and his purple Mohawk stood up like a porcupine on the dough-white bowl of his skull.

The guy was looking good, Bolan decided.

The guy was dogshit.

Bolan raised his hand cannon, and the pusher's eyes bulged. "That's only part of the problem," the Executioner growled. "This haircut's on me."

And Bolan shaved the token white Superfly with 240 grains of grim medicine.

As arms and legs twitched in the quagmire of muck behind him, Bolan swiftly checked his rear and flanks and stepped into the dimly lit hallway. The place reeked of sweat, puke, feces—the anything-but-subtle stink of human misery. And it reeked of fear. Cold, cold fear. The scum were being hit, and they knew it.

A door crashed open to Bolan's right. He saw the club headed for his face. Whirling, his right hand snaking out, Bolan caught and locked onto that club, an eight-inch steel spike quivering inches from his eye. The snarl on the face behind the club became surprise at the lightning reflexes that had abruptly ended the assault. Then the assailant's expression twisted into shock and agony as the Executioner plunged 6.5 inches of cold cannon steel into a soft beerbelly and squeezed the trigger. That .44 slug, married with a cut-down 7.62 mm NATO rifle cartridge, exploded like a land mine in the punk's abdomen, and he vomited out guts, blood and bone through the gaping maw in his lower back. The corpse sailed back into a dark tomb.

Bolan, still hanging on to the spiked club, wheeled as a skinny black with nunchaku in his hand charged out of the gloom. The punk howled, swinging the nunchaku around his head, behind his back, between his legs. A real showboat, yeah.

Bolan looked the punk in the eye. He might have laughed if the situation hadn't been so grim and ugly; for Bolan, death was never a joking matter. He figured the punk was either stupid or suffering from delusions of invincibility. Whichever, he was checking out. Bolan could have used the AutoMag, but he decided to let this guy's lamp blow out in true barbarian style. As soon as the nunchaku went behind the punk's back again, Bolan flattened the would-be Bruce Lee, burying the spike in the crown of the attacker's skull, wood cracking bone like eggshell. The martial-arts display was over. It was thumbs-down for that guy, who would have brought shame to the ancient samurai code of *bushido*.

Yeah, Bolan thought, there's kung-fu fighting all over the Big Apple tonight. He moved down the hallway, caving in doors with thunderous kicks, the Flesh Shredder sweeping the interior of each hellhole.

In every room on the first floor, Bolan found the same sight. Drugged-out zombies, shells of human beings. Drool running from vented mouths. Bloodshot eyes and expressionless faces. Crack pipes and needles. Bolan had seen a lot of hells during his long and unremitting war. But how, he wondered, did a warrior fight this kind of hell? Drugs had become the life's blood of the zombies under this roof. Insidious drugs were their idols, their gods. The highs had become more important than their lives, or than the lives of others. No amount of war or earth shaking was going to clean up their act. They would have to do it for themselves. They would have to *want* to do it for themselves. The users, he realized, were not the ultimate enemy. No. It was the heart of the beast that had to be cut out. The demand called up the supply, yeah. But if the poison wasn't supplied, pushed, in the first place, there would be no demand.

Bolan moved back down the hallway. It was time to put this hellhouse behind him. The word of the hit would spread, and the message would be clear. The Devil's Horn, Bolan knew, would start looking over their shoulders. Their cage had been rattled. And Bolan was determined that there was nowhere on the face of the earth they could run or hide from him.

He would find them. And he would crush the life out of them.

Back in the charnel room, Bolan scattered the white packets to the floor, crushed every last vial of crack under his foot. This was only the beginning, and he was far from satisfied.

Suddenly, ever alert, the warrior made out the faint whine of a distant siren.

Bolan quickly hauled the moaning ounce man to his feet, and ordered him to pick up his stash case. Then he shoved the miserable dealer out into the alley, and followed him.

The blitzkrieg was striking hard, and crackling blood and thunder. The war machine that was Mack Bolan was shifting into high gear.

It was no time to slow down.

Hell, no. It was time to take the war into the belly of the monster. It was time to cut the throat of the Hydra.

A pretty boy was next on the Executioner's hit list.

One Ronny Brennan. The cute one. The lapdog of the cannibals.

Bolan hoped the bloodsucker was throwing a party.

Because it would be the last one he ever threw.

3

Ronny "the Top Dog" Brennan threw a party every night. Come hell, high water or Viking women in black leather, he was always ready for a good time. Not even death or taxes would keep him from getting the party juices flowing. Well, maybe death, he reflected, but certainly never taxes. Hell, he hadn't paid Uncle Sam a dime in more than ten years. It was something he would have liked to boast about openly, but he was a slick dude in his eyes and in the eyes of all the broads who wanted to be part of his life, and he knew when to keep his mouth shut. Still, the urge was always there to let his circle know he was screwing the system and the system was helpless to stop him.

Yeah, he was a juggernaut, an underworld entrepreneur, damn straight. He was a top dog, *the* top dog. He might be on the short side of five foot six and look like some scrawny runt tipping the scales at one-forty sopping wet. But now as he eyeballed the beautiful Broadway starlets and the sleek wives of upper-crust dudes he'd bought and paid for who were strutting their wares in his sprawling penthouse suite, he had to smile to himself. He might be short and skinny, but he was big where it really counted. He was proud of that, and he'd take on all comers. He smiled again as he ran back that little play on words through his head. He'd sampled just about every woman there. They knew who he was. They knew he was a damned tiger in the sack.

Sipping at his glass of three-hundred-dollar French champagne, Ronny caught a glimpse of himself in the huge wall mirror behind the mahogany bar. A swarthy, dark-haired, dark-eyed Apollo, he thought. The Mediterranean blood ran thick in his family, and he had the image of a Caesar to uphold. He saw himself as a modern-day Alexander the Great—he caught himself just in time. It was good he hadn't let that one slip out—Alexander was a flaming faggot. Julius Caesar, maybe. Maybe even a Sicilian Hannibal.

Yeah, he was feeling great, a billion-dollar stud in a two-thousand-dollar white suit made of Thai silk. God, he was looking good. Life was beautiful, and he was at the pinnacle of the whole frigging world.

But it had been a hard climb to the top of his mountain. He owed his success to his late old man, but he defied the first son of a bitch to tell him that to his handsome face. Sure, Mario Bernelli had muscled out some of the stiffer drug competition in the old days, when heroin first hit the streets. Sure, Pop had commanded an army of soldiers that had bribed the big suits of the straight New York set into the alliance with the Devil's Horn, and bludgeoned any malcontents or deserters into a coma or black-bag city. If it hadn't been for the old man, some said, the kid wouldn't be shit.

Okay, Brennan thought, I'll show you shit.

And he had. The Devil's Horn had had some loose ends in the beginning. Guys running amok, doing their own thing on their own time and in their own way. Brennan had cleaned up the garbage quick, because he wasn't going to sit still for all that maverick crap. After all, it wasn't surprising to him, really, to have so easily herded up all the heavy muscle, be they crooked politico, bad cop, disgruntled mafioso. Whatever. The old man had had enough dirt on a lot of guys in the city, and on more than a few guys in Southeast Asia—the bad CIA apples and pissed-off Vietnam vets—to glue the Horn together. In his own mind Ronny had won the right to be top dog. And his was the hand that feeds, he thought.

Too bad the old man had just keeled over one day in his study in that Long Island mansion that God only knew how much blood had been spilled to buy. Heart attack, uh-huh. Too bad the old man hadn't had one of his gunsels check his medicine cabinet on occasion. Yeah, that was just too damn bad. The old man, Ronny reflected, wasn't always as slick as he thought he was. Sure, he had suspected there was a traitor in the ranks, but the old man had never suspected that his dear, his loving, his one and only son was playing Judas.

It paid, Ronny knew, to snowball people. Men, women, children, it was all the same to him. Men represented obstacles to be overcome, or money. Women were objects for his pleasure, either between the sheets or just stroking his ego; otherwise they got slapped around. Kids? Fuck 'em, he thought, who needs 'em? But kids were tools, too. Rebellious, disillusioned, know-it-all youth. Throw a little coke, crack, or some of the new smack their way, and they were his for life. When it came to dealing dope, that philosophy had cemented the golden crown right on his head. He briefed his cadre of pushers every week, without fail. If they missed a briefing, their ass was grass and he was the lawnmower. "You come away with every last dime these kids got," he always told his dealers. "You get 'em hooked anyway you can and keep 'em hooked. You guys are the doctors." And Ronny Brennan ran the hospital.

He was the doctor of love and good times.

He was the most beautiful guy in the whole world, and there wasn't a skirt chaser in his suite man enough to carry his jockstrap.

"Boss, we got a problem."

The deep rumbling voice snapped Brennan out of his thoughts. He jerked his head sideways, anger jolting through his bones. Pete Balducci, his *segundo*, had walked up on him from behind, and Brennan figured his second-in-command must have seen him with his head up his ass. Balducci was a six-foot-six block of granite with slate-gray eyes behind hooded lids that looked like the slits of a tank turret. He was a big, mean, cold-blooded killing son of a bitch, Brennan knew. But that didn't mean he couldn't kick his ass. A good shot to the nuts...what did they say? The bigger they come...?

Sizing guys up physically and deciding how he'd take them down if push came to shove was a habit Brennan had developed early in life. More than once in the old days he'd gone out with his old man's soldiers when a head needed busting, or a kneecap needed shattering, or a competitor needed cement shoes. Friend or foe, it didn't matter to Brennan. Every man was his enemy. And in his position, he thought, a lord overlooking an entire kingdom, could never be too careful.

"I thought I told you about walking up on me from behind like that," Brennan growled.

"Sorry, boss."

Brennan scowled. His *segundo* looked anything but frigging sorry, he decided. He was beginning to feel like he was surrounded by nothing but wiseasses.

"We've been hit—I just got word from the street. Somebody walked into one of our main houses, cool as the breeze, and started blowing heads off."

Brennan stared up at Balducci. It took a second for the shock to set in, then a ball of ice lodged in his gut. A feeling he hadn't known for some time. Panic.

"What the hell are you talkin' about?"

"Boss..."

"Yeah, yeah, I heard ya!" Quickly, Brennan scanned the room. People were dancing, and the music was loud enough so that no one could have heard the exchange. Since midnight, the coke had been flowing, and the mirror trays on the bar and the coffee table were kept heaped with the white god. Even at three o'clock in the morning the party was still going strong, and showed no sign of slowing down anytime soon. The women had been looking his way for the past hour, Brennan had noticed, and he was getting ready to score some ass. Now this! A hit. Who?

He ran the list of his enemies and would-be competitors through his mind, looking for that thorn in his side. Hell, he'd all but eliminated the competition in New York and New Jersey, and the families were playing ball with him. Somebody, though, had gotten cute.

Now he had a war on his hands.

Brennan cursed under his breath. He ordered his *segundo* into the conference room and followed him in quickly, his mind buzzing with fear and anger. As soon as Balducci shut the door, muffling the revelry beyond, Brennan started with the orders that would signal war. "Round up the boys, put the word out to your troops in the street. I want movement and I want ass kicked until there's some answers, understand?"

"I already did, boss. I got my hitters running down all our dealers now. There's a team on standby with the phones open. You got any ideas—"

"No, I don't got any ideas, goddammit!"

And Ronny Brennan didn't have the first inkling. Things had been running along smoothly, maybe too damn smoothly, he now reflected. Had the good life softened him up? Had he lost that mean edge that had won and secured his position at the top of the heap?

"Have you beefed up security on the floor?"

Balducci spread his hands, an imploring look in his narrowed gaze. "Well, boss, I just heard about it, and—"

"Yeah, yeah. Christ! I'll tell you what..."

Suddenly the intercom on Brennan's desk buzzed. The red light on the miniconsole was flashing, which warned Brennan there was trouble. Unexpected guests. Bad company. Brennan and Balducci looked at each other as if they'd just been shot. That bad company, they both knew, was now in the building, had gotten past the security guard in the lobby and was now on the upper floor. Some fucking security, Brennan thought. There was going to be hell to pay for this, and heads would roll. It was time to shake a few trees anyway.

"Well?" Brennan snapped at his *segundo*, silently cursing the soldier's hesitation. What the hell is this? he thought, a murderous rage burning through every limb. Is everyone going to come unglued on me now because some wiseass has thrown a monkey wrench into the juggernaut?

Balducci punched the intercom button. "Yeah?"

But the only sound that came out of the box was a harsh gurgle. Like someone was choking, fighting to get words out. Struggling to... *Damn!* The slobbering, strangling noise sent ice fingers down Brennan's spine. Then there was a sharp crack. It was a sound Brennan couldn't mistake, because he'd heard more than one neck snap during his reign, and had broken some vertebrae himself on occasion.

A Smith and Wesson .44 Magnum appeared in Balducci's big fist. The *segundo* was already moving toward the door, but Brennan hesitated, his mind tumbling with fear. Pull yourself together, he told himself. You're in charge. Get a grip on yourself, pal. You're the man. You're the top dog. The eyes of the world are on you now. The reassurance sounded flimsy to his mind, and he felt like a man walking on slowly cracking ice. Still, he summoned the courage of thirty-some mean years of violence and treachery and followed his *segundo* to the door. The unthinkable was now happening, Brennan knew, and he had to deal with it, he had to do something.

Walking on legs that suddenly seemed like deadweights, Brennan followed his hitter back into the big suite.

Then the unthinkable became reality.

The double doors to the foyer blew open and crashed into the walls like a thunderclap. Doors that were locked, bolted and chained. But the grim determination, the demonic fury that Brennan found in the eyes of the big man in blacksuit, who had breached his security and crashed his party, told him that there were few doors on the face of the earth that could hold him back.

The revelers in the suite froze, voices fell silent as all eyes turned toward the man in black. Rock music blared during the split second of mass paralysis. Then the late-night partyers saw the gun in the intruder's hand.

Balducci had spotted the Beretta 93-R before anyone else. He acted first, swinging his hand cannon toward the black-garbed invader. It was the last time he acted. The curtain of doom dropped over the *segundo*.

The intruder's Beretta chugged out a silenced round, and a 9 mm parabellum slug cored a third eye in Balducci's forehead. Blood and muck sprayed over Brennan's face, splashing his white suit like some bright abstract painting.

Several women screamed.

Brennan saw the only gun he had in that room topple to the plush brown carpet, glimpsed the blood on his suit, then looked across the room. Instantly, he recognized one of his top dealers out of New Jersey, though the man was trying to hide behind the intruder's bulk. An imploring look in the ounce man's eyes asked Brennan for forgiveness. Brennan swore to himself he'd kill that son of a bitch if it was the last thing he ever did.

The first shock of Balducci's slaying wore off within seconds, and Brennan was surprised at just how hard and mean he felt. He was going to deal with these two assholes himself. He was alone now. But hadn't it always been that way?

Brennan turned his outraged attention on the big invader. And the heart of Ronny Brennan skipped a couple of beats.

The invader was already halfway across the room.

Brennan stared at that death's-head expression, felt his knees turn to jelly. The invader's ice-blue eyes seemed to bore right through him like a drill. The searching look told Brennan this guy knew who and what he was and intended to punch his ticket. And Brennan would have sworn he knew that face.

Would have sworn he *should* know that face. But from where? And who was this . . .

Then it finally dawned on Ronny the Top Dog Brennan just who his uninvited guest was.

Mack Bolan. The Executioner. The one-man slayer of the Families.

Ronny the Top Dog Brennan suddenly felt very small. And limp.

4

Bolan was locked on to the drug czar with grim death sights. Crashing the party was a direct approach, but Bolan wanted it no other way, knew it could be no other way. Ronny Brennan's world was about to go up in flames. And, as far as the Executioner was concerned, there were no innocents in this den of vipers.

Damn right, Junior, Bolan thought. Your ass is fried bacon. And I'm the butcher.

Bolan sensed the fear he'd brought with him into the suite, saw that the way to Brennan was unobstructed at that moment by human obstacles. He had everyone's attention, and he seized the moment.

Breaching security had been easy. His blitzkrieg had taken the savages by storm, punched a gaping, bloody hole in their defenses. In the lobby he had taken out the security guard with a good right cross, damaging the man's ego more than his face. He had turned the top floor of the high rise into an open grave, drilling two 9 mm slugs through the foreheads of a pair of Brennan's goons, then snapping the neck of a soldier who had made a frenzied attempt to alert the drug-lord to the attack. Bolan's captive ounce man had come along for the ride. At this point, the dealer was nothing more than a shield against enemy fire, and no amount of sniveling or pleading for mercy would make the garbageman a breastplate of righteousness in Bolan's eyes.

Three long strides away from Brennan, Bolan saw that the druglord had decided to play it cute. Bolan let Brennan scoop up Slit Eyes's .44 Magnum, then he hammered a snapkick off the drug czar's jaw, hammering the king trashman into the wall like so much crumpled refuse.

It was then, too, that a lone wolf among the party-goers decided to bare his fangs. Out of the corner of his eye, Bolan saw the big hero lunge for his Beretta. A real good-looking guy, Bolan observed, a lady-killer with enough arrogance in his eyes and enough swagger in his step to shame any pretty boy. But if the hero was trying to impress the women, he came up limp. Bolan hit the dude with a straight right, a thunder-clapping shot to the chops. The fury that Bolan threw into that jawbreaker whipped the lady-killer's legs out from under him as if he'd slipped on a banana peel. Then another would-be David charged the Goliath. Bolan pistoned a sidekick into that clown's guts. The guy was poleaxed by the blow to his knees, and whatever he'd been drinking all night came out in one long gory spew.

Then Bolan's shield bolted. Bolan had known the ounce man would make another break for freedom at the slightest chink of daylight. With a sweeping right roundhouse he put out the lights on that garbage-man.

Again, everyone in the suite froze. Again, Bolan held everyone's undivided attention. The Executioner drilled a parabellum round through the compact-disc player, shattering glass and metal, dropping a cloak of silence over the paralyzed throng. The acrid smell of fear now cut through the thick flowery scent of perfume and cologne.

Quickly, Bolan swept up the .44 Magnum, tucking the hand cannon inside his combat webbing. Another piece of hardware, he knew, would come in handy, because this hit had gone hard in a hell of a hurry. Just in case the number of maggots multiplied too fast, Bolan had hooked two frag grenades to his webbing before entering the high rise.

"Anybody moves, joyboy here gets skinned," the Executioner growled, hauling Brennan to his feet by the scruff of his skinny neck. "Like a snake. Any more heroes?" he asked the partyers, raking an icy stare over the faces of all the guests.

There were no takers.

The party was over.

But Bolan had only begun to put the torch to the house. He was center stage, and his show was just getting on the road. He wanted to show these people just what Ronny Brennan was, just how little, weak and cowardly this lump of shit was when the chips were down. He wanted these people to know that when all else in their lives failed they'd better have something other than cannibalism to fall back on. And a piece of sewage like Ronny Brennan was not the answer. Brennan was now going to become the mirror image of their twisted passions.

"You're dead meat, smartass!" Brennan rasped, screwing up his face in pain as Bolan grabbed him by the hair, shoved him toward the coffee table near the bar. "I got thirty soldiers on the way. You'll never get outta here alive!"

Bolan picked up the stash case the dealer had dropped. "Watch me," he growled, then kicked

Brennan in the back of the knee, dropping him in front of his coffee table. As his eyes swept over the guests, challenging them to try to stop him, the party-crasher quickly opened the briefcase. He took out the packets of Brennan's smack and punched each one open on the coffee table with the butt of his Beretta, until a substantial pile of the poison powder was spread before Brennan's eyes. He wiped the butt of his Beretta on Brennan's suit to clean off the white junk, then fisted another handful of the druglord's hair.

"This is what you people have been living for," the Man from Ice rasped to Brennan's dumbstruck party guests. He pushed Brennan's head toward the smack pile, then violently thrust the guy's face into the heroin. "This is what you've sold your souls to. This is the guy who's bought you, who uses you like toilet paper. He's shit, and that's just what he's made you. You guys, this is the maggot that's probably been sleeping with your women and laughing behind your back the whole time. This is what owns you. And this is what the last stop will look like for you."

Brennan struggled to break free of Bolan's grasp. The Executioner slackened his hold, let Brennan lift his face a few inches, then plunged that white-powdered masklike face back into the smack. There was a crack of glass, and an even more audible and sickening crack of bone as blood sprayed from Brennan's pulped nose. The druglord sputtered, shaking his head like a wet dog, but Bolan held his face firmly planted in the fruits of his rotten harvest. Brennan coughed, choking on the powder that poured into his mouth and nose, and tears spouted from the creep's eyes.

"Take a good hard look at this, people," Bolan went on. "I'm not passing judgment on you; you've already passed judgment on yourselves."

They looked, all right. And Bolan could tell they believed. To further hammer home his message of doom, the Executioner pulled out his silver British lighter. With the flick of a finger, he torched the dirty money in the stash case.

Bolan hauled Brennan to his feet once more. With an upsweeping kick, the Executioner flipped over the coffee table, exploding the glass and littering the carpet with a snowy sprinkle and flaming wads of cash.

As Bolan jacked Brennan away from the mob, he heard a groan, then saw the ounce man stir to life.

"Get moving," the Executioner snarled. He kicked the dealer in the ass as he struggled to his feet, sending the ounce man reeling belly first toward the foyer.

"You b-bastard...I'll kill you, I s-swear to Christ," Brennan whined, stammering with hate and rage. Blood dappled red patches on the white mask of his face, crimson trickles leaking onto the lapels of his silk threads.

"Open that door," Bolan ordered the ounce man. He checked his rear, but found every hero there had already been driven into the ground.

"Think about what you saw here tonight," the Executioner said to them. "I'll remember your faces. And I may be coming back for some of you. You won't know when. You won't know where. But if I want you, you'd better learn to sleep with your eyes open."

Bolan was glad to get out of their reeking pit. He was tempted to kick the ounce man again, but instead exited to the corridor. Checking his corners, the Executioner found the hallway was just as he'd left it a few minutes earlier.

Dead men there had met the Grim One at the end of their ride into oblivion. Mack Bolan had only fulfilled their death wish.

Outside Ronny Brennan's fortress Bolan discovered the streets were coming alive with armed animals whose death wish had not been realized. Yet.

Brennan's ounce man exited first from the lobby doors just as a black Cadillac came to a halt directly across from the high rise with a squeal of rubber. Four grim-faced gunsels emerged from the Cadillac, and the dealer threw his hands up, shrieking, "Don't shoot! For God's—"

If the hitters heard that desperate plea, they didn't acknowledge it or seem to give a damn about that guy. Pencil-tip flashes stabbed the darkness around the Cadillac. Two slugs ripped open the dealer's chest with thundering lead hammers. Bolan instantly returned accurate and lethal fire, even though one arm was wrapped around Brennan's throat. The .44 Magnum revolver bucked in the Executioner's hand. Four rocketing headblasters found their mark, blasted apart faces and exploded skulls into fragments of bone like shards of pottery. Dead men spun, crumpled, flipped over the Cadillac's hood. Limbs twitched in death throes, and blood ran thick in the gutter.

Bolan dragged Brennan along the sidewalk, angling toward the commandeered BMW. "The Top Dog" was shaking in Bolan's grasp like a leaf in a windstorm. Then Bolan smelled the stench of urine as this tough darling of the jet set soaked his pants.

The engagement wasn't over yet, Bolan discovered a heartbeat later. Another carload of goons suddenly streaked onto the killing field. Before they could complete their tumble out of the Lincoln, Bolan pulled the pin on a frag grenade and hurled the doomsday numbers at their fancy wheels. As shoes hit the street and gunmetal swept into sight, the grenade bounced under the front end of the Lincoln. Brennan stared in fascinated horror as the fireball erupted and screams shrilled in the black night. Shrapnel and twisted metal razors shredded flesh like giant potato peelers. A solitary shadow propelled by the roaring explosion crashed through the plate-glass window of a department store.

Stunned at the sight of the flaming hulk across the street, Brennan hesitated. Bolan opened the door of the BMW and shoved him across the front seat of the car.

"Drive," Bolan ordered, his voice fire and steel as he slammed the door and jabbed Brennan in the ribs with the muzzle of the Magnum. "You make sure you get us across the George Washington Bridge. Or I'll drop you off in the Hudson."

Brennan didn't have to be told twice. His bloody, contorted face looking like a bizarre Halloween mask, the druglord fired up the engine and steered the BMW away from the curb.

"Where to?"

"I'll ask the questions," Bolan snapped.

"Fuck you!"

Bolan cracked a left off Brennan's cheek, punching the druglord's head against the window so hard the glass cracked.

"You're crazy!" Brennan squealed, blood streaming down his cheek where the shattered glass had gouged his face.

"No. You're a sick dog, Brennan. A rabid beast that I'm going to put to rest unless you get me where I'm going."

"Where is that?"

"The Devil's Horn."

The sounds of glass tinkling and wind whipping through the car were all that could be heard for a silent moment. Brennan looked at Bolan with renewed fear.

"What did you say?"

"You're going for a ride, pretty boy. All the way to the Golden Triangle." Bolan met Brennan's gaze with arctic ice in his eyes. "You're going to find out just how the other half lives."

Brennan appeared stunned, then a nervous laugh shook his body. "You are crazy, pal. You got guts, maybe, but you're stupid. I know who you are, Bolan. Yeah, you may have changed your face a little over the years with some plastic surgery. But there's only one smartass around with the MO I saw tonight."

Bolan wasn't surprised that the punk had figured out who he was; in fact, he had expected, had wanted as much. His methods of dealing with the Mob were well-known among the Families. After years of their being hit so hard in the guts by the Bolan blitz, their animal instinct for survival, he knew, made it critical that they look under each rock, scour every shadow each time one of their number took a hard fall into the inferno. He had given the Mafia scum good reason to sleep with one eye open. And hell, no, he wasn't the least bit sorry about that.

Brennan started to reach inside his jacket. Bolan dug the Magnum's muzzle into his ribs. "Easy, smartass," Brennan explained. "I got somethin' to show ya."

"Let's see it then. Take it out slow."

"Sure. Slow and easy."

Carefully Brennan pulled a small black box out of his jacket pocket. Bolan froze, grimly aware that he had bagged a cornered ferret, uncertain what that crazed animal would do next.

But Brennan just laughed. "Take a look behind you, smart guy."

Bolan sent a quick glance over his shoulder as the BMW headed into the dead zone of upper Manhattan. A block behind, two, then three Cadillacs shot into sight. Three's a good number, Bolan thought with grim humor. For the good and the bad.

"I told you, smart guy!" Brennan gloated with a sneer. "This here's a homing device. They'll find me no matter where you take me. There's three cars full of soldiers back there, and we'll pick up a few more before we hit the Parkway. You see, smart guy, I'm what you call an investment. I'm big money, and there's too many hotshots who want to make sure I stay in one piece. I wish the same could be said for you."

The Executioner showed Brennan his best graveyard smile. "You're pretty stupid for a guy who thinks he's so smart."

Then it dawned on Brennan just how dumb he'd been to show Bolan the ace up his sleeve.

"Keep it, playboy," Bolan told Brennan. "You may have just played your last hand. You'd better learn how to file for bankruptcy."

Brennan muttered a curse, hastily shoving the homing device back inside his jacket pocket.

But Bolan wasn't sure who was holding the losing cards at that moment. Would the ratpack now on his trail open fire indiscriminately? Would they risk knocking Brennan out of the picture just to lop off the Executioner's head?

Bolan, the lone crapshooter, was willing to gamble that they wouldn't.

At least not yet.

And he still held a big ace he was ready to deal their way.

He only hoped Jack Grimaldi was ready and waiting. If he wasn't, the hellhounds would come as a nasty surprise to Bolan's ace pilot.

The Executioner knew he would need all Grimaldi's firepower. To the hilt. To the blazing end.

The fires were raging to consume Bolan's search-and-destroy.

But he wasn't ready yet to see the darkness of his last blitzkrieg. No way.

5

Jack Grimaldi was worried. But, he reminded himself, he always worried whenever the big guy was scorching the hellfire trail, and here he was, merely an arm's length away from the fight.

Hell, even though he hadn't been there at the Pittsfield genesis, where Bolan had been baptized in the devil's fire storm against the Mafia, he still felt as if he'd known the guy all his life, instead of catching him more than a dozen campaigns into the war. Comrades, soldiers together in the War Everlasting. That was what they were, he knew, and that was what they would be until the end. Okay, so he felt like the warrior's blood brother, damn right, he told himself. More than once they'd been blooded together. More than once they'd pulled each other from the flames of the inferno. And they'd do it again.

Grimaldi smiled, but felt the nervous tension tugging at the corners of his mouth as he stared out into the darkness that enveloped the large field deep in western New Jersey. Damn, but he was glad Bolan had been brought back in from the cold. The guys in the white hats, he thought, had finally wised up. Again. Bolan was needed now, he knew, perhaps more than ever. Which meant there was too much for any one man to do. Maybe too damn much of a tab for any one man to pay. Even Mack Bolan. But Grimaldi knew better than all those guys in D.C. who had given Bolan back his white hat. He himself had seen Mack in action up close, with his nose grinding down into the muck and guts of the killing fields. One very good and very determined individual, Grimaldi believed, could and *would* make a difference in a world gone mad. By now, it was clear to everyone on either side of the Bolan guns just who that individual was.

Damn this waiting! How long had Bolan been gone? Grimaldi wondered. The big guy had been in that town for maybe two weeks, but he'd given Brognola the word that he was ready to move. And the big Fed had given Grimaldi the green light to move in with Skyhunter and stand by for an evacuation. But not for an escape, Grimaldi hoped. An escape flight meant trouble. An escape flight could signal disaster for this mission before it even got out of Jersey and on its way. But on its way to where? Mack had mentioned Southeast Asia, Thailand maybe. Something about the Devil's Horn, the Golden Triangle...

Damn! Grimaldi hated like hell waiting for Bolan when he'd been out of sight for so long. Thoughts of doom and disaster had a way of filtering into a mind normally steeled for quick and decisive action, chipping away at the hardened exterior of a soul committed to the good fight. The waiting, he thought, was killing him.

The ace pilot needed a cigarette. Smoking was a habit that had been growing on him insidiously lately. He loved and hated the damn cigarettes all at the same time. As he fired one up now with his lighter, he knew he was fooling himself that the nicotine would relax him. Like hell! The smoke only burned down into a belly already on fire, a harsh acid taste swelled his insides with a fever, sparking a flame his urge to get on with the battle.

Trying to get his mind off Bolan and his mission, Grimaldi forced himself to think of something else. He turned and looked at Skyhunter.

Skyhunter was the pet name he'd given to the modified, reconstructed Lear jet 25C. With the untiring help of the Army Corps of Engineers, brought in under Hal Brognola's umbrella, Grimaldi had designed and built this warbird. The work had begun some eight months ago at Stony Man Farm, and even now those engineers were putting the finishing touches to Condor, the backup 25C battle jet for Bolan's new war.

Grimaldi walked up the starboard side of the warbird, drawing on his cigarette, smiling to himself. Four 7.62 mm miniguns had been attached to the undersides of the warbird's wings, each capable of blazing out 18,000 rounds per minute. Also attached to each extended wing were two TOW missiles and two 7-tube 2.75 inch rockets. Kevlar protected the main and auxiliary fuel tanks and cockpit.

And that wasn't all. Behind the specially constructed windows in the aft section were two 40 mm modified Bofors cannons. In a split second, with the push of an electronic button, those windows would become portholes. A hell of a bird, Grimaldi thought as he admired it, a veritable flying battleship.

Grimaldi looked at the eagle insignia on the nose of the cockpit, a big white bird spreading its wings against an all-black camouflage paint job. The pilot patted the bird with affection; the paint job and the insignia had been his own final touches. Directly beneath the white eagle jutted the muzzle of a .50 caliber machine gun. Inside the cockpit, Grimaldi and those hand-picked engineers had installed the latest in sophisticated radar and tracking devices, infrared scanning equipment for reconnaissance and precision fire-control computers. With a nonstop range of 3,600 nautical miles and a maximum cruising speed of 492 knots at 45,000 feet, Skyhunter would get Bolan wherever he wanted to go fast, and with little concern about fuel stops.

Suddenly, Grimaldi heard his radio transmitter beep. It was Mack, he knew, and he feared a grim message.

Grimaldi pressed the Activate button on his transmitter. "Skyhunter here, come in."

"Iceman here. Burning shadow. I repeat, burning shadow. Copy, Skyhunter."

"Affirmative, Iceman. Burning shadow," Grimaldi answered, repeating the code word that meant immediate escape and evacuation.

"We're coming in off the main road now, Skyhunter. Prepare for the long run. Copy."

"Prepare for long run, roger that, Iceman. Over and out."

Signing off, Grimaldi ducked under the wing, giving one of the miniguns a pat on the muzzle. For good luck.

The big guy was coming in, he thought. And there was trouble on the way.

But Jack Grimaldi had expected as much.

This war was on. All systems go.

Grim-faced, Grimaldi set about putting Skyhunter into action. He was feeling the adrenaline rush.

"YOU GOT REAL TROUBLE now, smart guy. You're finished, pal, hear me?" The punk laughed. "You're just another swinging dick to me, Bolan," Brennan jeered, steering the BMW off the asphalt road and onto the narrow dirt strip. "And I'm gonna have your balls—"

"Shut up," Bolan growled, pinning the druglord with an icy stare. With his AutoMag he indicated that Brennan should head across the field toward the lone jet. As Bolan saw the warbird taxi to the end of the dirt runway and swing around for takeoff, he let out a pent-up breath in relief.

Bolan knew he wasn't going to get any information on the Devil's Horn out of Brennan at this point, and he hadn't tried to during the ninety-minute ride. The druglord was feeling good about the odds. And with good reason, Bolan knew. With eight carloads of hitters hard on their trail, strung out like a convoy behind them, Brennan had been gloating over how grim the Executioner's prospects looked. An interrogation, Bolan knew, would have to wait. Action was the only thing that was going to loosen Brennan's tongue.

"You get any ideas about running away from that jet," Bolan warned, fisting Little Lightning, "they'll be your last, and there'll be one less swinging dick around here."

Bolan heard Brennan mutter something, but the punk got the message. He angled the BMW on a direct line toward Skyhunter, the warbird's dark bulk looming in the night like some prehistoric bird of prey.

Bolan blazed into action. With a quick mini-Uzi burst, he knocked out the back windshield of the BMW. Glass chips fell around his head, nicking his face like tiny razors, as he palmed a frag grenade and pulled the pin. After estimating the distance between the BMW and the lead carload of gunners, he counted off two seconds in his head, then Bolan hurled the bomb. At the same time he began spraying the second car with sizzling 9 mm parabellum hornets.

The frag grenade detonated under the left front tire of the Lincoln. The earthshaking concussion and boiling fireball flipped the lead car over on its roof, metal rending and glass exploding. Emptying the 32-round clip into the second car, Bolan glimpsed naked terror on two faces before they were pulped into red mush. The lead car tumbled into a ditch, and the second assault vehicle clipped the back end of the flaming wreckage. A fountain of fire whooshed high in the air when the two cars collided, like metallic beasts locking horns inside a ring of flames. The six other assault vehicles skidded, slewed, then whipped past the fireball, their drivers handling Bolan's riposte with skillful evasive maneuvering. They were real pros, which didn't surprise Bolan. Nor was he worried. For every one of them, this night was going to last forever. An endless ride to hell for the cannibals.

"Brake it!" Bolan snarled. As Brennan stopped the BMW in front of the black warbird, Bolan slapped a fresh 32-round clip into Little Lightning, fisted Big Thunder. "Move it out!"

Tumbling out of the car right on Brennan's heels, Bolan cut loose with Little Lightning and Big Thunder. Fire and steel poured over that convoy, heavy screaming lead punching in windshields and windows with wrecking-ball tenacity. Two Cadillacs drilled into each other as the onslaught of lead chewed them up. As if they'd rehearsed the maneuver, the other cars formed a skirmish line, bore down on the BMW with reckless abandon.

Bolan sprayed those guys with a long raking mini-Uzi burst. But he saw heads duck beneath dashboards a millisecond before the lead typhoon washed through their cars.

Then, out of the corner of his eye, Bolan saw a sudden motion. He had expected the druglord to make a move on him, and was ready. Thrusting his right arm up, Bolan blocked the sweeping roundhouse, speared a knee deep into Brennan's gut. The punk doubled over, belching out air. Bolan corraled Brennan in a headlock and dragged him toward the warbird, where Grimaldi had opened the cabin door and lowered a ramp. This e and e, Bolan realized, wasn't going to come off easy.

The hunters were hungry. Brennan's hitters were on a march, and they weren't about to accept defeat without going down to the last man.

Bolan booted Brennan up the ramp to the doorway of the plane and climbed up behind him, then turned and cannoned a round from the AutoMag. The .44 headhunter decapitated the first goon in Bolan's field of fire. But the hitters were scrambling into position, falling out of their vehicles with shotguns, revolvers and assault rifles. Bolan shoved Brennan through the doorway, then laid down a suppressing line of fire with Little Lightning. One guy screamed, reeling away from a car door, clutching at kneecaps that were no longer there.

In a heartbeat, Bolan pulled up the ramp, shut the door. Behind him, slugs drilled the fuselage with a relentless pounding.

From the cockpit, Grimaldi called out, "Long time, no see, Striker. What kept you?"

"A party," the Executioner growled back. He grabbed a coil of rope, knocked Brennan to the floor with the butt of his AutoMag, and roped the punk like a steer. The turbofan engines whined, the floorboard vibrating as the warbird geared up for Mach speed.

As Bolan stepped into the cockpit, manned the armament controls, Grimaldi asked, "What do you think? Do we go the distance, or do you want to knock these guys out?"

"In the first round, guy. No dancing tonight."

Grimaldi cocked a half smile, lifted the warbird off the runway. "Roger. I always heard tough guys don't dance."

Grimaldi flipped on the computer-control switches on the console. The target screen lit up. The sky beyond the cockpit blurred as Grimaldi banked Skyhunter. Bolan knew the routine, had trained with Skyhunter on the range at Stony Man Farm. From the air, he knew, it could pick out enemy positions with ASQ Low Light Level Television(LLLTV), and APQ-133 Beacon Tracking sideview radar simply by locking onto engine and exhaust heat. The miniguns had a saturation factor that could put four hundred bullets in a circle 31.5 feet in diameter in a four-second burst. With that kind of firepower, it was hard to miss once the system locked onto target acquisition.

He'd seen the fearsome AC-130 fixed-wing gunships in action in Vietnam, knew Skyhunter would deliver fearsome death from above with the same earthshattering blows as the giant birds, even though its dimensions were much smaller. For guerrilla warfare, Spectre, Spooky, Dragonship had proven more than a match for the Vietcong. Although Bolan was fighting a new kind of war, a different foe from the one in the jungles of Southeast Asia, the enemy was still basically cut from the same cannibal cloth. Skyhunter was a formidable death dealer for waging war against that enemy, Bolan thought, a flying battleship, damn right.

Three hundred meters beyond and one hundred meters below the aircraft, muzzle-flashes stabbed the darkness. The enemy was taking potshots, but they didn't have a hope in hell. Doomsday was upon them.

The console beeped its signal once.

"Now!" Grimaldi said, his expression grim, tight-lipped.

Bolan squeezed the trigger of his firing stick. At the same time Grimaldi worked his minigun stick and unloaded the rocket pods. The warbird swooped over the enemy at two hundred knots. There was a brilliant flash of light one hundred meters in front of Skyhunter's nose. Like giant flares, four balls of fire lit the ground, meshing instantly into one wall of searing flames. Bolan heard the chatter of miniguns beyond the cockpit, but it was all over in the time it takes a lightning bolt to crackle across the sky.

"Insurance time," Grimaldi announced, as he banked Skyhunter, sending the warbird back for a cleanup strafe.

Skyhunter shrieked back over the killing field. Bolan made out the shadows of enemy numbers, running or limping away from the wall of fire. This time, the two warriors opened up at three-hundred-plus meters. Tracers blistered the darkness in front of the cockpit. Hailstorms of 7.62 lead dropped a flaming red curtain over the shattered enemy. One guy had been turned into a human torch by the fireballs, and Bolan clipped that demon with a tracking line of lead.

Seconds later, the sky opened up beyond the tree line, gray wedges of predawn light enfilading the black veil over the carnage.

"Where to?"

"Out to sea, Jack. I'll let you know the details in a minute," Bolan said, then moved out of the cockpit.

Back in the cabin, Brennan was groaning as he struggled to sit up and brace his back against a 40 mm Bofors cannon. Once upright, he found the Executioner looming over him, and his groans became edged with animallike fear.

Bolan leveled his AutoMag at Brennan. "Where is the Devil's Horn, playboy?"

Brennan hesitated. For a second, Bolan thought the druglord would sneer, but then he seemed to weigh the odds in his mind and come to the conclusion that Bolan was the blackjack dealer. And the house was almost always impossible to beat. Still, he wasn't about to make things easy for his abductor.

"You got all the answers, smart guy. You tell me."

Bolan was tired of dicking around with the creep. He snatched Brennan off the floor, mashed his face against the glass of the aft window. "Take a look out there, playboy. We're two thousand feet up and climbing. See those lights over there?"

Brennan stared through the glass. Perhaps four miles away, the lights of New York City gleamed against the murky sky.

"That's your town, playboy. Your home. Your fortress. And it'll be your graveyard in about five seconds unless you answer me. Because I'll open the door and send you on a swan dive."

Bolan let go of Brennan. The druglord's eyelids fluttered, then he closed his eyes as color drained from his cheeks. The soft flesh in his neck pulsed with his rapid heartbeat.

"Thailand."

At the moment, that was all Bolan needed to know.

The Executioner leathered Big Thunder.

"You heard him, Jack."

6

"It is time to eat, *ferangs. Vite! Vite!* Heh-heh."

Mike Tremain dropped his hoe in the sludge of the ankle-deep water and sighed. Food, he thought. Thank God. He was hungry, tired and angry as usual. Today was just a day like any other day, and anger toward and hatred for his captors was the only thing that kept him going. Indeed, he knew, it was the only thing that kept him from dying from the crushing despair that drove many prisoners there to suicide.

I must keep my heart black with vengeance for these bastards, he thought. *Someday...someday...I'll get my chance....* But when would that day of retribution come, if it came at all? How long was it since the Pathet Lao guerrillas had uncovered his covert operation to infiltrate the Devil's Horn? Eight years? Ten years? Perhaps time, he reasoned, didn't really matter anymore. Certainly the MIAs, the POWs there, had given up hope. He could understand their despair. Christ, Uncle Sam had written them off for good, he thought, and the politicians back home weren't about to kick up a bunch of shit in Southeast Asia again over a mere handful of dogfaces. So why should he be any different? He was CIA, after all, and in the eyes of even his own employers he had taken his chances and lost.

Escape from this jungle hell, deep in the bowels of the Thai peninsula, was impossible, he had been told by his captors, and he was beginning to believe it. The poppy fields were surrounded by a wall of forested mountains that formed a natural barrier against any escape that was less than brilliant. A barrier, yeah. Like a fortress. Like a prison. Still, as long as he was alive, there was hope—though daily that glimmer of hope was fading—and when despair threatened to break his will like glass, he turned his thoughts to revenge. To murder.

"Chien!"

The screaming of his overseers made everything seem worse. No matter how weak the slave labor became from lack of food and water, the workers were always screamed at as they were forced to move at a double-time pace. Everywhere they went they were driven by whips, from their cells, to the latrine ditch, to the fields, to mealtime. They were threatened with death if they stumbled from exhaustion or didn't move fast enough.

Now Tremain, formerly of the CIA, felt the inevitable scathing fire of the lash across his bared back. He was dreaming again, the overseer shrieked. He was loafing, and he would be punished severely if he did not move his filthy white carcass. *Fuck you!* Tremain screamed in his mind, though he knew he didn't dare say it.

"Vite! Vite!"

Tremain looked at the short, stocky Oriental. The hatred that blazed from his eyes did not escape Kam Chek. Indeed, his overseer seemed delighted that his brutality could stoke a seething fire of murderous rage in those he punished. The Pathet Lao soldier, Tremain thought, standing there in his dark green military uniform, his bullwhip dripping with blood, was a demon. A Hun. A Mongol. A Tartar.

What had Genghis Khan once said? Tremain asked himself racking his ironclad memory, recalling his study of the Mongol invasion of Europe. *The greatest pleasure is to vanquish your enemies and chase them before you, to rob them of their wealth and see those dear to them bathed in tears, to ride their horses and clasp to your bosom their wives and daughters.* Yeah, that was it. For some reason, those words had stayed branded on Tremain's mind. They described the savage nature of barbarian man, as he had come to know it so well from bitter experience.

And a barbarian was exactly what Kam Chek was, Tremain knew. A heartless butcher who could experience joy only when he was torturing, killing, raping, looting.

Kam Chek smiled. He had a sloping forehead, with high cheekbones that gave his oval face the sinister look of a death's-head. His eyelids formed narrow slits, but still they barely concealed the reptilian wariness of glittering dark orbs that hungered to see blood flow. His hair, black as coal, hung in a silken mane that brushed the knotted balls of muscle that formed his broad shoulders. His mustache, waxed at the ends to a fine needlelike point, drooped below his chinless jaw.

Tremain had seen the Oriental kill more than one man in the field. At his slightest whim, Kam Chek would decapitate a man with his samurai sword if so much as a speck of mud happened to splash his uniform or mar the sheen of his polished black jump boots. Jump boots that Kam Chek claimed to have stolen off a Special Forces paratrooper during the Vietnam War.

Kam Chek stood now on one of the walking boards that had been erected between the irrigation ditches. He rested his hand on the gold hilt of his samurai sword. The smile stretched his thin, bloodless lips. The breath that rasped out of his flared nostrils, blowing the mustache away from his lips, told Tremain that Kam Chek was anxious to use that sword. Again.

"Do you wish to say something, *ferang*?"

Tremain didn't want to say anything; he wanted to rip the monster's throat out with hands and teeth, spit the stinking blood and rotten flesh back into Kam Chek's face.

Tremain's defiant silence made Kam Chek tremble with fury. "Pick up your hoe, *ferang*. Now!"

Slowly, Tremain bent. As he scooped the hoe out of the mud, he glanced at the leeches clinging to his legs. Blood ran down his calves where the leeches had burst after sucking their fill. It was strange, he thought, how a man can get used to just about anything, no matter how horrible, no matter how degrading. The leeches were his constant companions, his silent, suckling enemy. Just as malaria, trench foot, beatings and insults were the only company of his time there in hell. These were things that he didn't, couldn't even think about anymore.

Things like death.

Death would be the final insult, he knew. Because death would deny him his vengeance.

His boots slogging through the syrupy mud, Tremain moved slowly toward the designated eating area. He felt the blood run, warm and sticky, down his back, seep into the coarse cotton cloth of his Bermuda shorts. Sweat burned into the gash on his back. Boots and shorts were the only attire the prisoners were allowed to wear when tilling either the rice or poppy fields. After toiling under a blistering sun in the fields every day without a shirt, Tremain was no longer white, but a *ferang*, a white foreigner. His skin had been charred black by the sun.

The conditions were the same for everybody, unless a man snitched on his fellow prisoners who might be contemplating a breakout. It had happened before, Tremain knew. The prisoners were sized up by their captors, who looked for any sign of weakness in a man that they could use for bribery. Brutality and treachery among the prisoners was not uncommon. Indeed, it was encouraged.

As Tremain looked at the gaunt, bearded faces of the other prisoners, he wondered who was being broken in by the guards as a snitch. It didn't matter really, he told himself, for he would keep his head, he would steel his heart. They wouldn't use him, and, by God, they wouldn't force his hand to betray the others.

Out of the corner of his eye, Tremain saw two guards hauling a body out of the muddy ditch. It was Maxwell. The POW from Miami, Oklahoma, had been suffering from malaria for the past two weeks. Finally, the man had dropped from exhaustion and sickness under the whip of Kam Chek. All of them had heard the terrible gurgling as Maxwell sucked in the mud and water, struggling feebly to claw himself out of the ditch, too weak to get up on his own. But the muzzles of AK-47s never wavered from the chests of the prisoners. And Tremain knew that if any of them had gone to Maxwell's aid, they would have been shot and left in the stinking pool to die alongside the suffocating POW.

Tremain's guts wrenched with pity for the other prisoners, even though he knew they hated his guts. He was a spook to them, considered a traitor because several renegade Company agents had devoted their time in Nam to building the Devil's Horn. But, in his mind, the suffering of the other men was his suffering, regardless of who or what he was. He understood their contempt, their hatred for anything that smacked of CIA; he felt hatred and contempt himself, too, because it was obvious to him that even his own people had abandoned him. Which gave him all the more reason to seek revenge, to prove to the other prisoners that he was unsoiled by the dirt that a few of his fellow agents had smeared the Agency with.

Kam Chek ordered Tremain to sit down in the mud. Three guards, dressed in spotless green uniforms, ladled the food from a rusty cast-iron vat. Seated, Tremain took his bowl. For a moment, he stared at the gummy slop. Clouds of flies and mosquitos swarmed around his head, dipping into the bowls, picking at the black chunks of meat.

Tremain ate. The meat had been charred black, and it stuck in his throat like glue. With the one cup of the brackish water that was issued at mealtime, it was impossible to rinse the bitter taste of the broth out of his mouth, much less wash the food down. He thought it was strange that their captors had stopped feeding the prisoners rice, instead replacing the daily meal with this thick, foul-smelling broth. Beef broth, Kam Chek called it. The change of menu had begun perhaps a month ago, at about the same time that the random killings of prisoners had started.

"Eat, eat, *ferangs*," Kam Chek said, standing in the shade of a tree beside the group of thirty-odd prisoners, his hands on his hips, the oily smile frozen on his lips. "Tomorrow, we begin the harvest. And you will need all your strength, *oui*. Heh-heh."

One of the prisoners groaned. They all knew what Kam Chek meant. Despair cut its razor-sharp edge through Tremain. He looked up, beyond the rice field. In the distance, near the foothills of the rolling green chain of mountains, stretched perhaps fifteen acres ready for the harvest. The poppy plants had reached maturity. The rainy season was over, and the time had come. It was what they spent all year working for. And dying for.

The sun, like some burning, hooded red eye, as much Tremain's enemy as Kam Chek, had slid halfway down behind the mountains of the Central Cordillera. Long shadows now stretched over the delta plain. A hot wind breathed in from the Gulf of Siam, gently swaying the acres of greenish poppy plants on their tubular stems.

Harvest time, Tremain thought, and understood completely the grim mood that had dropped like a shroud over the gathered prisoners. Harvest time meant twenty hours every day in the fields, scraping away the white sap of the green seed pods that were exposed after the brightly-colored petals had fallen off. Harvest time meant a two-hundred-mile forced march to Bangkok, carrying perhaps ten tons of compact morphine bricks and bundles of the pungent jellylike opium. Harvest time, he knew, meant death. As he looked at the heavily-lined, hollow-eyed faces of his fellow prisoners, he couldn't help but wonder who in the punished group would die this time, and who would survive. Survival, he knew, meant endurance. One way or another, he would make this march his last.

As the prisoners ate, Kam Chek walked out of the shade, and stood before the prisoners, smiling. Tremain noticed the strange laughter in the slave driver's eyes.

"Bastard," someone muttered under his breath.

"Eat, eat," Kam Chek urged. "It is good to see that you do your comrades justice, Kermin and Smith and the others, well, my friends. *Oui* they would be pleased if they could see you now, very happy, indeed. You do your comrades justice."

Tremain saw one of the prisoners, a black POW from Cleveland called Larry Jones, look up and level a stare of burning hatred on Kam Chek. Some of the other prisoners stopped eating at that moment, too. There was something particularly disturbing about Kam Check's manner, and Tremain sensed the hatred around him about to explode on this barbaric Oriental.

"What the hell's that s'pposed to mean?" Jones growled, referring to the prisoners Kam Chak had named, men who had recently died at the camp.

"Heh-heh. I am surprised none of you have asked about your comrades. Where is your *esprit de corps*, eh? Why have you not asked about the ceremony you are always allowed to perform in memory of your fallen comrades? Normally, you are allowed to bury them in the courtyard, *oui*?"

Tremain's stomach turned over. His hands began shaking violently. What in God's name . . .

Suddenly Kam Chek slid the samurai sword from its leather scabbard. He stood, legs splayed, as if daring someone to charge him.

"What . . . wh-what are you saying?" another prisoner croaked. "What did you do . . ."

"Ferang," Kam Chek hissed. "You are a fool."

Tremain's head spun as nausea seized him. He dropped the bowl into the mud, bile rising in his throat. He heard someone behind him gagging, retching, smelled the vomit as it splashed into the mud beside him.

Kam Chek's slitted gaze seemed to hide his eyes completely. "What do you think you have been eating for the past month?"

Dear Jesus, Tremain gasped. Kam Chek's harsh laughter rang through his head as his vision swam, and blackness engulfed him. He felt mud, cold and slimy, against his face where he fell. He puked his guts out.

My God, he cried inside in silence. *What madness is this?*

They had been eating human flesh.

For an entire month.

Then horror was temporarily obliterated as Mike Tremain passed out.

7

Bolan was interrogating his handle, and he didn't like what he was hearing. Already Brennan had given him plenty of food for grim thought.

After stops for refueling Skyhunter at a designated CIA-Mossad base outside Tel Aviv, and again at Calcutta, Bolan and Grimaldi were closing in on their objective, now having traveled more than halfway around the world since leaving New Jersey some twenty-five hours earlier. During this long flight, Bolan had pried the necessary information out of Brennan, had mentally outlined his plan of attack and had gauged his chances against the opposition.

It was going to be a shaky crapshoot, he knew. A black-dice affair.

Even though Brennan wasn't feeling like such a top dog anymore, the punk was still capable of gloating about the doomsday net his captors were flying into.

"If you know anything about Auschwitz or Dachau and you don't want to end up in that kind of shit, you'd be smart to head home while you still can," the druglord taunted. "But you're a freakin' Pole, Bolan. And everybody knows you people ain't too bright."

Bolan looked at this germ with ice in his eyes. A lesser man, he knew, might have felt the sting of

Brennan's insults. A lesser man might have become enraged, stepped all over this creep like the worm he was. But a good thrashing, Bolan suspected, was probably just what Brennan wanted. It would make the guy feel like a martyr, sure. And that was a privilege Bolan would deny him to the last breath.

As the drug czar ranted on about the dire fate awaiting his captors, Bolan pretended to ignore him. Bolan was busy, anyway, checking his armament, preparing himself for the death hunt that lay ahead. The M-60, cleaned and oiled, was now belted. The Executioner's dark green jungle fatigues were webbed and fitted with six frag grenades, garrote, commando knife, and the ever-present and formidable Beretta 93-R and .44 AutoMag. Little Lightning, filled with a 32-round clip, rested on the bench beside Bolan. In the lightweight aluminum weapons crate were two M-16 assault rifles fitted with M-203 grenade launchers and bayonets, an Uzi SMG, an MM-1 multiround projectile launcher and a LAWs rocket. After the final weapons inspection, Bolan began stuffing two rucksacks with the supplies the three of them would need for their journey to the Devil's Horn death camp once they hit the Thailand landing zone.

"This ain't no ordinary Southeast Asian hellhole," Brennan rasped. He was seated on a bench opposite Bolan, wiggling his tightly roped hands in a vain attempt to get the blood circulating through his wrists and arms. "When I told ya it was a death camp that wasn't no lie. Ya listenin' to me, Polack?"

"I hear you. And I'll tell you this—you get cute when we land, you'll end up rotting in the jungle. You'll be maggot food. I hope you're hearing that, loud and clear . . . maggot."

Brennan snorted. "Don't say I didn't warn you."

"I won't."

Brennan spit on the floor, his false pride suddenly bringing out the savage in him. "You ain't so tough, Bolan. Sure, you might've busted up some of my people back in New York, but they were punks and nothing else."

"Cut from the same garbage bag as you were?"

"Huh? What do you think you're gonna do anyway? March right into that camp and start blowin' heads off? Shit. You rattled a few cages back home, but you're stepping onto a whole new turf now. That camp is like a fortress."

"Every wall has its base."

"Yeah, well, this friggin' wall's gonna come crumblin' down on your fat head! You're lookin' to take on sixty, maybe seventy guns, smart guy, maybe hundreds. Khmer Rouge. Pathet Lao. Warlords who have shaved more ass in a month than you'd ever bag on a hundred killing fields. I've seen this place, wiseass. Your friggin' rep won't mean fuck-all to them."

"Tell me about the CIA's involvement."

Bolan looked Brennan dead in the eye now. The punk had mentioned CIA before, but Bolan hadn't pressed the issue then.

"Hell, you're the big Vietnam hero, you should know that scene. The spooks all had their hands in the black market heroin during that losing cause. I guess they figured if they couldn't fight the gooks and lop a few heads, they might as well get what they could out of that action."

"Speculation."

"Speculation, bull! Who do you think set up the Devil's Horn? A bunch of three-piece suits out of

Chicago? Smarten up, Bolan. Even the guys who are supposed to wear the white hats are dirty. You ain't in fantasyland anymore, ya jerk.''

Bolan cocked a graveyard smile at Brennan. That renegade CIA operatives were involved in the Devil's Horn came as no surprise to the Executioner. Brognola had already briefed him that errant Company operatives were at the head of the Hydra, outlaw agents who had been suspected of peddling black market heroin during the Vietnam war. It wouldn't be the first time, he knew, that he'd come up against soldiers who'd jumped the fence to land in the dungheap on the other side.

"That only means they aren't wearing white hats anymore, doesn't it?" Bolan cryptically replied.

Brennan shook his head. "Y'know, I just don't understand guys like you. You got guts, some savvy, some muscle. You got some things going for you, and what do you do? You piss it all away for some ideal that's been dead since the age of chivalry."

"You could never understand it in a million lifetimes, punk. But I understand you. And that's enough."

"You're a dead man, Bolan," Brennan snarled. "Don't that mean anything to you? You're fighting a losing cause for some extinct half-baked notion. This is the eighties, pal, and people want the good life. They wanna live and they wanna live it up. Hear me? You ain't normal. You're a bloody, twisted-up abortion, asshole! And if you go up against the Horn, I'll be right there, pal, dancing all over your corpse. You listenin'?" he screamed.

Bolan was listening, all right, but he wasn't about to give this human virus the time of day. No, the punk was right about one thing—he wasn't normal. Bolan often reflected on his life, on his War Everlasting, and had concluded that he was every bit the antithesis of normal. But what was a man, after all, if he did nothing except stand by and watch the world around him degenerate, crumble in the ashes of moral decay? Sure, it was easy, he thought, too damn easy to go along with the flow of the party crowd in life. Walk away from trouble. Turn your head and pretend your neighbor isn't suffering when the fight has broken his back, when he's too weak-willed to stand up and tackle the problems of life that every man, everywhere, has to face.

In Bolan's mind, Brennan wasn't tough, or smart, or even safe in the world he'd created. The guy was dumb. The guy was weak. His sales pitch was to offer the troubled, the weak-willed, the indifferent, the disillusioned a line of coke. *Take this, babe, and your troubles will be over.* Bull. When a guy stopped fighting, when a guy gave in and let his weakness control him completely, then from there it was all just a downhill slide over the jagged edge of the devil's razor.

Men are not born equal, Bolan believed, but they make themselves equal, or better, or worse, by what they do. By what they give. By what they take. He didn't expect a taker, a cannibal like Ronny Brennan, to understand that, and he wasn't about to explain it. The punk would just look at him as if he was some snot-nosed, mealymouthed TV preacher. In the end, a man was convincing only through his actions. Talk was cheap, damn right, and there were plenty of guys with diarrhea of the mouth.

"Striker."

Bolan turned his attention toward the cockpit. There was urgency in Grimaldi's voice. Alarm bells started to go off in Bolan's head. They were now deep in enemy territory, according to the coordinates Brennan had given them.

Combat instincts alerted, the Executioner moved into the cockpit. Four thousand feet below Skyhunter, the jungles of Thailand stretched out before them like an endless rolling green carpet. The sun had cleared the delta plain to the east, was warming up for the intense heat it would blaze down within hours over the ancient kingdom of Siam.

Bolan took a seat next to Grimaldi. "What do you have?"

"A situation, maybe. A flashpoint, definitely. Take a look at the radar screen."

Flashpoint, Bolan knew, meant that radar was picking up a large number of bodies and vehicles. Bolan looked at the screen, which was lighting up like the Fourth of July. Trouble.

"What's going on there?"

"Lock on, Striker, I'll take her down for a look."

Bolan manned the two gunsticks as Grimaldi plowed Skyhunter through a low cloud bank and angled the warbird's nose down. Within seconds Grimaldi cut the altitude to a thousand feet. Hard-eyed, combat senses on full alert, Bolan stared through the bullet-proof Plexiglas. Ahead, the delta plain petered out into a sprawling rice field.

Then they saw it. A firebase.

The compound was a whirlpool of frenzied activity, as the enemy scrambled into position. Soldiers were hopping over sandbags to man the big guns. Still more soldiers poured out of Quonset huts, fanning out in all directions, seeking cover behind walls of drums or securing deeper cover in the outlying bush of the jungle.

Bolan sized up the enemy. He could tell they weren't regular Thai infantry. Thai military uniforms were patterned after those of the United States military, and lower-ranking enlisted personnel wore uniforms resembling those worn by their French counterparts. But the soldiers at this outpost were wearing the dark green jungle fatigues of Khmer Rouge and Pathet Lao guerrillas.

The outpost had done everything but raise the hammer-and-sickle flag, Bolan thought.

"Looks like we've found something," Grimaldi said, tight-lipped. "What do you want to do?"

"Fly over once. If we draw fire, bank her and come back for the knockout punch."

"Roger."

Then, as Skyhunter shrieked over the compound, Bolan saw the multibarreled cannons open up. Smoke and fire flashed from the ground, melding into a twisted maze of belching flames. Thunder clapped above Skyhunter, time-delayed shrapnel bombs blazing into a giant boiling ball of firelead at ten o'clock one hundred yards above the cockpit. Bolan made a quick survey of the enemy numbers below as Skyhunter streaked past the danger zone and soared toward the jungle tree line. He figured about sixty guys with automatic weapons were opening fire on the warbird. So large a force at an outpost, Bolan reasoned, meant they had something important to protect.

The peal of the big guns boomed behind Skyhunter. The warbird shuddered from the rolling concussive blasts.

"What the fuck's goin' on up there, for Chrissakes?" Brennan screamed.

Bolan and Grimaldi ignored Brennan.

Grimaldi sent Skyhunter into a bank, rolling her over, heading back to the enemy garrison. "This is war," the ace pilot growled, his voice trembling slightly from fear and excitement.

The Executioner and his longtime comrade opened fire on the garrison at two thousand yards. Grimaldi plunged Skyhunter nose down into a steep dive, frag shells peppering the air far above the shrieking plane. The warbird raced toward the doomsday numbers, miniguns blazing, rocket pods belching deadly payloads. Bolan knew that this almost ground-level strafe was the safest possible attack run. Grimaldi brought the warbird out of its dive, searing over the enemy at three hundred knots. It would take a mighty lucky hit to knock Skyhunter out of action, Bolan knew, but luck is a tricky bitch. The fortunes of war favor no man.

Skyhunter's first strafe pounded the garrison with hellfire and a wall of lead that swept over the enemy like a tidal wave. Though the scene blurred below Bolan, he managed to see some of the devastation. Bodies jigged, like dancing bloody sieves, corkscrewed to the ground. Explosions uprooted thatched huts with jagged flaming tongues. Crushed debris seemed to float on a sea of flame for a split second, before gushing skyward in one roiling volcanic spray. One 2.75-inch rocket pulverized a deuce-and-a-half truck,

warped wreckage scissoring through limbs like a
chainsaw through balsa wood.

"Let's take it all out," Bolan ordered. "It looks like
an outpost, and I don't want our friends upriver
alerted by a quick radio SOS."

"You're the captain," Grimaldi answered, pulling
back on the stick, painting an azure sky across the
Plexiglas as Skyhunter shot up toward the heavens.

Then, within seconds, the warbird was back on its
kill course. Bolan could see racing flames lapping up
another transport truck, then the fire wall ripped apart
the deuce-and-a-half. Chaos had gripped the enemy
garrison. Bodies were strewed across the compound
and some guys were running pell-mell for the jungle,
having come to the realization that the battle was
about to be lost to the airborne attacker.

Despite the flight of some of the troops, the big enemy guns were still chugging out the heavy firepower.
In response, Grimaldi, who was aware of the fickle
nature of Lady Luck, launched a TOW missile. A
millisecond later, one firebase was vaporized, mangled corpses cartwheeling away from one of the two
sandbagged arenas.

Thunder then cannoned dangerously close to Skyhunter's cockpit. As the cabin shimmied and shook,
Bolan and Grimaldi triggered their gunsticks. Ty-
phoons of 7.62 mm lead blew over the fleeing soldiers. Long lines of coughing dirt were laid down
throughout that shattered enemy retreat, the heavy
slugs stitching up backs, punching open skulls, cutting legs out from beneath the running men.

Then fate took a hand to alter the apparently inevitable outcome of the firefight. Relentless shelling

from the remaining multibarreled cannon on the ground struck paydirt.

Along with a tremendous peal of thunder, a sudden explosive shock jarred Skyhunter, almost toppling Bolan and Grimaldi from their seats.

Grimaldi cursed, fighting the control stick, which was pulling to the right. The warbird, too, dipped to the right and threatened to roll over.

"They hit the right aileron!" Grimaldi shouted. "We're going down!"

Skyhunter shot away from the clouds of smoke and fire on both sides, the sound of rolling thunder trailing after it. As Grimaldi struggled with the controls, the plane cleared the line of trees. The control panel began to beep its danger signals.

"The engine's running hot, Striker!" Grimaldi cried. "We're going to stall out! We're going down!"

The rice paddy rushed up to meet the cockpit.

8

"Strap yourself in, Mack. We're making an unscheduled landing." Grimaldi chuckled grimly.

Bolan didn't have to be told to buckle up, hell no. The warbird's engines had stalled. Grimaldi was fighting the sluggishly bucking push stick in a desperate attempt to keep the tail rudder straight.

"You're gonna get me killed, you assholes, I knew you would!" Ronny Brennan whined from the cabin.

"Some guys just have no sense of humor," Grimaldi growled, tight-lipped.

But there was nothing funny about their predicament, Bolan knew. Skyhunter skimmed the paddy, bouncing like a bucking bronco in its own furious slipstream. As they sailed over a water buffalo and several workers, Grimaldi cleared the paddy and aimed the screaming warbird toward a narrow dirt road that cut through the jungle. Then Skyhunter's wheels hit dirt. Bolan and Grimaldi were jolted in their seats by the impact, almost as if dynamite had exploded beneath the plane. The tree line blurred past the cockpit, teak leaves and vines whiplashing the Plexiglas, scraping the fuselage with a grating sound.

Brennan's face hit the floorboard with a sickening crunch. Blood spurted from his pulped nose. He screamed in pain and terror.

A flock of birds flew screeching from the jungle trees as Skyhunter tore up the surface of the dirt lane.

Touchdown!

Skyhunter jounced along the road, one hundred, two hundred, three hundred yards. Dust plumed behind the skittering Lear jet.

Then, as if severed by some invisible giant steel wolf trap, the right wingtip was sheared off. Like a rhino dying at the end of its charge toward big game hunters, Skyhunter burrowed its nose into the road. The warbird's momentum flipped it over, and the entire right wing was clipped off with a rending scream as it crunched into the ground. Sparks shot from the instrument panel into Grimaldi's face as Skyhunter thudded down on its roof. When Bolan and Grimaldi unbuckled their seat belts they dropped headfirst against the cockpit ceiling. Seconds after they slid into the upside-down cabin, flames ignited in the cockpit.

In Skyhunter's cabin Bolan found Brennan lying on his back and groaning. The druglord looked up at Bolan with hate-filled eyes. Blood from a deep gash above his right eyebrow masked Brennan's face, running slick over the many other lumps and cuts his swarthy mug had sustained since he met the Executioner.

With the cockpit afire, there was no time to waste. Bolan dug a clawed hand into Brennan's shoulder, kicked out the mangled remains of the cabin door, then grabbed Brennan by the shoulder.

"You rotten bastard! Watch what you're—"

Bolan manhandled Brennan through the doorway, gave the punk a stiff boot in the ass to send him reeling into a cloud of dust. Quickly Bolan and Grimaldi gathered up the rucksacks and armament strewed around the cabin, then leaped from the doomed plane.

Bolan checked the road to the rice paddy as he unleathered Big Thunder. He knew the guerrillas would not give up so easily. Indeed, he expected the survivors to gather for a huntdown of the invaders.

And he did not have to wait long before the reinforcements showed. A second later the sound of grinding engines, angry shouts, and the crunch of stalks crushed underfoot reached Bolan's ears.

The Executioner grabbed one of the straps on the crate of arms, giving Grimaldi a much-needed hand. Then he kicked Brennan in the ass again, driving him toward the jungle.

"Get moving," Bolan snarled, "and keep your mouth shut."

"Fuck you," replied the drug czar. But he knew as well as his captors did that the warbird's gas tanks would explode any second, and he needed no more encouragement to put as much space as possible between himself and the impending conflagration.

Together, Bolan and Grimaldi hauled the weapons crate into the jungle. A black maze of teak trees, thorny vines and creepers enveloped the three men. With the muzzle of his AutoMag pressed against Brennan's spine, Bolan urged the druglord deeper into the dark labyrinth. The suffocating stench of rot, of things dead and dying, that had marked every jungle Bolan had ever ventured into was cloying in his nostrils.

Shadows danced on the branches above their heads, then he spotted several white-handed gibbons swinging from the vines. The monkeys screeched, hissed and spit at the intruders in their domain. Cicadas swarmed under the canopy of the treetops, chittering continuously like buzzsaws. Birds cawed from somewhere, but they were invisible to Bolan's searching scrutiny of the darker recesses. As he scraped against moss-covered tree trunks, Bolan glimpsed a giant gecko. The green-spotted lizard hung as if it were stuck to flypaper, its white eyes watching the invaders like the orbs of some mummy come to life.

Then they heard the thunder of the explosion they had been expecting. Grimaldi stopped suddenly, jerked his head sideways as the rumbling peal hammered through the jungle. The shattered wreckage of Skyhunter belched a firewall, and jagged chunks of flaming debris blazed into the foliage. As the concussive roar died away, shrieks cut the jungle air around the three men as panicked monkeys and squirrels flew from tree to tree.

"God!" Grimaldi rasped through gritted teeth. "The love of my life, gone forever."

"Ain't that tough?" Brennan spit.

Bolan had heard enough. Brennan, he realized, had become a serious liability now that guerrilla troops were on their trail. Before the punk knew what hit him, Bolan knocked him over the head with the butt of his AutoMag and dropped the guy into the brush, out cold.

Hastily, the two warriors buried the arms behind a cluster of vines and brush, putting aside those they intended to use immediately. Bolan then hefted the M-60, draped the cartridge belt over his shoulder. Grimaldi slapped a fresh clip into his M-16, cocked the bolt, loaded the M-203 launcher with a 40 mm grenade, slung the mini-Uzi around his shoulder. He was every bit as ready as the warrior beside him.

With grim resolve, they began cutting through the jungle. Thorny vines tore at their faces, slashed their fatigues; leeches clung to their exposed flesh. As they angled through the brush away from the flaming hulk of Skyhunter, they saw an amphibious armored transport truck lumber onto the road. Another vehicle slid in behind the troop column a moment later. Approximately thirty men in dark green camos then moved out in a skirmish line, AK-47s pointed toward the fiery ruins of the jet.

Bolan and Grimaldi slid into cover, crouching behind the thorny roadside brush. His heart hammering in his ears, Bolan waited until the last soldier in the column had moved past his position. He checked the rice paddy, saw no sign of a rear guard.

"You know what to do," the Executioner said to Grimaldi. "Work them from right to left. I'll go the other way."

"Gotcha."

"Let's do it," Bolan snarled, bursting out of the jungle, a panther lunging for its prey.

Bolan and Grimaldi opened up simultaneously, their weapons roaring, bucking, blazing out instant death. Sprinting across the road, Bolan swept his M-60 from left to right, rolling up the enemy's left flank in a red carpet of lightning carnage. As the Executioner's 7.62 mm flesh shredders tore through green camos, Grimaldi triggered the M-203. With a *whumph*, the 40 mm missile streaked away from the grenade launcher, sizzling on a direct line toward the Shortland Mk3 reconnaissance vehicle. The guerrillas, caught by surprise, toppled like bowling pins. A screaming hand of flame then shredded the Shortland.

Grimaldi unslung the mini-Uzi. Triggering it and the M-16, the two-fisted merchant of death moved away from Bolan, taking the mop-up into the enemy's rear and right flank. Like the jaws of a pincer, the two warriors crushed the enemy's flanks, driving soldiers into the center with their scissoring lead trap. Six men leaped from the back of the transport truck, but they were mowed down as soon as their boots hit the dirt. Blood sprayed through the air. Chunks of flesh sizzled as leaking, tattered corpses reeled into the flames.

Bolan pitched a frag grenade under the frame of the armored personnel carrier. The driver flung the door open and came out firing with a Soviet AKM. Bolan pinned the driver to the door with a gut-bursting roar, his M-60 flaming, spent shell casings twirling around his head. Then the frag bomb blew, lifting the transport truck off its wheels. Driver and wreckage meshed inside a flashing red-orange mushroom.

Debris banged off the ground near Grimaldi. Gritting his teeth, the ace-pilot-turned-hellscather emptied the clip of Little Lightning into three mangled guerrillas clawing for weapons. A line of 9 mm slugs stitched the militiamen, thrashing like fish out of water, driving them into dirt already stained black with running blood.

Bolan stood, his legs braced apart. He checked his comrade in arms, winked at him solemnly, then surveyed the slaughter field. Flames crackled. Blood formed pools beneath the shredded corpses. Several bodies, torched by licking flames, became shriveled black mummies within seconds.

It didn't take any genius, Bolan thought, to piece the parts of this puzzle together. Despite its constitutional monarchy and open friendly relations with other countries as a member of ASEAN, the Association of Southeast Asian Nations, Thailand was a hotbed of political unrest and military sabotage, because of its location, if nothing else. Communist insurgency was like a festering sore in the countries surrounding the former kingdom of Siam. And as Bolan knew from his grim experience in the Vietnam war, no border was safe from the iron claws of Igor. If the right people had been bought and paid for by the Devil's Horn, then the seat of political and military power in Bangkok would certainly turn its head away from their criminal activities.

Grimaldi broke in on Bolan's thoughts. With a glance toward the personnel carrier, he said, "We might've used that transport, Striker."

"No good, Jack," Bolan answered. He slung his M-60 around his shoulder and strode toward the outer ring of jungle. "We'd be too easy to spot from the air. And you can bet word's gone out about our arrival."

"Yeah, you're right," Grimaldi acknowledged as he sheathed Little Lightning in a special shoulder rig. "I just don't like the idea of tromping through the jungle when we don't know where the hell it is we're going."

"That's why we've got the playboy."

Swiftly, silently, under the jungle canopy where animals and insects chattered and rustled, Bolan and Grimaldi made their way back to where they had left the unconscious Ronny Brennan.

Parting the shadows, sweeping aside the vines, Bolan approached the druglord just as Brennan pushed himself up onto his elbows.

Then Bolan froze in his tracks.

At first, Bolan had thought it was a branch, but then the king cobra had slithered out of the brush, gliding across the jungle floor toward Brennan. Then the punk saw the serpent, too. His jaw hung agape, his eyes widened in terror at the sight of the black ten-foot-long king cobra.

In a blur of motion, Bolan whipped Big Thunder from its hip holster. *Nyuh-tyong-ahn*, as the Thai Buddhists called the most feared and revered creature in that part of the world, lifted its gleaming, metallic-looking head. With its tongue darting like a red pencil tip of flame, the cobra lunged for Brennan's face.

Brennan screamed.

Bolan triggered the AutoMag.

The cobra's hooded head vanished in a podburst of muck and flesh. The headless body convulsed in death throes, a long, thick whip lashing around in the brush.

Bolan didn't waste a second trying to calm down Brennan, who was still shaking violently. Instead, he just hauled him to his feet by the collar and shoved him toward the dirt road. A second later, he thought, and we'd be on our own right now.

Grimaldi, stopping behind Bolan, looked at the decapitated serpent and muttered, "Jesus!" Then he pulled the LAWs, the MM-1, and a satchel of projectiles out of the brush.

Brennan's indignation at Bolan's manhandling overcame the shock and horror of his narrow escape from the deadly cobra. "You guys are crazy. I ain't goin' nowhere with you!"

"The hell you're not," Bolan rasped, pushing Brennan out onto the road. "You're the big production manager here. You're our ticket into the Horn. And you, Ronny, are going to be the star of the show."

Already stumbling down the road on rubbery legs, Brennan looked behind him at the flaming killzone. He teetered suddenly.

But Ronny Brennan looked like he believed.

Bolan could understand the punk's anxiety. He'd been living that good life at the expense of others for every second of every day of his stinking life. He'd jerked the strings of his puppets, made others dance to his tune, while he was safe inside the walls of his fortress. But Bolan had shown the creep just how flimsy his house of cards was, and just how easily that house could be blown down.

Now the guy was being asked to pay up. And Ronny Brennan, Bolan could tell, didn't like it. Too bad.

If their welcome to Thailand at this outpost was a taste of what was to come, Bolan decided, Ronny Brennan had better toughen up.

In one hell of a hurry.

9

"Then it is agreed, gentlemen. We are the masters of our own destiny. We are the Devil's Horn, and there will be no others. There is no competition outside of us, and there is to be none as long as I am head of this organization. This year, gentlemen, will be a big winner. A very big winner, indeed. To us."

Jonathan Torquemandan raised his glass of Clos de Vougeot to the twelve men gathered before him around the long oak table. They echoed, "To us." The table, heaped with plates of lamb, veal, and steak, trays of cheese and fresh vegetables and bowls of fruit, looked like a feast prepared for a king. And as Torquemandan, smiling, held his salute to his soldiers of the Devil's Horn, a king was exactly what he considered himself to be. No, not just a king, and not just any king, he decided. Hell, no. He was a king among kings. His smile broadened as his people joined in the toast to their success, and showered words of praise upon him.

Like most of his "generals," Torquemandan was dressed in a white three-piece suit made of Thai silk. He wore a diamond ring from South Africa, smelled of four-hundred-dollar-an-ounce Belgian cologne. A handsome, dark-haired, lean-bodied man, Torquemandan was proud of the way he looked. And, as the

king of kings, he was as pleased with the success of his
opium empire as he was proud of his appearance. Indeed, he had come a long way, he reflected, in just
twenty years—from the rice paddies of Vietnam and
the shadowy black-market underworlds of Hanoi and
Saigon, where, as a CIA paramilitary operative, he
had created his pipeline, playing the heroin off against
both the Viet Cong and the American dogfaces.
Reaping profit and expanding his trade. Cutting down
his enemies, while forming formidable alliances.

But recently one of those alliances had been
crushed. Several of his people had begun to echo the
fears that sounded alarm bells in his own mind. And
what had happened to that former alliance was no
mystery to Torquemandan.

"Have you investigated the Engels matter, Jonathan, as you said you would?"

Torquemandan looked at the enquirer, Tuhban
Mongkut, a short, stocky, and very wealthy Thai
businessman who pulled the strings inside the Bangkok government, kept the pipeline open to Turkey and
Germany and France. Mongkut, Torquemandan
knew, was a shrewd, cunning and dangerous man.
Torquemandan recalled more than one story about the
fate of competitors who had crossed Mongkut up.
Torquemandan knew there would be no competition
as long as Mongkut was one of the top two or three
"entrepreneurs" at that table. At last count, Torquemandan thought, Mongkut had a ninth-degree black
belt, and it was rumored that he could kill a man
merely by flicking his middle finger. But Torquemandan would believe that when he saw it.

Still, Mongkut was different from the other men at
his table, Torquemandan knew. Although none of the

generals was enthusiastic about coming to the farm-compound for the annual conference and harvest—even though they stayed in large luxurious suites at the organization's Thai palace—Mongkut seemed to hold a special disdain for the palace grounds and all its comforts and lavish material trappings. No, Mongkut liked to be out in the field, beneath the broiling sun, overseeing the prisoners, working the harvest, demanding the labor force pick up the pace in his own peculiar but brutal way.

Mongkut, Torquemandan reflected, would even march alongside the prisoners on the terrible two-hundred mile journey to Bangkok, the death march, as it had become known on the peninsula. In some ways, Mongkut claimed, the master should appear no better than the slave; that was why he insisted on walking the death march with the prisoners. He maintained that he solidified his status as "a better specimen of manhood" by showing both captives and captors that he was able to share the burden and suffering of a lesser man. Indeed, Mongkut's march was intended to show that he deserved his superior position, that he was a superman who had not forgotten his humble origins.

Torquemandan didn't understand this philosophy at all. In his mind it was a jumble of macho bullshit. But then again, he reasoned, the Asian mind was a strange and twisted maze of ideas based on half-baked myths and legends. He had walked among the yellow men for the better part of forty-five years, and still he didn't understand them. What he did know was that Asians were not to be trusted. They were cunning, underhanded, and would slit a man's throat from behind in a flash if it worked to their advantage. They had a sense of honor and nobility, and they worked hard, sure, and that was why so many of them succeeded so admirably in the United States. Yet at the slightest whim, it seemed, they could turn into devils, barbarians. Strange, he thought, very strange, indeed.

Suddenly Torquemandan realized that he had been staring at Mongkut for several seconds rather than replying to his question. Can this Asian devil read minds? he wondered.

Torquemandan chose his words carefully. "Yes, the incident has been investigated, Tuhban. It was not the work of any legitimate law-enforcement agency, I can assure you all. In fact, it is believed that John Engels, who was a longtime friend and associate of mine, was murdered by a man named Mack Bolan."

Torquemandan got the reaction he expected. Silence froze the twelve men into statues. The pudgy pink hand of Rolly Woods, the three-hundred pound ex-CIA case officer for Thailand and Burma, buried among the strawberries in a fruit bowl, as if the hand were case-hardened in cement.

"Bolan?"

Torquemandan looked at Charlie Wells, another errant Company operative left over from those early days in Nam. Wells was a tall, skinny, hook-nosed guy who was always fidgeting with something in his hands or cracking his knuckles.

"I thought Bolan was dead," Wells said, and cracked a knuckle.

"You heard all wrong, Charlie," Ken Carson, another renegade paramilitary operative, told Wells. "Bolan went AWOL again, the lone wolf on the run from every gun on both sides of the Iron Curtain. Last

I heard from our source in Washington is that Bolan's been brought in from the cold again."

"Hurrah," Wells muttered sarcastically. "So what's to keep this Bolan nut from coming here and climbing our tree, tell me that?"

Torquemandan held up a hand in a gesture of restraint. There was a patronizing expression on his face. Suddenly, the members of the Devil's Horn reminded him of children who had misbehaved for their babysitter and were fearfully awaiting the wrath of a returning parent. Torquemandan could see where this discussion was headed, and he didn't like it.

"Gentlemen, gentlemen, please. Let me refresh your memories. First of all, thanks to Mr. Mongkut, we have the backing, the unofficial support, of key government and military officials in Bangkok. Therefore, we are allowed to work free and undisturbed here. Secondly, we have more than three hundred, mind you, three hundred Khmer Rouge and Pathet Lao guerrillas in our employ, not to mention soldiers of our own placed strategically in Turkey, Beirut and Marseilles—the French Connection, gentlemen, as you know, is no misnomer.

"We own, we control, we dominate, an empire that reaches across Asia and Europe, which extends across the entire continent of North America. This empire nets us close to thirty billion dollars a year. Gentlemen, the projected estimate for this year's harvest is fifty tons, from this field only. At the present rate of production in the Triangle alone, we stand to double our profits in six months."

Ken Carson whistled.

"That's right, Ken," Torquemandan said, smiling, nodding. "Our biggest harvest to date."

"What about the march?" Mongkut asked, his gaze narrowing. "How will a little more than a hundred men carry fifty tons of uncut scag?"

"Each man will carry one hundred pounds," Torquemandan explained, then held up his hand to silence Rolly Woods. "I know, I know. That's far short of the manpower needed. We will use oxen, mules, transport trucks, whatever. The road is rough, it's long and treacherous, cutting through some of the worst terrain in Thailand. Many of you have ridden on the march before...you know how it goes. I daresay that about three-quarters of the prisoners will not make it this time out. Therefore, as you will soon see, nothing has really changed since last year, gentlemen.

"Many of these prisoners are Americans, POWs, MIAs taken away from the Vietcong by myself, specifically to work the crop. The march is the culmination of their effort. To test their strength of character—" *I've got to stroke Mongkut's ego a little,* he thought, *you never know* "—will be their reward. Some are tough and strong, and will last. Others are weak, and will not be able to bear their own cross. Once again we shall see who will survive this test of character."

"You make it sound like some kind of game, Johnny."

Torquemandan leveled a hard-eyed gaze on Carson. The ex-case officer could be an arrogant fool at times, Torquemandan believed. He had warned Carson more than once not to refer to him as "Johnny." If a man could not command respect from his peers, then just what the hell good was he, Torquemandan wondered.

"I am from the Darwinian school of thought, gentlemen. Only the strong will inherit the earth. Whoever drops on the march to our processing laboratories in Bangkok...well, he will be left where he dies. As usual. And there will be no exceptions."

Silence. Torquemandan searched their faces. Some of them, he knew, didn't have the stomach for the march. There would be torture. There would be killing. There would be horrible suffering, and the guards would degrade the prisoners in ways that very few human minds could conceive of. Many at that table would avoid witnessing the march, would fly on ahead to Bangkok. Some would ride in the transport trucks alongside the prisoner column, sitting in the shade of the cabs, sipping ice water, perhaps reading a book or a magazine, or simply mentally tabulating the profits they would reap from this year's harvest.

And then there would be Mongkut. Yes, Mongkut. He would walk. Perhaps this year, Torquemandan hoped, Mongkut would not last through the entire two-hundred-mile march. Perhaps Mongkut would quit, fall out, hop on a truck. Perhaps Mongkut would simply drop dead. This year's march was going to be very interesting, Torquemandan decided.

Suddenly, the double doors behind Torquemandan burst inward. The generals' stares shot past Torquemandan, who whipped sideways toward the doorway, glowering in sudden anger.

The intruder was the Khmer Rouge General Chaika Kan Khang. The short, lean, dark-haired, dark-eyed Khang came to an abrupt stop before Torquemandan. The silver and gold medallions on Khang's military blouse gleamed, rattled, as he snapped to attention. A hideous scar ran down the side of his face from temple to jaw. Torquemandan had never got used to the camp commandant's scar. He had heard that Khang received it in the ugliest knife and sword fight that Bangkok, indeed all of Southeast Asia, had ever witnessed. It was rumored that Khang had killed thirteen men during that battle, which had started in a crowded whorehouse, then spilled out into the streets. Thirteen men, Torquemandan thought, thirteen was an unlucky number. But no, thirteen men represented the Devil's Horn. Reassured, he forced the grim feeling aside, concentrating instead on his anger over Khang's sudden intrusion.

"What is it, Khang, that you have to barge in here and interrupt a very important meeting?"

"Sir, I have some disturbing news."

Khang had a high-pitched, nasal voice, snapped his words out in a way that irritated Torquemandan. Torquemandan saw Khang glance past him toward the table, as if the Khmer Rouge warlord was silently suggesting that they should talk in private.

"Speak up, man. What is it?"

"We have been attacked."

Torquemandan's heart fluttered. Worried voices were grumbling behind him. "What? When?" he asked.

"Our outpost was hit by an unknown attacker, ten minutes ago. Some kind of jet fighter, sir. A black warbird with a white eagle. There were only three survivors from the outpost. It seems our men hit the wingtip of the jet, forcing it to land. Kamdang set out after the invaders with those who had survived the first hit, but they were ambushed and killed.

"The situation demands our immediate response, sir. Kam Chek has assembled a large force and is ready to move out in a chopper and armored truck. The outpost is only three kilometers west, and..."

"Yes, yes, Khang. Take as many men as you need. But, if at all possible, I want the invaders, whoever they are, brought in alive. Do you understand?"

Khang jerked a curt nod. "Perfectly, sir. I know exactly what must be done. I will call up our reserve from the north. That will triple our force. They will be here within the hour. You will have the invaders very soon after."

"Very well, Khang. Take care of it. Dismissed."

Khang bowed, wheeled, left the conference room.

What the hell was going on? Torquemandan wondered.

It was a question he was suddenly hearing from those at his table, too.

Torquemandan rubbed his chin, lost in thought, feeling a stab of fear. He thought he heard some of his associates groan, *Bolan.*

Then he looked at the anxious expressions on the faces of the Devil's Horn.

He did not like to see fear on the faces of men who were supposed to be his allies. Ice pricked his guts suddenly, his heart beat faster in a chest that felt as if it was wrapped in a plaster cast. Goddammit, they're infecting me with their weakness! he thought.

For once, Torquemandan didn't know what to say to them.

10

Bolan, Grimaldi and Brennan moved away from the outlying ring of trees on the jungle's edge. Their clothes were torn, the flesh beneath scratched; their faces were slick with sweat. M-16 in hand, Grimaldi led the way across the savanna, angling west, skirting the marshy edge of a mangrove swamp. Brennan trudged along between his captors, his roped hands holding the large satchel of projectiles for the LAW 80 and MM-1. The druglord grunted beneath his burden, frequently cursing Grimaldi and Bolan as he hefted the heavy sack up closer to his shoulder.

Bolan brought up the rear. The M-60 was strapped around his shoulder, and he toted an Uzi SMG. Twice during the past hour he had called a halt to their northward march so that they could burn the leeches off their bodies with cigarette tips. During both stops he had also further interrogated Brennan about the Devil's Horn prison camp. Unwilling, but afraid to refuse, Brennan had drawn a rough diagram of the compound and the surrounding terrain. According to the druglord, the compound and prison camp and the poppy fields that surrounded them were in a large valley just beyond the next chain of hills. Bolan had originally planned to climb that hill to scout out the enemy base. When night fell, he would have penetrated the hellhole, slain the enemy in silence, one by one, then freed the prisoners. He figured he could have pulled it off without too much sweat under other circumstances. But he hadn't counted on the heavy engagement with the Horn's outpost. Security would have been beefed up by now all around the Devil's Horn prison camp. Worse still, he was sure a full-scale hunting party had already been turned loose to track them down.

Bolan stopped pushing through the thick grass and motioned to the others to stand still. He scanned the savanna and listened. There was a leaden silence over the forested hills and the grassy plain that Bolan didn't trust. It felt too much like the calm before the storm. The complete absence of activity reminded him of death. It was as if death had claimed for itself this chunk of the Thai peninsula.

If the chain of hills ahead did indeed form a natural barrier around the prison camp, as Brennan claimed, then sentries could be watching them right now, Bolan knew, waiting until the three of them walked right into their arms.

Fifty yards ahead and to the west, the plain edged off into more teak trees, some mangroves and brush. Bolan gave the go-ahead, and while Grimaldi led the way into the cover off the plain, he checked their rear and flanks. Just ahead were the hills.

Suddenly, blinking sweat out of his eyes, his teeth gritted from exertion, Ronny Brennan chuckled. "Well, you guys'll be just in time to help reap the harvest. You jerks shouldn't feel too bad, after all, 'cause you didn't come all this way for nothing."

"Ronny," Bolan said in a patronizing voice, knowing he was just one word away from kicking the punk's butt into the middle of next week, "do yourself a favor. Keep your lips pressed together and your eyes peeled."

Brennan cursed. "Yeah, sure. Christ, everybody's a tough guy."

Grimaldi started to forge the way up the hillside, carefully avoiding any obvious paths. It took a full thirty minutes for them to climb the three-hundred-foot slope; their route had been twisting and roundabout and often they had had to hack their way through the brush. Finally, they reached the top of the hill, Bolan and Grimaldi flanking Brennan. Bolan shoved the druglord down onto his stomach, then he and Grimaldi assumed the same position just behind the ridge. Both Bolan and Grimaldi pulled high-powered binoculars out of their rucksacks.

Bolan adjusted his binocs to the five-hundred-yard distance, and swept his gaze slowly and steadily over the scene below him. Quickly he came to the grim realization that Ronny Brennan had not been exaggerating the facts about the prison camp.

From all outward appearances, the camp was indeed a hellhole. A thirteen-foot-high wall of bamboo and barbed wire surrounded the prisoner's quarters. Bamboo sentry towers, placed strategically at the four corners of the compound, loomed some forty feet over the thatch-roofed huts below them. Scanning the compound, Bolan noted very little activity inside the prison walls—only the sentries in the towers smoking cigarettes as they stood guard behind machine guns mounted on tripods. The real activity was taking place in the poppy fields beyond the prison. There, about one hundred half-naked men appeared to be harvesting the poppies, scraping the bulbs of the plants with long flat knives. Bolan counted fifteen guards, stationed to form a tight ring around the slave labor. They all brandished AK-47s. Bolan read the lips of the guards as they cursed and shouted at the prisoners.

Then the sound of a whip lashing flesh stung the air, and one of the prisoners fell under a punishing beating by an irate guard.

Grimaldi flinched as he laid down his binoculars. "Jesus! What have we walked into, Striker?"

Bolan knew, for damn sure. "Hell, friend, we've walked right into hell."

"Those look like they might be Americans down there," Grimaldi said. "POWs, maybe? MIAs?"

"If they are, Jack, they're going home." He turned to Brennan. "Well, Ronny, how about it? You've been here before. Just where do your bosses get their help?"

"I told ya, jerk. From all over. Yeah, there's American dogfaces down there, left over from Nam. With all the flak that's been goin' on about our boys being left behind in Southeast Asia, Saigon got the perfect alibi delivered right on their doorstep, courtesy of the Devil's Horn. For a few dollars more and a little cut of the opium trade, Saigon hand-delivers whatever Americans survived their camps. The rest of those people...hell, I dunno. Peasants, maybe. Kidnap victims, for sure. Diplomats or Thais who maybe ran off at the mouth, tried to rock the boat. This, pal, is their reform school."

"Well, school's just about to be let out," Bolan said, tight-lipped. He could only begin to imagine the horror, the years of suffering those men down there had lived through—those who had been fortunate enough to live. Or was it the ones who had escaped through death who were fortunate? Being imprisoned

by one's enemies, stripped of any means with which to
fight back, was an experience that Bolan was all too
familiar with, an experience in futility and desperation that he didn't care to know ever again.

Returning his attention to the valley below, Bolan
spotted a huge, white-walled palace, perched on a hill
at the far northern edge of the valley. He felt his teeth
set on edge. So near to all that squalor and suffering,
the fat cats of the Horn overlooked hell from some
artificial heaven, some ivory tower, keeping themselves shielded from the misery they inflicted on others. Bolan's guts twisted with rage. He wanted a piece
of those guys. In the worst way.

Brennan must have seen the expression on Bolan's
face. He gestured in the direction of the distant palace. "That's where the bigtimers are, jerks. That's
where the king sits on his throne—Jonathan Torquemandan."

"Torquemandan?" Grimaldi queried.

"Yeah, you heard me right. Like Frey Tomas de
Torquemada, the famed Spanish Inquisitor."

"I wasn't aware you knew so much about the history of torture, you creep," Grimaldi commented.

"Hey, what the hell? You think I'm stupid, or
somethin'? I know a lot of stuff. I know Torquemandan ain't the guy's real name, you know. He's a former spook, he established the Horn about the time of
the fall of Saigon. I've met the guy. Spook ain't no—
whattaya call it—misnomer, yeah. The guy's a ghoul.
He makes like a big Inquisitor in his own right. Likes
to see guys bleed, squirm. He's big on statistics, too.
He can tell ya how many men died in all the big wars.

"But he sure does like Torquemada for some reason. Hell," Brennan continued with a chuckle, "you

get the feeling if there were posters of that guy at work
in his torture chamber, old Johnny would snatch up
every last one of them to decorate his walls. Whatever you wanna know about Torquemada, old Johnny
can tell ya. He says Torquemada burned 10,220 people, that the inquisitors killed a total of 200,000 people during the witch hunts of the sixteenth and
seventeenth centuries. He makes it all sound like some
kind of sport. Yeah, he's real big on that Spanish in-
quisition shit, and if you're around him for a while,
you'll have to listen to it.''

"Like hell," Bolan muttered, knowing right away
just what kind of cannibal he was dealing with in
Torquemandan. The kind who would make turkeys
out of innocents, carve the flesh off a victim's skin
until there was nothing left but a raw, quivering mass,
something that was unrecognizable as a human being.
Yeah, Bolan had seen that more than once, too. People he'd loved and cared about. He wanted to rip the
memory out of his mind with his own two hands—like
the removal of a foreign object that's causing some
festering sore—if only he could. And now, this bag of
slime, this piece of human shit that was Ronny Brennan was sitting there talking about torture as if murder and mutilation were pastimes reserved for a
privileged few to inflict on their victims.

A sudden, though faint whapping bleat roused Bolan from the rage Brennan's recital had aroused.

"Striker!" Grimaldi cried out.

Bolan snapped his head sideways, his ears pin-
pointing the source of the noise instantly. The source
of the danger.

An American-made UH-1H was flying in from the south. From the scene of slaughter at the outpost, Bolan knew. From the direction of their march.

They'd been found out and tracked.

But not spotted. Yet.

The chopper banked, arcing a wide circle over the savanna to the south. A reconnaissance maneuver, Bolan knew. Then the bird straightened out its course, soared nose down toward their hilltop position.

A killing run, Bolan suspected.

"C'mon, let's move it down into the brush!" he growled. He grabbed Brennan, yanked the druglord to his feet.

The chopper lowered, angling over the treetops that patched the foothills.

Bolan looked up, saw the M-60 and its gunner in the doorway of the fuselage.

Brennan twisted violently, wrenching himself away from Bolan's grasp. The druglord ran to the crest of the hill, waving his arms wildly. "Hey! Hey! Up here! Up here!"

Bolan cursed. Like a bolt of lightning, he dashed after Brennan. With all the pent-up anger he'd been feeling toward the punk since their first encounter, the Executioner buried a pile-driving fist into Brennan's midriff. The punk belched air, doubled over.

Bolan heard the whine of rotor blades. It was too late. They'd been spotted.

A staccato burst of M-60 fire opened up from the Huey's doorway. Bolan dragged Brennan off the crest of the hill, shoving him so that he rolled head-over-heels down the slope and tumbled into the cover of brush. A line of 7.62 slugs stitched the rise behind Bolan, missing him.

The Huey angled, strafed down over the crest. Grimaldi opened up with his M-16, tattooed the hull of the Huey with 7.62 mm NATO slugs, sending the warbird screaming, nose-heavy, away from his deadly line of raking fire. It hovered at a point near the end of the ridge.

Meanwhile Bolan jumped down behind the cover of a cluster of bushes and fallen trees. Looking up, he saw a short figure in dark green step into the Huey's doorway, holding a mike. A megaphone boomed out the angry demand of surrender.

"*Ferang!* Give up! It is no use! One hundred soldiers are now on the way. They will begin climbing the hill any second from both sides. You will be surrounded. If you do not surrender immediately, you will be annihilated. This is your only warning. You have five seconds to throw down your weapons and step up to the ridge. Do not be stupid!"

Beads of sweat broke from Grimaldi's forehead as he turned and looked at Bolan. "What now, Mack? We can't do those prisoners any good out here."

"Or if we're dead," Brennan rasped, gasping for breath. "Do like he says, damn you! Give up. Don't be stupid."

Bolan knew Jack was right. On the other hand, what was to stop the warlord and his mercenary army from torturing, then killing, both of them as soon as they surrendered? As for Brennan...well, that guy just wanted to save his own rotten skin. At this point, the creep had gotten them as far as he could, and Bolan could not have cared less about what happened to Brennan now. Still, there was the mission, the destruction of the Devil's Horn, the removal of their pipeline and its poison from the face of the earth forever. There would be no recon or hard probe from here on in, Bolan knew. Hell no. So as far as he was concerned, there was only one possible alternative.

Fight it out. Strike the enemy dead. Punch a gaping hole in that offensive ring of guns. Breakout. Retreat. Regroup. Riposte.

Bolan looked Grimaldi dead in the eye. "I think you know the answer already, Jack."

A grim smile cut Grimaldi's lips. He nodded.

Brennan snarled. "You stupid asses!" He whipped his head around, looked out across the savanna. "Look at that, you fuckin' heroes!"

Bolan was already looking. And he had the numbers sized up.

Two armored personnel carriers with mounted machine guns and recoilless rifles on the turrets surged across the grassy plain. Sixty or seventy soldiers of the Devil's Horn mercenary army swept across the savanna, spreading out in a ragged skirmish line. Bolan spotted three more APCs and supporting infantry cutting through the wide break in the chain of hills to the east, moving into position to storm the hill from behind. AK-47s held at port arms, the mercenary army looked to Bolan as if they were waiting for word from the guy in the Huey. It was obvious to Bolan, at any rate, that the mercenaries' objective was the hill. Already the first wave of that force had reached the foothills. Bolan heard the snap of twigs, the crackle of underbrush being trampled under boots.

The enemy would be there within minutes.

Bolan handed Grimaldi the sack of projectiles and the MM-1. "Hit the ridge, Jack, when I tell you. If they're coming up the other side..."

"Gotcha, big guy. Mow 'em down. I wonder if this is how Napoleon felt at Waterloo?"

"Or maybe the friggin' Duke at the Alamo," Brennan rasped. "This ain't playtime, ya dicks! This ain't no history lesson! Christ, you guys make me sick! My ass is on the line! My..."

The megaphone boomed again. "*Ferang!* Your answer! Now!"

Bolan cut loose with his Uzi SMG, gave that guy his only, his final answer. The line of 9 mm parabellum slugs whined off the Huey's fuselage. Instantly, the guy with the mike flung himself behind the doorway. A second later, the Huey soared away from the ridge like a petulant sparrow whose nest had been violated.

"Now!"

Grimaldi bolted away from cover, charged up the hill.

Bolan turned. He had secure cover behind the grove of trees, the clump of brush, yeah, but that cover quickly petered out, giving way to a series of trails.

Shadows slithered up those trails.

Muzzle-flashes stabbed through the cover from down the hillside.

Brennan howled in terror as slugs whined off bark around his head.

Bolan knocked the guy out with a good right to the jaw.

It was war.

Bolan lifted the LAW 80 to his shoulder and lined up the sights on the dozen figures bursting through the brush on the trail, AK-47s blazing.

11

The Huey hovered at four hundred feet. Chaika Kan Khang stood in the fuselage doorway, the whiplash of hot air fanning his face as he looked down at the hills below. The *ferangs* were scrambling into position along the ridge of the hill. There were three of them.

Fools, he thought. Two forces of his mercenary army were now converging on the enemy, moving up both sides of that hill, like the prongs of a giant pincer. The white invaders would be squeezed inside those prongs, crushed like insects in those mighty jaws. They will be squashed beneath my boot heel, he thought. Or will they?

The pang of doubt that sprang up in Khang's mind was squelched almost at once. Now was the time to watch the drama unfold, to direct the battle, he thought. This was no time for uncertainties and fear.

But the nagging doubt kept trying to filter into Khang's consciousness. Who were these *ferangs*? What did they want? Yes, he had seen the carnage, the utter death and destruction that they had wreaked on his outpost and on the road, trampling his soldiers underfoot like so much powder. Whoever these *ferangs* were, they were good, he had to admit, and they were not just going to lie down and die. Still, they were not invincible. More than a hundred against three

would be a massacre; indeed, the enemy seemed prepared to commit suicide. Even more confusing to
Khang was the fact that one of the *ferangs* appeared
to be bound, as if he was a hostage.

Kam Chek, his hand wrapped around the gold hilt
of his samurai sword, his long black hair tousled by
the rotor wash, approached and stood behind Khang.
His eyelids mere slits, Kam Chek stared down at the
foothills where their men dispersed from the armored
trucks, sliding between the trees like ants scurrying
back into their holes.

"What are we to do next, if the *ferangs* do not surrender?" the second-in-command asked.

"I have already given the order," Khang answered,
forced nearly to shout in order to be heard above the
rotor wash. "The first wave of our troops is to assault. If the enemy engages us, we will encircle and
overwhelm them with our superior numbers and firepower. But I have given express orders not to shoot to
kill."

"How can that happen, sir? If our men come under fire, surely they will not care if the enemy is taken
alive or dead—so long as to kill the enemy means saving their lives."

A thin smile slashed Khang's lips. "You did not
hear my orders then. The enemy is to be wounded, or
at the worst crippled. But they are to be taken alive.
Our men have already been warned that whoever fires
the killing shot will not live to see the sunset. We must
find out who the enemy is, and what they are doing
here. The entire operation here is now jeopardized by
their presence. Only a thorough interrogation and
imprisonment, and perhaps later their deaths, will
satisfy the great white lord on the hill."

Kam Chek nodded, understanding now. Torque-mandan. Kam Chek didn't really like to think of the *ferang* as the "lord on the hill," but he had no choice. Torquemandan was all-powerful on the peninsula. He was master of the Devil's Horn, yes, and his money was all-powerful, too, and plentiful. No, neither Kam Chek nor Kan Khang could argue with the hand that fed them. Nor were they about to bite that hand off.

"In the event that they cannot be taken alive immediately..." Khang began, then turned to look behind him.

Behind Khang and Kam Chek, a group of eight prisoners sat on the bench along the wall. With eyelids drooping over bloodshot eyes, faces bruised and battered, torsos streaked with black lines of dried blood, the prisoners looked back at their tormentors with empty stares. Only one prisoner injected defiant hatred into his eyes, spit on the floor. Khang decided that *ferang* would be the first to die. Khang could not tolerate impudence.

"They are worse than dead now as it is," Khang coldly continued, returning his attention to the hill. "If the enemy has come here to free these men, as I suspect they have, then we will begin a new line of bargaining. I will accept only an unconditional surrender. Nothing else."

Kam Chek nodded. A smile stretched his lips. A low chuckle escaped his tightly compressed lips as he patted the golden hilt of his sword. Yes. He understood perfectly now.

And Kam Chek hoped that the enemy below would, indeed, hold out and force Khang's hand.

MACK BOLAN WAS NOT about to simply hold out.

Trapped in the unenviable position of possible encirclement and annihilation, the Executioner began the breakout.

With a vengeance.

The first wave of Devil's Horn mercs streamed up the trio of trails. They howled, screeched like banshees, triggering their Soviet assault rifles. It was a reckless, pell-mell charge, meant to bewilder, frighten, then paralyze the enemy.

Only the enemy happened to be Mack Bolan.

As lead burned the air around Bolan, he triggered the LAW 80. The round sizzled down the hillside, coasting toward target acquisition. A millisecond later, the 94 mm warhead detonated, a direct hit on the middle trail. The fireball consumed a dozen men, cleaving limbs, shredding flesh. The blast uprooted rotten trees, hurling debris and bodies down the trail. Smoke and fire boiled over the mercs, and flying rubble pounded into the second wave of the enemy.

Bolan gave his opponents no time to lick their wounds.

Like a wraith, the Executioner streaked down the hillside, pitching a frag grenade, then unslinging his M-60. As the shrapnel bomb ripped through the left flank of the enemy and shrill cries of agony pierced the air, Bolan began hosing down the green-garbed mercs with a hellstorm of 7.62 mm lead.

One guy hollered something in Thai. Most likely signaling for a retreat, Bolan reasoned.

And the Executioner turned their retreat into a landslide of tumbling death. Swinging the chattering M-60 back and forth, Bolan chewed the mercs apart. Heads burst open like ripe fruit. Guts spilled from abdomens and lower backs were skewered open by sizzling lead tumblers. The Devil's Horn mercenaries reeled down the hillside, crumpling, slamming face first into tree trunks, hammering head down against rocks and boulders. Men screamed and died. Blood sprayed, and bones shattered like pretzels.

Releasing the trigger, Bolan watched as the survivors fled. Then he listened to the steady *whumphing* from behind.

Jack Grimaldi raked the squat, fearsome-looking MM-1 back and forth. The enemy charge up the other side of the hill seemed to ram head-on into an invisible wall. Then that wall collapsed on the mercenaries like a tidal wave. Within five seconds, Grimaldi had triggered all twelve rounds from the MM-1. The dozen 38 mm warheads cratered the hillside with a series of earthshaking, vomiting blasts. Bodies flew skyward like crimson stick figures. Smoke and flame blazed one searing line across the wave of the enemy's attack, decimated their numbers, crushing them into the ground as if they'd been run over by a giant steamroller.

Grimaldi watched the few survivors retreat down the hillside. He was satisfied. The attack had been repulsed. For the moment.

Looking down toward the prison camp and the field surrounding it, Grimaldi noted that all activity had ceased. As the smoke and haze curled down the hillside toward the compound, he felt as if he was looking at some ghostly tableau of frozen death out there on the poppy fields.

"FERANGS!" BOLAN HEARD the Oriental warlord in the Huey scream through the megaphone in an enraged voice. "You have been warned. Resistance is

useless. You will see that you cannot deny Chaika Kan Khang, warlord of Thailand, indeed of all of Southeast Asia.''

Bolan froze, then crouched behind the brush beside the unconscious Brennan. He looked up at the suspended Huey and cocked his head sideways for a moment. Checking on Grimaldi, he could see him still in one piece, crouched behind the ridge, M-16 in his hands. Ready and waiting in case of another charge.

''*Ferangs*, watch. Watch what your resistance has done.''

Brennan groaned, stirred to life. His eye lids fluttered open, and he struggled to sit up, bracing his back against a tree trunk. ''What the hell's going on....''

''Shut up,'' Bolan growled.

The Huey was almost directly above Bolan now at twelve o'clock. He could see the doorway clearly, but the figures that hung back from the opening were mere shadows. Still, what happened next took little imagination and no binoculars to understand.

A human figure was suddenly, forcibly thrust into the doorway of the Huey's fuselage and pummeled about the head until it dropped to its knees.

''*Ferangs*, I know you have come here to rescue these men, no? They are Americans. POWs. MIAs that your country has forsaken and forgotten. These are your people. Their blood is on your hands for your resistance.''

Bolan saw another person, a man with shoulder-length black hair step into the doorway. For a second, Bolan thought that long-haired figure looked down at him, caught his eye and smiled. Then the man drew a sword, lifted the big blade above his shoulder.

''My God, no,'' Bolan heard Grimaldi growl.

Bolan clenched his teeth, felt the air rasp through his nostrils, hot and stinging with the acid bile of the rage that churned in his guts. He saw the blow delivered.

Then the head sailed away from the Huey, plunged on a straight line for the hillside. A second later, the body tumbled out of the Huey.

Bolan heard someone chuckle over the loud-speaker.

"There are seven more Americans here. You have thirty seconds to throw down your weapons and move with your hands up to the ridge. If you do not...one man will die for every thirty seconds that you do not obey."

Bolan hung his head, screwed his eyes shut. The mission had gone to hell. The cannibals had already sharpened their claws, and their fangs were now pressed to his throat. It was one thing, Bolan knew, to fight on and to wage war fiercely for his life, even if the situation appeared hopeless. It was quite another matter to let innocent men die because of his actions. That, he couldn't let happen.

Grimaldi, he knew, believed this, too.

Ronny Brennan also sensed the inevitable. The druglord smiled through his punished mouth, his grin lopsided on his pummeled, blood-caked face.

Bolan couldn't bear to look at that guy right then. If he did, he knew he might kill Brennan. The maggot was about to claim victory.

Bolan turned away from Brennan, slowly walked up the hill. At the crest, he looked into Grimaldi's eyes. His friend, he saw, was sharing his moment of pain. It was over. They had to surrender. There was no choice. There was no need for words. The silence spoke their personal devastation. Neither one of them could possibly have anticipated such a cold-blooded play on the part of their enemies. Had they, then, underestimated their opponents? It seemed that they had, Bolan thought. Perhaps they had made a fatal error in judgment.

The Huey descended, landed on the ridge.

Ronny Brennan needed no urging to get up the hill. With a smile lighting up his battered face, the drug czar hastened his strides to greet Kam Chek and Khang as the two warlords stepped out of the fuselage.

Bolan and Grimaldi faced their captors. Bolan looked first at the blood of the executed man on the landing skid of the Huey, then at the haunted faces of the rest of the prisoners, still inside the chopper. How long would it be, he wondered, before he looked like they did, beaten, battered, dispirited, curled up at death's door? Hell, in a way, he was already one of them. How long would he and Grimaldi survive? he asked himself. Certainly they faced interrogation by their captors. And torture.

The nightmare had only begun.

Khang squared his shoulders. Somberly, he looked at Bolan and Grimaldi. "It was the honorable thing that you did," he barked in his clipped tone.

No, Bolan thought, it was the *only* thing they could do.

Out of nowhere, it seemed to Bolan, the surviving mercenaries of the attack force converged on the ridge.

Breathless, Brennan finally reached the crest and pulled up before Kam Chek and Khang. He held his bound hands out to them, as if silently beseeching them to cut the ropes off. "Hey, c'mon. You guys know me. It's me, Ronny Brennan. Torquemandan's head cock."

Kam Chek and Khang looked at Brennan as if he was some parasite that would cling to the ass of a water buffalo.

Brennan appeared confused, then angry. "For Chrissake, cut these ropes off me! I ain't with these two jerks. They kidnapped me back in the States. Hey, I'm—"

"Silence, *ferang*!" Khang snapped. His voice was raspy, nasal. "You are as nothing to me at this moment. I will let Torquemandan decide your fate. For now, not another word out of you, or I shall kill you!"

Brennan looked dumbfounded. "Jesus!" he muttered as Khang wheeled, hopped up into the Huey.

"Into the chopper with them!" Kam Chek ordered his surviving soldiers.

The mercs jabbed their rifles into the spines of their new prisoners.

Kam Chek had a final word for the man who appeared to be the intruders' leader. He looked at Bolan and smiled. "You will be very sorry, *ferang*, that I promise. By tomorrow, you and your comrade here will be longing for death. You will beg for it. But it will not come. We will deny you the pleasure of simply dying."

Kam Chek laughed.

An icy chill went down Bolan's spine.

12

The Huey landed in a clearing north of the poppy fields. As Bolan and Grimaldi, their hands tied with rope, stepped out of the fuselage, several of the prisoners stopped scraping the poppy bulbs, looked toward the chopper and its passengers. But the workers' scrutiny of Bolan and Grimaldi ended with the sharp crack of whips flaying their flesh, driving them back to work.

Bolan froze, grimaced in anger and sorrow. He felt as if the rotor wash pounding over him held him rooted to the spot. The cruel slave drivers went about screaming at the workers, striking their exposed backs with lashes. Bolan wanted to wrap his hands around the throats of the bastards with the whips. Damn! If only he could . . .

But Bolan had caught a glimpse of the look in several pairs of those tortured eyes. He recalled the fleeting defiance and hatred he'd seen in the stares of the imprisoned men who now filed out of the Huey. No matter what their suffering, they were still alive. And, yeah, where there was life there was still hope. At the moment, that was all these men had to cling to. Hope, and a burning desire for revenge.

And it was all he and Grimaldi had, Bolan knew.

"Move!" Kam Chek snarled at Bolan, shoving his new prisoners ahead.

Bolan, Grimaldi and Brennan, accompanied by a cadre of twelve AK-47-toting guards, were led up a steep trail. At the top of the trail were massive stone steps, a statue of a three-headed dragon, and a stone railing that surrounded what Bolan guessed was a pool. The palace loomed beyond the dragon statue, gleaming white, majestic.

"I don't understand you guys," Brennan whined at Kam Chek and Kan Khang. "You gotta know who I am. You can't treat me like I'm one of these jerks. You just can't, for Chrissakes, you just..."

"Silence, *ferang*!" Khang barked menacingly. "I will not warn you again. You are wearing my patience thin. I would just as soon kill you, you filthy, cowardly *ferang*. I am a good judge of men. And you are a germ. You are dirt. You are no good."

Brennan looked away from Khang. "Fuckin' gook," he muttered under his breath.

"Did you say something?" Khang snarled.

Fear flashed through Brennan's eyes. "Naw, I didn't say nothin'..."

Boot heels clicked on stone as the three captives were ushered up the steps.

Moments later, as he reached the top of the steps, Bolan faced the principal target of this search and destroy mission against the Devil's Horn. Jonathan Torquemandan. Fanatic admirer of the infamous Spanish inquisitor. Butcher. Cannibal. Human poison. Although there were four other guys in white suits beside the stone railing, it wasn't hard for Bolan to pick out the head cannibal. Torquemandan was all arrogance and self-importance. Bolan got the impression that the guy wanted to burst out laughing when he saw the new captives.

Brennan instantly began whining his case. "Mr. Torquemandan, hey, it's me, Ronny Brennan. From New York. I was here a coupla years ago. You remember? Hell, how ya been?"

Bolan could tell that Torquemandan was not impressed; indeed, the butcher looked threateningly at Brennan.

But the druglord continued to make explanations as the three of them were halted in front of Torquemandan.

"These two jerks hit me, Mr. Torquemandan. Busted up a coupla my places and then kidnapped me."

"So is that how they found me here? Did you lead my enemies to me?"

Bolan saw Brennan go limp with sudden fear, the bombast driven out of him by a few accusatory words.

"It's B-Bolan, Mr. Torquemandan. The fucking bastard, Mack Bolan. You got him. I got him here for you!"

Brennan paused, as if to let the news, which he obviously hoped would be startling, sink in to Torquemandan. But the warlord of Thailand betrayed his surprise by only a flicker of his eyes as his cold stare fell on Bolan for a second.

"If you please, Mr. Brennan," Torquemandan chided him. "We do not use that kind of language here."

"Y-yeah, sure, Mr. Torquemandan, whatever you say."

Brennan held out his hands. Torquemandan looked at the ropes around the New York druglord's hands, then raked a gaze over his soiled clothes, his battered, bloodied face. Torquemandan's nostrils twitched as if some stench was assaulting his nose, then coughed. Finally, he jerked a nod at Kam Chek.

Kam Chek grunted, slid his samurai sword from its scabbard. Wheeling in front of Brennan, Kam Chek bared his teeth in a feral snarl, raised the sword above his head and brought it down before Brennan in the blink of an eye. Brennan shut his eyes, screaming in terror, certain his head was about to be split open. Then Ronny the Top Dog Brennan opened his eyes, saw the shredded ends of rope dangling from his wrists. The space between Brennan's hands had been less than a half-inch. Kam Chek had driven the sword through the ropes without drawing a drop of blood. His mouth agape, Brennan stared at his hands, astonished, then relieved.

Kam Chek burst out in laughter, then stopped laughing just as abruptly.

Torquemandan smiled at Bolan. "So, this is Mack Bolan. The feared Executioner. Sergeant Mercy, I believe they called you in Vietnam . . . hmm. And who is this?" he asked, looking at Grimaldi.

Grimaldi stood in silence.

"That's his fu-pilot, Mr. Torquemandan," Brennan answered, rubbing his wrists. "His name's Grimaldi, big hotshot fly-boy. Thinks he's the Red Baron or somethin'. Until you guys blew the wing off his pet project. Some kind of warbird, a Lear jet, I think. Yeah, they busted me up in New York, all right, thought they were real tough. Look at 'em now, huh. Heroes. Big, tough guys, yeah."

Torquemandan drew a breath. In a patronizing voice, he told the New York drug czar, "Mr. Brennan, you are excused. There is a servant there on the patio. He will show you to your room. Get cleaned up and I shall speak with you later.''

Brennan appeared to shrink at Torquemandan's words of dismissal. Like a whelp, Bolan thought, that's just been beaten by its master. Without protest, Brennan departed.

Torquemandan turned his attention to Bolan but remained silent for a moment as if considering what he should do with the Executioner and Grimaldi.

Bolan read the madness in Torquemandan's eyes. He had seen that look many times before. The look of a ravager, a cannibal who has built an empire, a house of cards on the flesh and blood of other people. Such a guy cherished what he had, kept a tight grip on his life—which he believed was more valuable and worthy than other men's lives—but suspected, feared, that in the end he would be less worthy than the poorest of men.

Yeah, Bolan knew the look, all right. How many Mafia thieves and butchers had he sent into the void wearing that plastic face? When a man lived like shit, Bolan had observed over and over again, in the end that was all he would be. Shit. Gloss over the manipulations with an infinite bank account, shield the house of cards with material wealth, cover the fakery and arrogance with the peacock feathers of one who has degraded others to enrich himself. Without backbone, without the will to do the right thing, Bolan knew, power or material success, all meant nothing. In fact, they meant less than nothing. In the meantime, though, a proud, ball-less peacock like Torquemandan would keep on savaging the good and the decent and the innocent. He would keep piling cards on top of his roof. One of these days, though, Bolan thought, such a man would draw the joker. The joker in the deck with the death's head and the maggot-dripping sickle.

Torquemandan clasped his hands behind his back. "Tales of your exploits, Mack Bolan, reach far and wide. I have followed your, uh, crusade through my contacts in the CIA. In fact, I have always hoped that someday our paths would cross. Particularly after the unfortunate affair with John Engels."

Bolan remembered well the renegade CIA operative who had run a drugs-and-arms pipeline from his stronghold in the wastelands of New Mexico. Bolan had dealt Engels the grim joker. If he had suspected that Torquemandan was the mastermind behind the Engels pipeline, Bolan would have gotten to Thailand sooner. A lot sooner.

"You are a man of great strength and courage, Bolan," Torquemandan continued. "I wish I had more like you under my employ. Perhaps, in time, you will come to change your allegiance?"

"I doubt it."

Torquemandan flashed Bolan a crooked grin. "I see. Very well. I've been considering what to do about the two of you and have now reached a decision. It's harvest time for our poppy crop, gentlemen, and we need all the help we can get to work the fields. You will join the other prisoners in the work of the harvest, under the supervision of Khang and Kam Chek here. You will be treated like the rest, or rather, you will be treated worse than they are. In several days, you will march with the others to Bangkok, carrying the harvest to our laboratories there.

"Do not, I repeat, *do not* attempt to escape. Several have tried, and they all have met the most unfortunate of ends. For the rebels among our inmate population we have reserved a very special place. It is called, simply, the Black Room. See that you obey. See to it that you do not cause any trouble at all. If a man survives to leave the Black Room alive, then he has been reduced to something less than a vegetable. Useless. Mindless. He is usually shot, or impaled, shortly thereafter.

"I do not kill you right away for one very good reason, Bolan, and one reason only. Your crusade has damaged links in my pipeline, has created something of a panic in the less stout-hearted individuals within the Devil's Horn organization. I mean that you have cost me men, time and money. Harvesting the crop will be your temporary reprieve from a worse punishment. In blood, sweat and pain, you will earn me back what you have cost me by your crusade."

Torquemandan suddenly turned to Khang and snapped, "Khang, casualty report."

"We do not know yet, sir," came the reply. "My guess is between one hundred and one hundred and fifty killed and wounded."

A dangerous rage burned in Torquemandan's eyes. "Find out the numbers before sundown, Khang. When you do, take Bolan and Grimaldi. Tie them up in the square, then assemble the other prisoners. You know how it is always done. For every man that has been killed or wounded, you will administer a blow to Bolan and Grimaldi in turn. Use both whip and fist."

"Yes, sir!"

Torquemandan looked at Bolan for another stretched second. "I don't like what I see in your eyes,

Bolan. I suspect you are harboring thoughts of vengeance. You won't, uh, be feeling so heroic come sundown, I assure you. Get them out of my sight!'' he growled at Khang.

The guards closed on Bolan and Grimaldi, grabbed them by the shoulders and shoved them toward the steps.

Bolan clenched his teeth. He would bide his time, he vowed. At the moment, he was just another card in Torquemandan's house.

But that was going to change, he told himself.

A black storm began to build in Mack Bolan's heart.

BOLAN AND GRIMALDI GOT a taste of prison life under the scourge of Kam Chek's whip right away. As soon as the captives were ushered between the rows of poppy plants, guards descended on them like vultures on carrion. Savagely, the guards ripped the shirts off the backs of the two new prisoners, their long-fingernailed, dirt-grimed fingers slicing over flesh like talons, gouging out skin from the backs of Bolan and Grimaldi.

Rage continued burning ever hotter in Bolan's guts. He looked at the six Oriental mercs, their AK-47s trained toward his chest. There was no way out, he told himself, calming his fury to cold steel in his belly. It looked bad. In Grimaldi's eyes he saw the same impotent wrath he himself was experiencing. He could feel the eyes of the other prisoners on his bared, bleeding back.

Kam Chek screamed at the prisoners to return to their work.

Whips cracked through the air.

Bolan winced as the metal-studded tip of the whip tore into his back between his shoulder blades. He turned, hate blazing in his eyes as he looked at Kam Chek.

"Ferang!" the long-haired Oriental thug shouted. "Get to work. There is no loafing here. We give you no time to stand around and feel sorry for yourself, you miserable white pig!"

A warm trickle of blood rolled down Bolan's back. The sun blazed, sinking on its waning arc toward the mountains in the west. Bolan felt the sun's fire on his shoulders already—like knives digging into his skin.

A guard threw two knives between Bolan and Grimaldi.

"Ferangs!" Kam Chek barked. "You will be shown only once what to do. Listen."

Bolan and Grimaldi picked up the knives.

"What I wouldn't give to drive this through his guts!" Grimaldi whispered to Bolan.

Kam Chek's whip sizzled through the air, cracked off Grimaldi's cheek like a pistol shot. Blood welled up in the welt on Grimaldi's face, then burst like a bubble and poured down his cheek.

With an iron will hardened by years of suffering and hardship, Bolan kept a tight rein on his impulse to charge at Kam Chek and rip his throat out. Grimaldi trembled with rage, took a half step toward Kam Chek. Bolan dropped a hand over Grimaldi's shoulder. It was enough. Grimaldi got his anger under control. He was not about to commit suicide, as a half-dozen AK-47s swung his way.

"Watch!" Kam Chek shouted in his usual staccato manner.

One of the prisoners, a tall man whose skin hung in folds off his protruding bones, was shoved toward Bolan and Grimaldi. Quickly, with fingers that worked with a speed and dexterity that surprised Bolan, the prisoner demonstrated the technique of harvesting the poppy plants. He began cutting a series of shallow incisions across a poppy bulb with his curved knife. A white sap began to seep out of the slits, congealing on the surface of the bulb, where its white color changed to a brownish-black. Swiftly but carefully, the prisoner scraped the seepage off the bulb and into a large bucket.

"You must scrape the bulbs completely dry, *ferangs*!" Kam Chek rasped. "The first time that you let the sap miss the bucket, it is the whip. The second time, it is two lashes, and so on. We do not tolerate sloppiness. Prisoners who are sloppy do not last long around here. Understand?"

Bolan and Grimaldi stood in defiant silence as the prisoner who had given them the demonstration was pushed back to his place in the row.

Kam Chek's gaze narrowed. He squared his shoulders, sucked in a deep breath. "I can see," he said in a low voice, his tone edged with menace, "that I am going to have trouble with you two right away, *oui*. I will be watching you very carefully, *ferangs*. Get to work!"

With their curved knives, Bolan and Grimaldi began cutting incisions on the poppy bulbs. Bolan listened attentively as he worked. Apart from the scraping of knives, the scratching of buckets being dragged over dirt, a heavy silence prevailed. A silence that hung in the air with all the oppressive weight that had accumulated on the shoulders of these enslaved men over the years. How in the hell could this place have existed for so long? Bolan wondered. But he knew the answer right away. Somebody had been bought out to keep his mouth shut.

The rage continued to knot Bolan's guts tighter and tighter. While Ronny Brennan had been living like a king in New York City, men had been suffering and dying here in this poppy field. Hardship, grief and, ultimately, death had kept Ronny Brennan in his big penthouse suite, put the fancy expensive threads on his back, imported the finest champagne and wine from France. It was bloodsucking at its ugliest, its vilest. If Mack Bolan had ever had a reason to crush men for their cannibalism, this was it. Here, under the broiling sun of Thailand, with the blood flowing freely down his back, with the threat of constant death held over his head, with the humiliation of imprisonment and the certainty of torture ahead, this was it. Because whatever he suffered, Bolan knew that many others here had gone before him.

There were a lot of tabs that needed paying up.

An hour passed. Time, though, Bolan sensed, meant very little here. Every minute of every hour of every day would be filled with the same routine. Violent death and torture would be the only break in that routine. He found his mind becoming shrouded with gloom. There would be a way out, he told himself. The time would come. He would know when the time was right. And he would act. But first he would have to reach some of the other prisoners. He could not revolt against Kam Chek and his mercenaries alone, and hope to win.

Suddenly, Bolan heard a groan, a pitiful but piercing sound, like that of a wounded animal slumping down in its death throes. He looked up and saw a prisoner topple to the ground. The man was four feet away, between Bolan and three other prisoners in front, behind and on the other side of him. Not one of the three moved to help their fallen comrade, didn't even look at the motionless, emaciated, sun-blackened heap. What the hell is this? Bolan wondered. But he knew. Through fear of death, the brutal guards had crushed even the last crumbs of humanity out of these men. They had been reduced to something below the level of animals; they had become automatons.

Bolan dropped his knife. He bent over the fallen man, whose shriveled lips trembled open.

"W-water...p-please...w-water..."

"Easy, guy," Bolan said, biting down a curse. He could tell that this man was going to die soon, very soon. Dehydration. Heatstroke. The prisoner's skin was hot and dry to Bolan's touch, his pulse rapid. The guy was burning up. He needed shade, had to be wetted down.

Bolan looked up, about to ask one of the guards to give him a hand. Then he saw Kam Chek striding toward him, realized at last just how naive his actions must have looked to the other prisoners. But as far as Bolan was concerned, when a man stopped caring he was better off dead.

"Ferang!" Kam Chek screamed. "Get away from him! Get away!"

The whip cracked through the air behind Bolan. It bit like a snakebite into his flesh, once, twice.

Three times was enough.

Bolan sprung, his hand snapping out in a blur of speed. He caught the whip in one hand, a move that left the guard holding it frozen in astonishment. And fear. Bolan looked that guard dead in the eye, and the guy seemed to shrivel up inside of himself.

His arm muscles ripped and rippling, Bolan tugged on the whip, drew the guard a half step toward him. The guard's jaw went slack, as if he was about to scream for mercy, for rescue before being hurled into the abyss.

Steel flashed through the air.

Out of the corner of his eye, Bolan saw the blade streaking toward him, falling, it seemed, straight from the sky. He knew he couldn't react fast enough to avoid the death blow.

"Mack! No!" Grimaldi hollered.

The sword sliced through the strained leather of the whip. Bolan toppled backward into the poppy plants. He looked up at Kam Chek, who wore an expression of demonic fury. AK-47 toting guards swarmed behind Kam Chek.

"I could just as easily have killed you, *ferang*. Next time, I will. You get one warning. A man falls in the field, you are to leave him where he lies. Do not touch him. Do not even look at him. The second offense is punishable by death. Get up, *ferang*," Kam Chek whispered menacingly.

Slowly, Bolan stood. He glimpsed the relief on Grimaldi's face, heard his sigh.

Then a strange gleam lit up Kam Chek's eyes. The long-haired Oriental mercenary smiled. "General Khang has returned. You and your friend are to accompany me. Now."

Kam Chek chuckled.

Bolan felt blood from the new welts on his back dribbling under the waistband of his pants. He looked at the fallen prisoner.

Vacant eyes stared back at him. Flies buzzed in and out of the man's open mouth.

13

Shortly after sundown, four guards marched Bolan and Grimaldi into the prison courtyard. Kam Chek had ordered that all the prisoners be assembled, and his soldiers had rounded up the inmate population and lined them up in front of their thatch-roofed huts. They were now shackled, hand and foot, in chains. They stood slouched, slumped, utterly still. They were shells of the men they had once been, so very long ago.

With the setting of the sun, deep shadows had begun stretching over the prison. Klieg lights had been turned on, bathing the bamboo, barbed wire and huts in a pale white sheen. Birds chirped and cawed from the surrounding jungle. The sky, fading slowly from gray to black, hung over the prison like some misty velvet curtain.

As he was led to the bamboo stakes, Bolan expected the worst, steeled himself for the inevitable agony of the punishment that was to be meted out. He wouldn't be spared, he knew.

Roughly, cursing Bolan and Grimaldi, the overseers roped the hands of the two men to the poles. Bolan noted the despondency that was beginning to creep into Grimaldi's eyes. He could offer his friend no words of comfort, only a look that he hoped Grimaldi would interpret as *stay hard*.

Grimaldi gave Bolan a shallow nod, letting Bolan know that the message was received and appreciated.

Chaika Kan Khang, dressed in a spotless green military uniform, stood beside the line of prisoners. He clasped his hands behind his back, jerked a nod at Kam Chek to begin.

"It has been determined by the Khang Imperial Revolutionary Army of All Enslaved Oriental Peoples of Southeast Asia," Kam Chek announced to Bolan and Grimaldi, "that one hundred and six of our comrades have been killed, wounded or are missing." Kam Chek glared grimly at Bolan and Grimaldi.

Bolan thought he heard someone mutter, "Bullshit," but if Kam Chek heard the remark he chose to ignore it.

"We will round off the number of blows to a nice even figure—one hundred, to be divided between the two of you." Kam Chek looked at the prisoners, seemed to search their faces for a moment. "I need volunteers. You. And you." He gestured at two men who were hanging their heads as if in shame. "Step forward."

Guards grabbed the two men he had appointed, shoved them toward Kam Chek. Bolan read the fear in the eyes of those men and saw something else, too. Pity. Bolan knew how the torture would go, and the reasons why it was to be delivered in that way; it was one of the oldest methods of breaking the spirit of an enslaved or imprisoned man. The captors forced their captives to brutalize one another—perhaps hoping to set them at each other's throats, perhaps in an effort to weed out the weak ones, the prisoners that Kam Chek considered inferior, deadweight. It was also a way to let new arrivals to this hell know that they had no friends there, that they could expect no sympathy, no mercy, no consolation or help from the others.

Kam Chek held out a leather belt to one of the two men. When the man didn't take the belt immediately a guard clubbed him over the head with the butt of his rifle. The man dropped to his knees, vomited.

Livid with rage, Kam Chek screamed at the man, kicked him in the ribs. "Get up! Get up! Have you no pride, *ferang*? Sniveling like some worm before your master!"

Bolan's teeth were set on edge. Out of the corner of his eye, he saw a look of depthless pity and sorrow shadow Grimaldi's face. Grimaldi, he knew, was a man of great courage. The guy was bleeding inside. Not for himself, hell no.

The second prisoner took the belt that was handed to him, but the other wretch had to be hauled to his feet by the guards. Shaking in terror, that man, too, reached for his belt, as a tear broke from his eye.

"You disgust me," Kam Chek snarled when he noticed the man's emotion. Then he stepped behind the two prisoners, shoving them one at a time behind Bolan and Grimaldi. "You are no man. I have seen little girls with more courage than you. If you do not stop your sniveling, I will cut off your balls right here! Do you understand?"

Kam Chek spit on the back of the man's head, and continued to hurl insults at the prisoner for a full thirty seconds. Then he shouted, "Begin!"

Bolan clenched his fists. He heard a belt crack flesh, saw Grimaldi flinch.

The man behind Bolan whipped his belt through the air, slapped Bolan on the shoulder with the thick leather.

"Harder!" Kam Chek screamed.

Again, Bolan took the belt on his shoulder. But the second time the blow merely grazed his skin, rolling off him like the fluttery edge of a feather.

"Harder! Harder, you coward, harder! Those blows do not count! Harder!"

Bolan heard a sob break from the throat of the prisoner behind him, a strangled cry for deliverance.

The wretched prisoner fell to his knees. He buried his face in his hands and wept. "I can't . . . I can't do it . . . I . . ."

Furious, Kam Chek screamed something in his native tongue.

Bolan felt the anguish, the hatred burn through his guts. He knew with a terrible certainty what was going to happen next.

"I can't . . . I can't . . ."

The samurai sword sprang from its scabbard. Snarling, Kam Chek fisted the hilt with both hands.

Bolan heard the decapitating blow, a wet dull sound, followed by a thud. Bolan looked down and saw the severed head roll between his legs. Dead eyes stared up at Bolan, white orbs frozen forever in horror and grief.

Bolan's throat constricted, his heart felt like a block of ice in his chest. He would be free again, he told himself. He would escape. He must. *There will be vengeance,* he vowed. *And it will be a terrible vengeance on you, Kam Chek, you goddamn soulless butcher.*

Kam Chek now directed his rage toward the other prisoners, seeking in vain for a volunteer to replace the beheaded man. "Are there no men among you? Are you all women, cowering in fear of pain? I will kill you all, if that's what it takes.''

When no one volunteered, another prisoner was selected and pushed bodily into position behind Bolan.

The headless body was left where it lay.

The belt-wielding prisoners needed no more urging. They flayed Bolan and Grimaldi with all the strength they could muster in their weakened condition. After a dozen blows, long welts streaked the backs of Bolan and Grimaldi. Then the blistered skin broke open. Blood began to trickle, then stream down their backs.

Kam Chek still screamed, ''Harder!''

Fire raced through every inch of Bolan's body. His muscles felt as if they were being torn open by razors. His head swam with nausea, an acid taste filling his mouth as he choked back the bile. He felt himself slipping into unconsciousness; the screaming, the cursing, the crackle of leather as it struck his flesh became a distant, distorted jumble of noise in his ears.

Then the guards threw buckets of salty water over Bolan and Grimaldi.

With a jolt, Bolan felt his strength return with the fire of the salt water sinking into his stripped flesh. Then he shivered, an icy chill running down his spine, a white light flashing before his eyes.

Urged on by the screaming Kam Chek, the prisoners began pummeling Bolan and Grimaldi about the face, head and back with their fists. Kam Chek spurred the prisoners on with his whip, lashing them front and back, directing their blows with his stinging leather. For a full two minutes, Bolan and Grimaldi were punching bags. And, within a matter of seconds, their faces and torso were turned into something that resembled raw hamburger.

Bolan tried to roll with each punch, but each blow that connected brought him that much closer to unconsciousness. He could tell that the prisoners inflicting his punishment were aiming their blows carefully, staying clear of the nose, the ribs, any bone that could be easily broken, any soft area that could be crushed; they were avoiding lethal strikes that could send bone splinters into the brain or rupture vital organs. And this fact told Bolan that he and Grimaldi were meant to survive this beating. In the mind of someone like Kam Chek, Bolan realized, death would seem to be too easy an escape. No, the cannibal wanted the two of them to live with the pain and the humiliation, wanted them to feel the sucking fires of their own hatred, to taste the bitterness of their impotent rage.

Kam Chek kept screaming at the men not to hold back on their punches, but at this point not even the brutal master's whip could force the emaciated prisoners to do what their failing strength would not let them do. Finally, the two prisoners collapsed in exhaustion.

Blood poured out of the mouths of Bolan and Grimaldi. Bolan slumped, his vision fading in and out, the ropes biting into his wrists. Grimaldi heaved a ragged breath, then his head lolled to the side and he went limp in his bondage.

Disgusted, Kam Chek kicked his forced torturers in the face. Then the whipmaster unsheathed his samurai sword. With four lightning strokes, he sliced through the ropes that bound the hands of Bolan and Grimaldi. Both men toppled face first into the dust.

Blood formed a puddle beneath their faces, blackened the dirt.

Bolan felt a boot plunge into his gut. With a stubborn effort, he let the momentum of the kick flip him onto his back.

There was a terrible ringing in Bolan's ears, a sound that pierced his throbbing brain as if an ice pick had been lanced through his eardrums. Through a gray fog, he saw Kam Chek loom over him, resting clenched fists on his hips. If only he had the strength, Bolan thought, he would drive his boot through the guy's nuts. If only... if only...

Then he thought about Grimaldi, wondered if his friend had survived. If he hadn't, Bolan vowed there would be hell to pay.

Kam Chek smiled. To Bolan the expression looked like a vision from his worst nightmare. The Oriental barbarian spoke, in a gloating voice that stirred Bolan's rage like a stick in smoldering ashes.

"Ferang."

That word again, Bolan thought. That voice... It echoed through his head, a swirling, swollen heat.

Dimly, Bolan saw Kam Chek's smile disappear. Before he lapsed into blackness, he heard the final words.

"Welcome to hell."

14

Ronny Brennan felt as if he was back at the top. Feeling good. Looking like a million bucks. Absolutely a prize-winning stallion in white silk threads, ready for the women. He had survived the crisis of being captured and used like a pawn by Bolan, and he felt that once again his world was back in order.

Hell, he thought, this could turn out to be his return to triumph. He was back among the kind of people who appreciated him, not the gung ho, moronically idealistic psychos like that Bolan and Grimaldi. He hoped they were eating shit right now. If only they could see him here in the banquet hall, in all his glory. Solid gold incarnate. What was it his favorite late-night talk-show host said? "It's going to be a magic night." Yeah, that was it. A magic night. Brennan said those words to himself a few times, relishing their sound.

Seated at the opposite end of the table from Torquemandan, Brennan was stuffing his belly with lamb, pork, an assortment of cheeses, fruit, caviar, smoked salmon, shrimp. God, he thought, this Torquemandan knows how to live. If there's one thing this Italian boy can appreciate, it's good eating. Brennan almost said, Hey, Torquee, baby, pass the spaghetti, the vino, will ya, then remembered where he was. And who he was. And what he was. No. Ronny Brennan was not the top dog here. Ronny Brennan was strictly small potatoes, a mere page at the foot of the king's throne. Suddenly that feeling of smallness and unimportance dampened his sense of well-being and made him very uncomfortable indeed. And just a touch angry.

Adding to his discomfort was the look in Torquemandan's eyes. Cold. Distant. Brooding. Like the guy wanted to devour something, or somebody, Brennan thought. How come I get the feeling I'm being set up for some kind of fall, huh? All Ronny wanted to do then was make tracks for Bangkok and get on the next plane for the States. What was going on in the weird bastard's head, anyway? Brennan wondered. But he forced a smile at Torquemandan when he realized suddenly that his host had caught him staring.

Torquemandan cleared his throat loudly, formed a steeple with his hands. "Ronald. There are some things that we need to discuss. Serious matters, which, uh, need some clearing up. We must talk."

Brennan looked at Torquemandan carefully. What's with this Ronald shit? he thought. Nobody talked to him like that. Like he was some kind of snot-nosed kid. Some kind of frigging dog that got patted on the head when it fetched the master's bone.

"Okay. Shoot, Mr. Torquemandan," he replied, hoping he was hiding his misgivings.

Torquemandan nodded, smiled. "Yes. Shoot, indeed. It's been what, two years since I last saw you, Ronald? Our only meeting ever, as I recall."

"Yeah." What the hell's the point, Brennan wondered.

"The presence, indeed the violent intrusion, of Mack Bolan here at the headquarters of our Devil's Horn organization has caused some of our more prominent members to become a little . . . edgy."

Brennan shrugged, as if he didn't understand what Torquemandan was talking about. But he knew. The so-called prominent members of the Horn were the guys in suits within the legitimate circles of the established Thai government. He figured some of them had been dining with Torquemandan at this very table earlier, though when he had been conducted by guards to the banquet hall, no one was there but Torquemandan. Those guys were useful up to a point, Brennan thought, but when the heat came down they weren't worth a shit. They would be the first ones to run and hide. And, if worse came to worst, they would merely start pointing fingers, naming names, they would cut their losses and seek out the next rainbow. Brennan had no use for chickenshits like that.

Torquemandan rested a large hand on the table. A dark look shadowed his face. "Ronald . . . we need to know just how badly this Bolan has damaged your New York operation. And why he would pick on you so suddenly."

Accusation time, huh. Brennan felt the anger slice through his guts, but made a conscious effort not to appear defensive or resentful. Torquemandan was, after all, a businessman, and his gripes, if he had any, were legitimate, Brennan reasoned, the guy was just trying to serve the best interests of the Horn.

"I'm not sure why this Bolan came after me, Mr. Torquemandan, honest."

Torquemandan smiled patronizingly. "I am not disputing your honesty, Ronald. Feel free to correct me if I am wrong."

Brennan didn't know what to make of that statement. Hurriedly, he continued, "Bolan busted up a crack house of mine, Mr. Torquemandan. He bagged one of my top dealers, an ounce man who'd just about outlived his usefulness anyway. Well, this ounce man squawked, it seems, to save his own skin. He was nothing but a street punk, an easy mark...."

Torquemandan interrupted. "I trust your judgment of men will be better in the future."

Brennan fought the urge to jump out of his seat and grab the smug bastard by the throat. Who the hell did he think he was anyway, questioning his judgment? But Brennan merely spread his hands, an apologetic look on his face. "A mistake. It won't happen again."

"Rest assured, Ronald."

"We only survive in the business, Mr. Torquemandan, if we learn from our mistakes, as I'm sure you know."

"Indeed."

"Sometimes, it's learning the hard way, unfortunately. Anyway...Bolan roughed up this guy to get to me, and the creep caved in. He had no guts doing that, after everything I'd done for him."

"Precisely, Ronald. Exactly how I would feel."

Brennan looked at Torquemandan for a moment, hoping he was concealing his confusion, the bad gut feeling that was choking him.

"If you're saying there's a leak at my end, Mr. Torquemandan, well, the best thing for me to do would be to check it out as soon as I get back."

Torquemandan nodded, rested his hands in his lap. "I hope there's no confusion here, Ronald."

"How's that, Mr. Torquemandan?"

"Well...let's call it a matter of organizational priorities, status, if you will."

What the fuck's with all this double-talk? Brennan thought. Let's cut the crap here, buddy.

"You see, Ronald, I am well aware that in the early years, when I sent some of my men to you, more precisely to your deceased father, you were ready and willing to help me set up the Horn. And you proved very capable. I could have no personal contact with you at that time, which was unfortunate. That left some rough edges...my CIA past, you understand. I became a wanted man near the end of the Vietnam debacle, Ronald. Company orders were to terminate me with extreme prejudice on sight." Torquemandan chuckled. "Over the past decade, I have had so much plastic surgery done that I can't even remember what I looked like six months ago."

Brennan nodded, chuckling at the guy's bad attempt at humor. "As far as I'm concerned, Mr. Torquemandan, you've always been the top do—top man."

"That's good to hear, Ronald. I have heard rumors that you've been spreading your feathers far and wide back in the States. Certain people were beginning to get the impression that the Devil's Horn was your creation, thus your property. Would you like to be sitting where I am, Ronald?"

Brennan had to think about that. The guy was halfway across the frigging world, hiding out in the jungle with a CIA contract out on his head. But, then again, Torquemandan had the power that he wanted.

He had the wealth, the contacts. Hell, he had every-thing. Except for the price on his head, perhaps. Maybe all that material jazz, Brennan thought, wasn't really worth spit if a man didn't have freedom of movement. What good was money if a man didn't have the security to enjoy all the pleasures that money could acquire for him?

"I'm not sure, Mr. Torquemandan."

"That was an honest answer, Ronald. I could see you were thinking about it."

What is this guy—psychic? Brennan asked himself. And did he think Brennan's earlier statements were *not* honest? It was time to wrap this up.

"Look, Mr. Torquemandan..."

"Call me Jonathan, Ronald."

"Okay, Jonathan. A while back I sent some specialists in the trade to you. They helped you out, but you ran the risks, ultimately, of getting burned. I can respect and admire a man who takes the kinds of risks you have. You've won. We've all won. I've es-tablished a big... hell, a massive operation for you at the other end in the States—"

"And for that, you feel you deserve some respect. Correct, Ronald?"

You'd better fucking believe it, dude. Brennan shrugged. "Well... let's just say I've taken consider-able risks, too. I've pulled my weight and kept up my end, Mr. Torque—Jonathan. I believe every man gets what he deserves in the end."

Torquemandan nodded thoughtfully. "Yes. Yes, indeed you have, Ronald. And you're absolutely right, Ronald. Every man gets what he deserves in the end."

Brennan didn't like the way that was said.

"Look, Jonathan. All I want to do right now is get a good night's sleep and get back to New York tomorrow. The past day or so has been a frigging nightmare for me. I just want to leave it all behind. I've got to get back to business as usual, you understand?"

"Of course." Torquemandan stood and half-turned, gesturing toward the giant oak double doors behind him. "And you will be free to leave it all behind, Ronald. Yes, I'm feeling better about our situation already. Much, much better. Now that we've cleared the air, shall we take a walk?"

Brennan hesitated, then rose from his chair. Why was Torquemandan grinning at him like that? he wondered.

Slowly, Brennan walked toward Torquemandan. The New York druglord felt an icy chill go down his spine, a tremor in his legs. He was getting bad vibes about Torquemandan. In fact, the CIA renegade suddenly looked terrifying to Brennan.

"Come, Ronald. I have something for you to see."

TORQUEMANDAN KNEW exactly what he had to do. And that was to make an example of Ronald Brennan, for the inmate population as well as for the gathered members of the Devil's Horn. The inflicting of pain, intense, horrible pain was the only clear-cut solution to this crisis. There was simply too much to gain, or lose, at this point. Torquemandan could not afford to leave any loose ends dangling. And Brennan was clearly a loose end, hanging all the way down to his shoes. A definite and very serious liability to the organization.

If Brennan returned to the States, the local and federal law would be all over him like a cheap suit,

Torquemandan knew. He did not believe that Brennan could hold out against constant harassment or tough questioning by the law. One thing would lead to another, and there would be more intruders like Bolan. Yes, Brennan had already shown that he couldn't handle the pressure at his end. The man simply crumbled during a crisis.

It was time for Torquemandan to reassert his absolute hold on power. There could be no treacherous scheming, no shadowy power struggle within the ranks. History, he recalled, was full of black examples of how powerful regimes disintegrated because of disaffection within. The Third Reich was one such regime.

Not only did Torquemandan need to make an example of the New York druglord, but he was certain that Brennan had been mocking him back in the banquet hall, that he had been thinking treacherous and derisive thoughts right under this very roof. The arrogance of the man infuriated Torquemandan. And Torquemandan needed to salve his bruised ego. In Torquemandan's mind Brennan was no guest of honor; he was a peasant, a small-timer, an opportunist who'd been riding the coattails of the organization's success.

"If you don't mind me asking, what are we doing out here, Jonathan?" Brennan asked, somewhat winded from his effort to keep up with the other man's long strides.

Torquemandan smiled, leading the way to a small stone hut on a knoll directly above the prison compound. A lone kerosene lantern hung from a bamboo post beside the hut; it bathed the stark blackness of the hut's front wall in a pale yellow light.

Torquemandan twisted the iron knob on the door of the hut, pushed the door inward with a squeal of rusty hinges. He held out his arm, motioning for Brennan to go inside.

Brennan hesitated, looking with an anxious gaze into the pitch-blackness beyond the doorway.

Torquemandan reached inside the doorway and flicked a switch on the wall. A solitary naked bulb hung from the low ceiling of the room, its white light striking against the coal-blackness of the inner walls.

Brennan looked past Torquemandan. In the middle of the room was a chair, which appeared to be bolted down. Something jutted above the back of the chair, some kind of leather headgear, maybe? Brennan noticed the straps on the chair's thick arms. Beads of sweat broke out on his forehead. Bewildered, he looked at Torquemandan.

A rustling noise broke the silence of the night.

Brennan snapped his head sideways just as Kam Chek and three guards with AK-47s stepped off the trail that led from the palace to the hut. Brennan's jaw went slack as it dawned on him what was going to happen.

Before Brennan could bolt, Torquemandan's hand shot out, grabbed the lapel of the New York druglord's expensive white suit.

The terror that Torquemandan read in Brennan's eyes excited him. A herculean strength seemed to explode through his arms as he effortlessly flung Brennan into the black room. It was always like this, Torquemandan knew; he always felt an enormous surge of power when he was about to play God with someone else's life.

Stumbling, Brennan crashed into the black chair face first, two of his front teeth snapping off as his open mouth cracked against the edge. Stunned, petrified by fear, Brennan braced his hands on the floor. Cold stone. He gave a little whimper.

Torquemandan stepped into the room. He loomed over Brennan. The sight of the man on his hands and knees below him, filled him with violent contempt. He watched as Brennan looked at the chair, raked his desperate stare around the barren room, as if searching for some way out. But there was no way out. The pure blackness of the walls always had that effect of freezing a victim with panic, Torquemandan knew. There was a stench of blood, sweat, fear, in the room that seemed to ooze from the very walls, a cloying, sickening smell that worked on a victim's senses instantly, making him wonder just what had happened here before. They always found out, Torquemandan thought.

Brennan's eyes fell on the large black chest in the far corner of the room.

"Is it making any sense to you now, Ronald?" Torquemandan asked with a smile.

Shaking, Brennan looked up at Torquemandan. "Why? Why are you doing this?"

Torquemandan's smile vanished as he drilled a front snapkick off Brennan's jaw. His foot smacked Brennan's head off the edge of the chair, and the trembling druglord dropped to the floor on his back.

Kam Chek and his men walked into the room. Kam Chek grinned.

"Leave the door open," Torquemandan ordered Kam Chek. "I have work to do. No one must sleep tonight."

Torquemandan took a step toward Brennan.
He knew that no one would sleep that night.
The night belonged to pain. To suffering.

15

Voices seemed to echo through Bolan's mind. They were just a faint hum at first, then the noise grew louder to become a relentless drumbeat pounding through the depths of his unconscious mind. Pain, sense-shattering, fiery, all-consuming pain unlike any he'd ever experienced, dragged Bolan back to the hellish awareness of grim reality. With an effort of iron will, fueled by rage and a heart full of vengeance, Bolan opened his eyes. He tasted the blood and bile in his mouth. His eyes opened, their lids tugging away from the dried crust of his life's juices that had hardened on his face like weathered glue.

Bolan groaned as he took in his surroundings. He was in a hut with some other prisoners. Eight men, he counted. They were watching him with fear, pity and silent despair written on their faces.

Bolan struggled to sit up, raw fire surging across the slashed flesh of his back with every inch he moved. He propped himself against a wooden pole, savored for a moment the sensation of the wood's coolness against his punished flesh, then checked his injuries. Every muscle in his body ached, throbbed. He hurt bad, right to the marrow of his bones. But nothing appeared broken. He was lucky, he thought. But just how lucky was he?

Bolan's eyes anxiously swept over the hut seeking Grimaldi. He spotted his friend stretched out on a straw mat on the other side of the hut. Bolan stood, lost his balance for a second, then willed strength into his rubbery legs. Ignoring the solemn scrutiny of the other prisoners, Bolan moved painfully across the hut. He knelt beside Grimaldi, checked his pulse, found a heartbeat, faint but steady. A pang of grief stabbed Bolan as he examined his friend. From face to waist Grimaldi was one mass of black, blue and purple welts and bruises. Flies crawled on the patches of congealed blood on his face and arms. A lump the size of a golf ball lodged in Bolan's throat.

Gently, Bolan shook Grimaldi. "Jack? Jack?"

Grimaldi stirred, groaned, winced. Opening his eyes, he stared up at Bolan for a stretched second. He blinked several times, then forced a half smile. "Damn, Striker, did you get the number of the train that ran over us?"

"Does it feel like anything's broken, Jack?"

Grimaldi clenched his teeth. Bolan helped him to sit up.

"Just my pride and dignity," Grimaldi answered.

"Then consider yourself lucky, friend. Genghis Khan was in a good mood tonight." The comment came from one of the other prisoners nearby.

"If this is luck," Grimaldi replied in a scratchy voice, "I'd better stay away from the tables at Vegas, pal."

Bolan turned, looked at the man who'd spoken. Like all the captives there, the man looked like little more than a skeleton. Gaunt-faced. Hollow-eyed. Emaciated. In the flickering orange glow from a torch directly over their heads, they resembled scarecrows.

Bolan knew that in a matter of days both he and Jack would look like them—walking dead men.

"Allow me to introduce myself and your other roomies, friends," the man said, his voice edged with bitterness. "I'm Mike Tremain." He pointed at a black man. "That's Larry Jones." He indicated the other six men in turn. "Bill Carver. Pete Struber. Aaron Ribitowitz. Harry Karn. Jim Sellers. Paul Polanski, or Bruno, as we call 'im.'"

"I'm Bolan. And this is Jack Grimaldi," Bolan said curtly, forcing the words past swollen, split lips.

"Yeah, we know who you are, man," Jones said. "We was all there in Nam, Sergeant, soldiers for the cause, y'know—except the spook here, he didn't have no cause, 'cept maybe a little lust for a piece of the black market." He threw Tremain a hostile glance. "We were in the twenty-second Marines, fourth division. Our Huey was shot down on recon near Da Nang in '72. We been under Charlie's tender lovin' care ever since."

The bitterness in the black soldier's voice didn't escape Bolan. The memory of the harsh ordeal these vets had endured seemed to live in their eyes, like a broken headstone, Bolan thought, a sorry tribute to what these men believed was a dirty war, a lousy damn joke that had been played on them. But Bolan saw, too, the strength in those watchful eyes, sensed the courage in this group of soldiers. Hell, he knew, they had to be good, hard as rock to have survived their fate this long.

"You can forget about all that pride and dignity stuff, Sergeant," Pete Struber said. "It's the first thing they take away from you here."

"And we're long since out of sympathy," Ribito-witz added with a deadpan delivery.

"Believe me, soldier," Bolan said, his eyelids slit-ted as the fire continued to race like molten lava through his veins, "I can understand that."

Grimacing for a moment, Bolan stooped, perched himself against the wall beside Grimaldi.

Grimaldi touched his bruised jaw, screwing his eyes shut for a second. "Any of you guys got a ciga-rette?" he asked, then, as Bruno snorted, Grimaldi gave the guy a lame nod. "Guess not. Dumb ques-tion. Just tryin' to lighten the mood a little, huh."

"And they don't serve up surf 'n' turf here neither, funny man," Struber growled.

Carver added with a bitter chuckle, "You get two meals a day, friends, one in the morning, one at night. If you get a bowl of slop that looks like ground-up meat, don't touch it."

Bolan didn't like the sound of that. His suspicions about what the man was driving at triggered a new wave of rage in his belly. "Why's that?"

"You know that guy you tried to help out there to-day?" Karn said.

"What about him?"

Seller's mouth twisted in an ugly sneer. "'Cause he'll come back, served up as ground meat. That's fuckin' why, Sergeant."

"Christ!" Grimaldi groaned. For a moment he hung his head.

Bolan's jaw muscles tightened, his guts knotted up into a coil.

"You can eat the rice," Jones said.

"But don't bitch about the gourmet cooking," Struber supplemented in grim mirth. "You two guys got off easy today. You knocked off most of the cream of their troops, took out a big chunk of their friggin' mercenary cutthroat outfit. Thank your lucky stars that your reputations preceded you, or you'd be dead meat already and some poor bastard would be spooning you out of a bowl in the morning.''

Tremain snorted. "Don't worry, I think that little practice is pretty much over. Genghis started his cannibal routine about a month ago. The other day Torquemandan got wind of it, we heard, and put a stop to that bullshit right away."

"It seems the head creep," Seller interjected, "is afraid of an epidemic breaking out. Imagine that. They'll cut your guts out and tie 'em around your neck for talking back. But a little plague scares 'em to death."

"Don't worry 'bout no plague, Sergeant," Jones said. "If you survive this next week you'll get all your shots."

"I suggest you two get a good night's sleep," Carver told Bolan and Grimaldi. "Today we got off with a short work day, because of the ceremony for our new arrivals—that's you. We got four more days to finish scraping the plants. Deadline, deadline, deadline. Timetable, timetable, timetable. That's all you'll be hearin' from now till then. And the whip'll bite harder every day from here on in. By tomorrow afternoon you'll think a friggin' viper's biting at your back."

"Twenty-hour work days coming up, friends," Ribitowitz rasped. "The ones who don't get worked or whipped to death will wish they had."

Struber jerked a nod at Ribitowitz. "He's talking about the big parade, Sergeant, in case you didn't know."

"The death march," Jones acknowledged. He shook his head wearily, anger creeping into his eyes. "Two hundred miles to Bangkok with maybe a hundred pounds of scag on our backs. Then it's a two-hundred-mile hike back. You drop out, they leave you right where you are. If you're still breathin' and don't get up, Genghis'll put a bullet in your brain and roll ya off the trail into the ditch. And you try not to be the first few sorry suckers to fall out, either. They'll have one of these Mongols carryin' a flamethrower, and they'll put the torch to ya. Fuckin' Genghis gets a big kick when he sees the first few dudes drop from exhaustion. He likes watchin' guys burn up almost as much as he likes whippin' all the skin off them."

"Shades of Bataan, huh," Bruno Polanski growled, looking Bolan dead in the eye.

Bolan thought about the forced march that awaited all of them. No, he had never experienced the hell that those American and Filipinio GIs had suffered at the hands of their Japanese captors, after Wainwright ordered the island abandoned. But Polanski's words reminded him of the reason for his being there.

"What are the chances for an escape?" Bolan asked, point-blank.

Carver let out a soft whistle. "Boy, you don't waste any time, do you?"

Bolan ignored the man's cynicism. "There has to be some point on this march where it could be pulled off. Maybe the midway point. At night. The guards will be just as tired as the prisoners, just a little better nourished, that's all. What about it?"

Tremain looked at Bolan with astonishment, then anger. Yeah, Bolan figured these guys would have hashed over the idea of escape before this, and they

had obviously arrived at a dead end. But even though
a mass breakout would be a last desperate act, having
perhaps a one-in-a-thousand chance of succeeding and
leading to inevitable death if it failed, there was still
that hope. Bolan could see their minds were chewing
over the possibility. The prisoners realized the odds,
though still incredibly long, had shortened slightly
with the arrival of the two tough though battered
newcomers.

Struber was the first to voice an objection. "Nah.
No way, Sergeant. It hasn't even been tried, not in the
terms of one mass uprising by all of us, anyway. We'd
be shot dead before we ever got out of the friggin'
starting gate."

"With that kind of thinking, Struber," Bolan said,
"you're beaten already."

Struber stiffened but backed off, and fell into a
brooding silence. Bolan didn't have time to worry
about wounded pride. He needed winners from that
moment on. Any doubts at all about their chances of
success meant doom. It was time to start separating
the fat from the lean.

"I suggest you keep your voice down, Bolan," Tremain said, then jerked a thumb at the bamboo wall
that supported his back. "The walls, friend—they
have ears. Big ones."

"We got us some real bad apples in here, pal," Karn
said. "Camp snitches. They'd turn you in for a pack
of cigarettes."

"We got us one pigeon here in particular, man,"
Jones said his dark eyes still lit with anger. "A dude
by the name of Davis. He's already turned in a dozen
mates. Every time he does he gets a carton of smokes,

a bottle of Burgundy and a fuckin' ten-course meal from the Mongol himself.''

Sellers snorted. The hatred in his bloodshot eyes seemed to further inflame the redness of those sunken orbs. "We call the SOB Virginia Slim. Christ help me if I ever get my hands on him...."

"Virginia Slim," Tremain added, "will turn you over to Genghis if he even thinks he smells an escape attempt. You can kiss your raggedy ass goodbye if that happens. It'll be the black room for you."

Bolan had known from the moment of his capture that he would have to watch his step, that certain inmates could prove deadly in their cowardly treachery toward the others, just for some special privileges granted them by the hand of the whipmasters. Pigeons were always damn sorry excuses for men, any way you sliced it, Bolan knew. A Judas goat among their ranks here could be the worst enemy of the whole savage lot.

Bolan decided to carry on working up an escape attempt, though he might have to go about it in a different way. Time was wasting, indeed time was killing them all. Bolan had to win their confidence now, and begin laying the foundations for the breakout. When the attempt was made, it would have to be fast, brutally violent, and would have to make use of the element of surprise. And most, if not all, of the prisoners would have to act together as one body of lightning fury during the initial seconds of the breakout. First, though, Bolan needed more facts about the march.

Bolan had noticed something else about his fellow prisoners. Though they knew there were spies among them, these inmates made no attempt to lower their voices, nor did they seem concerned that snitches were roving about the hut, listening to their conversation. No, these soldiers had reluctantly but angrily accepted their fate. Their attitude was that what would happen would just have to happen. Death hung over every head there for every second of every day. Dying seemed to mean very little to these men anymore. If the opportunity for escape presented itself, or if someone presented it to them, men with so little to lose would bite, he knew. They would surely go down fighting, screaming out all their pent-up rage and frustration in the obscene face of death, seizing the moment to pay back the men who had enslaved, tortured and dehumanized them. Bolan sensed that the hope to break free of their bonds still rested in their hearts. Once a good soldier, always a fighter. These prisoners were broken in many ways, on the verge of total defeat. But maybe, Bolan thought, just maybe...the light would shine. It would have to, he knew. Doing nothing meant certain death, or long-term enslavement and torture, which, in his mind, were the same thing.

"What about this forced march?" he queried. "Tell me about it."

The eight men exchanged glances. Bolan read in their hesitation a sudden fear. Judging by the anxious expressions on their faces, he could guess they felt as if they were being pushed into something they all wanted, but were afraid to put into motion themselves. Hell, yes, he was about to open a potential Pandora's box, and they were being asked to act, to begin to make their dreams of freedom a reality.

"Let's tighten up this circle," Bolan suggested, and waited for a response.

Then Bolan noticed the hostile glances the others directed at Tremain.

"What makes you think everybody here can be trusted, Sergeant?" Struber said.

"What's to make me think that they can't?"

Jones looked at Tremain. "This dude here's CIA for starters. It's thanks to his buddies that we're rotting here in the first place, man."

Tremain shook his head, disgusted. "You believe these guys?" the CIA man growled at Bolan. "I've been here for seven years, I've made it through seven marches side by side with each and every one of them. I'm beginning to think their bitterness is matched only by their stupidity and naïveté."

"Fuck you, pal," Struber quietly snarled.

"I was never involved in any black-market operations, assholes," Tremain rasped. "I've told you that before. You can believe it or not. I don't give a shit anymore what you think."

Bolan knew where this talk was headed and decided he'd better throw some ice over the emotional sparks right away.

"If Tremain's been here that long, I think you soldiers better take another look at him. And at yourselves. Now, what's it going to be?"

Again, the soldiers and the CIA op hesitated, looked at one another as if each was waiting for another guy to speak up. Bruno Polanski stood first, moved to the center of the hut, crouched on his knees. The others stood, moved in behind Polanski.

For a moment Bolan looked at the eight men in the dim, wavering torchlight. The years of suffering and hardship that had worn them down to skeletons had left few distinctive physical features to separate one man from the others. They all had scars from the whip on their bare backs, arms and chests. Several of them had patches of dead purple skin where they had either been burned deliberately, or shot. Their mistreatment had been the same for all. And they had all better start believing, Bolan thought, that their destiny was the same, too. The bellyaching, the individual crap, had to go. Fast.

In every pair of their eyes Bolan saw something that he was very familiar with. Death. Death's haunting shadow seemed set deep in their gazes, a black pool of terrible memories.

"Don't leave me out of the powwow, Striker," Grimaldi said, bracing an arm against the wall as he tried to stand. Bolan helped him to his feet.

The ten men now formed a ring. And this time when they spoke, they lowered their voices so as not to be overheard.

"Okay," Bolan began. "Give it to me. Everything you can tell me about the march: formations, guard duty, vehicles, weapons, terrain."

"They march us in a close column," Tremain answered. "There's usually a hundred to a hundred and fifty prisoners. Most are Caucasians, but there's a lot of Asians, too, stolen out of Cambodia, Laos, Burma, Vietnam. They chain us together for the duration of the march. Hand and foot."

"Problem number one, Sergeant," Carver announced. "You can't run too far in chains."

"Keys," Bolan shot back. "Who has them?"

"Genghis," Tremain said. "Khang keeps a set for himself and distributes a set to each of six guards. Always six."

"Those guards will be the principal marks," Bolan informed. "Pick them out right away, because they'll be some of the first ones hit. Is the column single or double file?"

"Triple file," Polanski replied.

"Makes sense," Grimaldi chipped in. "Shortens the column. Brings it in tight so that the guards can watch everyone better."

"This year was a good harvest for the big boys," Tremain informed, one side of his mouth twisted in sarcasm. "We're looking at anywhere from fifteen to twenty tons."

"So there're vehicles to carry the bulk of the heroin?" Bolan asked.

"Yeah, and horses and oxen," Jones said. "There's one armoured personnel carrier at the front of the column, the fuckin' spearhead, and one more at the rear. Both rigs have fifty-calibers mounted on the turret. There'll be three, maybe four other transport-type trucks loaded down with scag. And, of course, don't forget the fat cats of the Horn."

"You mean all the members of the Horn will be riding along?" Bolan asked, and he received a hard nod from Ribitowitz. That might work to the prisoners' advantage, Bolan thought. A nice, tight package, all wrapped up in one. Maybe a hostage or two could be seized to help them get clear.

"Most of the fat cats will come along on the big trip," Jones went on. "Mister Clean, too. S'ppose you've already met the big man in the white suit?"

"Torquemandan. Yeah, we've met."

"Right," Jones said. "Well, aside from the transport trucks, there'll also be a jeep with a fifty-caliber mutha' that'll ride along about the middle of the column.''

"Okay. We'll have to take the armed vehicles right away to man the guns." Bolan directed his next question to Tremain. "How about guards? How many?"

Tremain shrugged. "Roughly fifty, sixty. They're staggered along the flanks. Most of them, though, will be packed in the rear with Genghis. They'll all carry AK-47s."

"And the routine? How many hours a day do you march? Any meal breaks?"

"You march from just before dawn to maybe three, four hours past sundown," Sellers answered. "One meal a day, if you can call it that. A handful of rice and a cup of water, at night. That's it."

"The terrain?"

"The peninsula's almost all mountains and jungle," Karn said. "No rivers that we've seen. But the monsoon season has just ended, so there'll be water holes, some swampy marshes, a stream running down from the mountains."

"Over the years," Tremain added, "they've made us hack out a trail for the march."

"For every hundred feet of jungle that's been hacked out," Ribitowitz said, "one of us has died doing it."

"And that ain't no bull, Sarge," Jones said, mean-faced, grim.

"Any villages along the way where a rest stop might be ordered?"

"Yeah, there's three," Tremain said. "Small ones. One at the fifty-mile point, another just over the hundred-mile mark, and the last one about thirty miles south of Bangkok. Genghis always orders a stop at all three. He and his hordes are always greeted with open arms by the villagers. They seize whatever food and water is available. I've only seen villagers resist once, and there was another time when a village didn't have anything for Genghis. I say once, because those people who resisted never got the chance to disappoint Genghis again."

"There ain't nothin' left for those folks once we pull out," Jones added bitterly. "Genghis and his punks clean them out like a swarm of locusts."

"And the Mongol usually takes a sampling of the women," Karn said. "When that happens, it means a few hours holdup, you can bank on it."

Bolan's mind was racing. Possibilities were beginning to reveal themselves. Suddenly an escape attempt didn't look as hopeless as these men had thought. There was a good chance at least of making the attempt. Damn right. Bolan vowed to himself right then that there would be a breakout.

"Okay. Now, one very important item," Bolan said. "Somehow we have to get word to the other prisoners. If the ten of us attempt a breakout on our own, there will be confusion and the guards will just start slaughtering everybody."

"I follow ya, man," Jones said. "I tell ya what. For the next few nights before the march, one of us could fall in with the mates at another hut."

"Yeah, right after we break at night," Polanski said, his eyes lighting up. "We could spread the word that way. Then a guy from another hut could move into another bunch the next night. Pass the word on. Or we could all just take turns, maybe two guys a night, each man to a hut."

"It could work," Grimaldi said, his gaze narrowing with determination.

"It's a good plan," Bolan assured. "It'll have to work. Do we have to get a man from the other hut to take the place of whoever leaves here? Do the guards take a head count at night?"

Tremain shook his head. "No. Just a quick look to make sure we're all there, then they separate us into our groups."

"We may have to chance the replacement the first night," Bolan said, "until we can get word to the next group. I think our best bet is to let the breakout rip at one of those villages, probably the second one at the hundred-mile point. The guards will be tired by then, and from the sound of things, hungry for a little R and R. That'll be our chance. Let's think it over. Let me know if you can think of anything else you've forgotten to tell me. Any more breaks in the routine, anything like that. Sleep on it for a couple of hours. We'll work out the finer details in the morning before the guards come and round us up."

"You know, I like it," Bruno Polanski said, his eyes hard with sudden conviction. "I think we can do it."

"You're damn right we can do it," Bolan acknowledged. "We're *going* to do it. No ifs, ands or buts about it. Agreed?"

Bolan met each man's gaze. He found steel in every pair of eyes that stared back at him. Carver and Tremain nodded. Only Struber looked doubtful to Bolan. The Executioner made a mental note to watch that guy. It would only take one man to screw everything up.

"We're with ya, man," Jones said, "we can—"

Jones broke off abruptly when a sudden scream ripped through the night beyond the hut. Bolan and the circle of men snapped their startled attention toward the doorway.

"No-o-o-o! No-o-o-o! Don't!"

Bolan recognized that voice, even as the words shattered the night, twisting into the scream of a man in terrible agony. A scream of pure terror and pain.

Grimaldi knew the voice, too. "Brennan," he murmured.

"Jesus!" Tremain breathed into the taut silence. "The black room...the poor bastard..."

Again, the bone-chilling shriek for mercy split the night. The cry seemed to linger in the air, envelop the hut as if that doomed soul was hanging just above the roof.

Carver looked pointedly at Grimaldi. "Brennan? Is that the other one that came in with you?"

"Yeah," Bolan answered, tight-lipped, his cold stare riveted on the doorway. "Brennan."

"Who is he?" Sellers wanted to know.

"A pusher. A smart guy who wasn't as smart as he thought he was," Bolan said.

Rititowitz snorted, seemed to find something amusing in what he heard. "A pusher, huh," he said, acid in his voice. "I hope he gets it good. It'll be just what he deserves."

"When Genghis told you, 'welcome to hell,' friends," Tremain said, "he wasn't just talking to hear himself."

Bolan didn't have to be told that, as he listened to another bloodcurdling scream. He had a gut feeling that the harrowing cries were going to go on all night long. And he had to wonder if a man deserved the fate Ronny Brennan was suffering.

But he knew the answer before he even formed the question.

Bolan spotted the pigeons the next morning out in the field. It didn't take much imagination on his part to size up the camp stoolies, to determine what they'd gained by their betrayal of their fellow inmates. Yeah, Bolan had seen their rotten ilk many times before. They were the kind of human virus that lived, indeed thrived on the host body of others' suffering. Here, though, these rats openly flaunted the privileges they had acquired through their guile and treachery. The physical appearance of the scum was as starkly different from that of the other prisoners as night is from day. They were like a roadside billboard advertising beer on an empty desert highway.

Jones, scraping poppy bulbs beside Bolan, glanced at the Executioner with contempt in his eyes, then jerked a nod at the three rats, who were several rows of plants beyond them. Then, Jones shook his head. Bolan read the gesture as an expression of Jones's personal frustration at not being able to kick the hell out of those bastards.

Their clothing was the first thing Bolan noted that set them apart from the others; they were dressed in light gray silk shirts and slacks. But what really made them different, on a closer appraisal, was the fullness of their well-nourished faces and figures, the scrubbed, damn-near-pink freshness of their skin. Indeed, their bodies were padded with fat from excessive eating. Every thirty minutes, the three snitches took a cigarette break, talked and laughed with the guards. The only work they did was to carry the wooden buckets of raw opium to the edge of the field, where they dumped the sap into black drums. The vermin even had the gall to demand angrily that the other prisoners work faster.

Bolan had learned that the pigeons were protected by Kam Chek and his cannibals. If any of the three rats was harmed by another prisoner, the offender was immediately hauled away to the black room. His screams of agony would be the last thing anyone in the inmate population would ever hear from that man again. Bolan knew he would have to work his plan past them, somehow avoid the ever-present threat that the plan would be discovered by the spies. But he already had that angle covered. The three rats had their own hut, powered by a generator. The rats had light, even a refrigerator, and were allowed magazines and books of their choosing. It was even rumored that they received a salary, supplemented by a commission for every inmate they sent to the black room. Eavesdropping, Bolan's circle of captives had informed him, was the rats' most effective method of picking up information damaging to the prisoners. A second method was to buy out inmates within other circles.

Bolan was grimly aware that his proposed breakout plan was full of risks, with holes that could be punched gaping wide by an unforeseen twist of fate. He was going to have to mix chance with daring.

Bolan caught the eye of a pigeon. The rage that burned inside Bolan hardened his stare, so that his eyes were like two glittering diamonds behind narrowed slits.

For a moment the rat seemed frozen by Bolan's graveyard expression. Bolan read the fear in the guy's eyes; all of a sudden the punk looked as if he wanted to crawl into the nearest hole. To Mack Bolan there were few savages worse than a traitor in the ranks. He believed this kind of cannibal deserved nothing but sudden death.

Just then Kam Chek, who had been making the rounds of the work party with his threats and insults, approached the area where Bolan was working.

"Back to work, *ferang*!" Kam Chek screamed. "You are daydreaming. You are feeling sorry for yourself. I tolerate no loafing! I have a deadline to meet. I have a timetable!"

Kam Chek shrieked insults at Bolan for several moments, finally moved on to the next group of prisoners. From the corner of his eye, Bolan saw the pigeon smile at him. The smile was a sneer, a look of such arrogance that Bolan wanted to carve it off the rat's face with the edge of a very dull knife.

Bolan went back to work, all right. Quickly but carefully he continued cutting incisions into the poppy bulbs with his knife, then scraping away the bleeding brown-black sap. At this point, it was important that he not draw unnecessary attention to himself. As it was, Kam Chek and the other guards were watching his every move with the predatory wariness of hawks. He could feel their eyes boring into the back of his head at all times.

As the sun climbed across the burning blue sky, it seemed to suck the air away from the field, straight up into the vortex of a furnace. That time of the year in

Southeast Asia, Bolan knew, was always hot, but he suspected that day was unusually hot. But the heat had only begun to stoke his fury. The more he suffered now, the better, he reasoned. Perhaps pain would give him all the edge he needed.

Just before dawn that morning, Bolan, Grimaldi and their eight accomplices had gone over the plan again, smoothed out the rough edges. They decided that the attempt would take place at the village that marked the halfway point of the march. Before setting out, Bolan, Grimaldi and the eight prisoners of their circle would stumble into the column, assume strategic positions in the front, rear and middle of the marching prisoners. The veterans of the march didn't think this would be a problem, for the assembly and file of the prisoners at the outset was always a mass of crowded flesh and huddled misery. Kam Chek's screaming for the men to fall into place and pick up their sacks of heroin always added to the confusion, panic and terror.

Once the march got under way, Bolan intended to keep as low a profile as possible, though gut feeling told him he would be the center of Kam Chek's cruel attention.

At the midway rest point Bolan would give the signal, a look and a shallow nod that would be passed on down the line. Because of the possibility of spies in the ranks, none of the other prisoners beyond his circle would know the exact moment that the breakout attempt would be staged. It would take daring, grim resolve and speedy maneuvering to pull it off, he knew. He had stressed this to Tremain and the seven soldiers. Together, the ten of them would have to carry off the brutal force of a shocking initiative, and take the brunt of the cannibals' resistance.

Bolan had also learned from the veteran marchers that many of Kam Chek's cutthroats got drunk at the halfway rest stop. They did this every year without fail. An orgy, Bolan hoped, would seal the fate of their tormentors. In fact, he saw this as a very fitting end to their savagery and brutality.

In the event that it appeared they were going to be overwhelmed and massacred by Kam Chek and his cutthroats, Bolan had ordered the rebels should instantly bolt into the jungle surrounding the village. He didn't think this would happen, but he had to cover all contingencies. What he wanted, he thought as vengeance pumped hot blood through his heart, and a sudden feverish rage spread a fire through his brain, was for the prisoners to stand their ground and annihilate their captors. Completely. Totally. Without mercy or hesitation. But he knew there was the strong possibility that some prisoners might fail to seize the initiative. And, of course, their weakness from undernourishment, their exhaustion from the punishing march and their lack of firearms put them at a disadvantage. There would be casualties, Bolan was certain of that.

But there was no alternative.

Strike first. Strike hard. Strike with twice the ruthlessness and viciousness that their captors had used on them over the years.

Bolan knew that he didn't have to drive the men of his circle into a state of frenzy; their rage and hatred were fueled by the terrible memories of their enslavement. When the time came, they would act. They would have to. Their lives depended on it.

During the next few hours in the poppy field, Bolan became the object of intense observation by the pigeons. He saw them pointing his way, talking, as if trying to decide some issue that had suddenly arisen. Then one of the pigeons broke away from the others, walked up to one of the guards.

Bolan looked at Jones, and nodded at the pigeon.

"Davis," Jones whispered.

The King Rat, Bolan thought.

Kam Chek walked over to Davis and they conferred for several moments. Davis did most of the talking, while Kam Chek nodded repeatedly. Finally, the whipmaster turned, looked at Bolan.

Bolan ignored Kam Chek, busied himself with his endless task of scraping the poppy bulbs. But a warning bell was sounding in his head. Now what? he wondered.

"Ferang."

Slowly, acting as if he couldn't be bothered by an interruption, Bolan straightened, looked at Kam Chek. The whipmaster stood less than four feet away, legs planted far apart, clenched fists on his hips.

"Something has come to my attention, Bo-leen."

"Yeah. Like what?"

Jones, Grimaldi, and the other prisoners in Bolan's group suddenly stopped working to watch the exchange.

Kam Chek glared at the prisoners behind Bolan. "Work!" he barked. "Back to work, you filthy *ferangs*!"

Kam Chek summoned some guards who ran up behind the prisoners. Whips cracked through the air like lightning, lashed flesh with several strokes.

The beaten prisoners grunted and moaned. Bolan pinned Kam Chek with an icy stare. *You're going to be the first, pal. I swear...* Kam Chek could beat him. Kam Chek could thrash him to within a breath away from death. But Kam Chek, Bolan knew, would never break his will. Never.

"As I was saying, Bo-leen. A certain look has been noted on your face. A most suspicious look, I may add. It is a look we have seen before. Many, many times, *oui*. It is the look of a man who still has plenty of fight left in him. It is the look of a man who will defy his superiors at all cost.

"Bo-leen, listen to me, *s'il vous plaît*," Kam Chek said in an almost imploring voice. Then came a shrug and a mocking grin. "Have you no respect for us? Have you no wish to cooperate and accept your lot of suffering, deprivation and pain? Bo-leen, you must cheer up, you must. You are becoming a morale problem, *oui*? Perhaps this morale problem will become infectious. Perhaps, Bo-leen, this morale problem will turn itself into an escape attempt? Eh?"

Bolan cursed silently, but his eyes did not show Kam Chek the first flicker of surprise he felt. If the SOB had any positive proof about the breakout plan, Bolan suspected, he would have been whisked off to the black room by now.

Or would he have been taken at all? he asked himself. Maybe Kam Chek knew the whole plan. Maybe Davis or one of the other rats had been eavesdropping around the hut. Maybe Kam Chek would take no action yet, would let Bolan make the first move in the planned escape, then slaughter any prisoner who dared to join in the attempt. A lot of maybes, Bolan thought. The attempt, when it came—and Bolan determined right then to go ahead with the plan—would be touch and go. If Kam Chek knew about the plan, Bolan was willing to gamble that the whipmaster would announce this to the prisoners before the march set out, just to show the inmate populace how smart and cunning he was, to show them that escape would be a dismal exercise in utter futility, ending in bloody disaster, to prove that freedom away from the stinging bite of his whip was impossible.

"What the hell are you talking about?" Bolan grunted.

Kam Chek chuckled. "Nothing, I hope. Perhaps, nothing at all, Bo-leen. For your sake, let us hope it is nothing, eh?" His eyes were nearly hidden behind hooded lids. *"Oui?"*

Kam Chek started to turn away from Bolan, then he stopped suddenly and turned to face the Executioner. Kam Chek smiled. "We were talking about you this morning, Bo-leen. Would you like to know what I heard about you?"

Bolan's spine stiffened. At that moment there was something particularly ugly about the laughter in Kam Chek's dark eyes. What was the savage going to come up with now? Bolan wondered uneasily.

Kam Chek draped his hand over the hilt of his samurai sword. "I see you are pretending to have no curiosity about what it was I heard about you. Never mind, I will tell you the story anyway. I understand your family was killed in a most tragic incident ... in a city called Pittsfield, I believe the *ferangs* of the Horn said."

Grimaldi stopped working, looked up at Kam Chek, his gaze cold.

Rage twisted Bolan's guts. He knew where Kam Chek's "story" was leading. Stay hard, he told himself. This bastard's day is coming.

"I believe your father went berserk, as I heard it, *oui*," Kam Chek went on. "He shot your sister, your mother and your brother, a Donny or Johnny, I believe. And all because your sister was selling her body? A most regrettable reaction on your father's part. To me, such an act of barbarism shows a decided lack of willpower. A decided lack of character, *oui*? Perhaps this deficiency in strength is inherent in your blood. Perhaps you suffer from it yourself." Kam Chek looked at Bolan with a level stare, then he laughed scornfully.

Grief tore through Bolan. The horror of the past...the moment he had learned the nightmarish truth...a truth that had changed the course of his destiny. His throat went dry, tightened up, was suddenly raw and burning. Kam Chek's derisive laughter fired the murderous wrath that was searing through every muscle in Bolan's body. No! he silently cried. Kam Chek was wrong about his father. Dead wrong, goddammit. Bolan's father, he knew, had been driven over the edge by the savage cunning of bloodsuckers, driven beyond the point that any man could be asked to endure. What would he have done if he had been in his father's shoes? he asked himself. He knew exactly what he would have done. He would have crushed the bloodsuckers beneath the heel of his shoe. Squashed the life out of their twisted souls.

With a determined effort, Bolan steadied the trembling of his hands, and went back to work. But he could still hear Kam Chek's laughter ringing in his ears.

The sweat rolled down Bolan's back, burned into the raw slashes. Fire. Agony. Hate.

The edge. Yeah, Bolan thought. The final, cutting edge.

Someone was going to pay. Pay hard. Pay in pain, then death.

And this time the judgment was going to be meted out differently.

With a Sadeian twist. With the very righteous, steely edge of the blade.

THE INFILTRATION OF ANOTHER circle of prisoners by Carver seemed to go off without a hitch. But Bolan wasn't about to become overconfident at this early sign of success. The whole enterprise was a crapshoot. The dice were rolling.

Bolan had selected Carver to move into another hut and spread the word about the escape attempt because the man was fluent in Thai, Burmese and Hmong. There were some twenty-plus Southeast-Asian men among the captives who spoke these languages. Of course, some of the Asians spoke English, but Bolan wanted them to know exactly what was going to happen, which made it desirable to brief them in their native tongue.

Bolan particularly wanted the Montagnards on his side. He had worked with Montagnard tribesmen—the Meos—before, in behind-the-lines search-and-destroy operations during the war. They were not only excellent guides and accurate interpreters for seventeen different tongues, but they were also fierce fighters. Better still, he knew, they were loyal, would fight to the last man, to the bitter end, their allegiance to a chosen ally incorruptible. Bolan remembered them

with warm feeling, affection, yeah. The Montagnard
tribesman had been best friends to the Special Forces,
many of them earning the 101st Airborne Division
patch, some three dozen of them qualifying to wear
U.S. airborne jump wings. And they had been the fe-
rocious, hated enemy of the Vietcong. Yes, Bolan
thought, he had great respect for the Montagnards.

After the prisoners received their bowl of rice and a
cup of water, they had split up and moved to their
huts. Bolan had trailed Grimaldi and the other prisoners of his group into the hut. He was exhausted, still
aching and burning from his beating and whipping.
The strain of the long hours in the field, the physical
punishment of the beatings and lack of food and water were wearing down his strength, dangerously fast.
It seemed that every step he took now was made possible only through sheer willpower.

Bolan looked back at the guards, who were watching as the prisoners filed into their huts. Nobody
stopped Carver when he entered a different hut than
usual. Kam Chek, Bolan noticed, was nowhere to be
seen at the moment.

As Bolan walked into the hut and seated himself
beside Grimaldi, he looked at the ravaged faces
around him. He spotted the telltale shadows of fear in
every pair of eyes. And he spotted wonder, too. And
hope.

"Mack."

Bolan looked at Grimaldi. His friend's voice was
one rasping scratch of pain. There was deep sympathy in Grimaldi's eyes. Bolan looked away. He knew
what was on Jack's mind.

"Mack, I . . . I . . ."

"Forget it, Jack. It's all part of the sickness here."
And Bolan believed what he told Jack, knew he should
put Kam Chek's spiteful needling out of his mind. But
Bolan still felt the hurt, the rage over Kam Chek's
mockery of his family's tragedy.

There was a sudden scuffling sound beyond the
doorway. Bolan, Grimaldi, and the other seven prisoners looked toward the hut's opening. A second later,
a man was tossed into the hut.

Not a man, Bolan saw. No, nothing human could
possibly look like the lump of blackened, twisted flesh
that sprawled on the dirt floor.

Someone muttered an oath. Bolan looked at the
guard in the doorway, but Kam Chek's tool of enslavement wheeled away from the opening, seemed to
melt back into the night.

Bolan's gaze fell on the lump of flesh on the floor.

On Ronny Brennan.

Slick crimson drool spilled from Brennan's mouth
as he lifted his head, looked at the faces around him.
He looked as if he wanted to curse them all, then he
seemed silently to implore someone to help him.

No one did.

"Jesus!" Mike Tremain murmured.

For just a second, Bolan experienced a stab of pity
for Brennan. Since the man wore only a pair of shorts,
the scars of his torture left very little to Bolan's imagination. The guy had just come from hell. The drug
pusher had been mutilated, disfigured beyond recog-
nition. His face was a mask of raw meat; the skin appeared to have been scraped, or perhaps clawed off.
There were black burn marks, purple lumps and long
pink streaks on every visible inch of Brennan's body.

But the worst sight was his hands. Several fingers had been chopped off. The other fingers were crooked at impossible angles, broken, crushed by some instrument of torture. His fists appeared to be swollen to twice their normal size and looked more like clubs than hands.

Ronny Brennan looked Bolan in the eye, with a stare of pure hate at first, then depthless misery.

Then a sob broke from Brennan's mouth. He wept, let his head fall to the floor again, face first.

No one moved.

17

On the third day of Bolan and Grimaldi's imprisonment, Kam Chek made a sudden and unexpected announcement. It was midmorning, and the sun burned its fire down on the slave-labor force from a cloudless sky.

"*Ferangs*, and other workers of the Imperial Revolutionary Army. Listen!"

Bolan, Grimaldi, and the more than one hundred other prisoners straightened from stooping over the poppy plants. Everyone gave Kam Chek his undivided attention as the warlord addressed them from the far eastern edge of the field. Kam Chek shouted, though that wasn't necessary; his voice would have carried easily enough in the oppressive silence that gripped the prisoners in exhaustion and despair.

As he looked at the other prisoners, Bolan wondered how these men kept going. It was hard to believe that many of these same prisoners had lived in this appalling slave-labor camp year after year, and survived. Why, under these conditions, did they even bother to live? He knew why. Damn right he knew why. Because in the back of the mind of each and every prisoner, there was hope. The belief that they would someday be free again. No one was going to take that belief away. A man might seem to give up under these conditions, he knew, might even appear totally defeated. But somewhere in his heart there was still that belief. If there wasn't, only then would that man give in, just lie down and die.

"We are ahead of schedule, workers of the Imperial Revolutionary Army!" Kam Chek announced.

"Cut the crap, Genghis, will ya," Tremain muttered from the bank rank.

"You have done well," Kam Chek continued. "The harvest, it appears, will be completed by the end of this day's work, perhaps as early as this afternoon. I congratulate you. Half of you will then begin to bundle your harvest. You will complete this chore today..."

Kam Chek left the warning unfinished. Bolan suspected what the veterans knew: what would happen to prisoners who did not finish wrapping the raw opium for transport. Most likely those prisoners would be the first ones to die on the march, forced by beating and starvation to drop out.

"Therefore, workers, we will set out in the morning. Early. Prepare yourselves for the journey. Rid your minds this instant of any foolish thoughts of escape."

Bolan would have sworn Kam Chek looked his way. Did he know? And what if he did? he asked himself. Or had Bolan imagined that warning glance?

"Strip yourselves of any weakness, particularly the loathsome baggage of self-pity."

"I didn't know ol' Genghis was such a poet," Larry Jones growled under his breath.

"You will need all of your strength this year. The haul is much larger than usual. We do not have sufficient transport for one march alone." Kam Chek paused, smiled. "It will be necessary, then, to make two marches. Heh-heh."

Bolan could feel the despair building among the captives around him, like some clutching, suffocating force. Then he heard a groan, a plaintive cry from somewhere in the field. Two rows down from where Bolan stood, a prisoner dropped to his knees. The man was weeping.

Kam Chek barked an order in Thai at his guards. Seconds later, a guard stood behind the sobbing prisoner. The guard pulled a Tokarev 9 mm pistol, placed the muzzle against the prisoner's temple, squeezed the trigger. The Russian pistol cracked once. The prisoner disappeared from Bolan's sight, dropping behind the plants like a stone.

Bolan's teeth were clenched, his jaw tight.

A prisoner a few rows away from Bolan cursed Kam Chek softly.

"Workers!" Kam Chek bellowed. "That weakling was a coward. What happened to him is what will happen to you if you show such weakness. Only your punishment will be worse. See that you remain strong. See that you act like men and not like women and children. You are, after all, men, aren't you?"

Bolan was sure now that Kam Chek was looking directly at him, as if the butcher was challenging him.

"Back to work!"

As the prisoners returned to scraping the poppy bulbs, Bolan observed Davis approaching Kam Chek. The pigeon and the warlord began to talk. Even at a distance of more than one hundred feet, Bolan could see the rapid rise and fall of Kam Chek's chest, the anger that blazed in his stare.

Moments later, Kam Chek and "Virginia Slim" walked toward Bolan and the prisoners in his circle. The captives froze in the act of cutting the bulbs.

"Which one?" Kam Chek snapped.

Davis, a cigarette dangling from the corner of his mouth, pointed at Carver.

No, Bolan groaned soundlessly. Not now. *Damn!*

But it was too late.

Three guards encircled Carver, their AK-47s trained on his chest.

Bolan read the naked terror in Carver's eyes. Carver was doomed, and he knew it, Bolan could tell. Then something steeled Carver's expression. Defiance. Carver looked at Kam Chek, as if to say, take me. Go ahead. Beat me. I'll tell you nothing.

"Why were you in another prisoners' quarters last night?" Kam Chek rasped at Carver. The warlord stood menacingly before the prisoner, his legs apart, his hand wrapped around the hilt of his sword. "You were heard discussing something with the prisoners last night. What was the subject of your discussion?"

Carver held his ground in silence, his eyes hardened with hatred.

The guy was going to hang tough to protect the plan, Bolan thought. But he knew where Carver would end up. The black room. Would the soldier endure the hell that Ronny Brennan had suffered? Would he break, save himself by talking, or would he sacrifice his life so that the others might have a chance to attempt the escape?

"No matter," Kam Chek said, softening his tone. "I should interrogate the other prisoners as well, but I cannot afford to spare the manpower at this time. But, you...you, Carver, are expendable!" he rasped.

"You will talk. Or you will cry out for death and welcome her. Take him!" he ordered the guards.

As the guards dragged Carver away from the field, Kam Chek walked up to Bolan. The warlord shook with suppressed rage.

"Bo-leen...understand that I will be watching you very carefully from now on. You will march the entire time in front of me. I will disperse the men of your hut throughout the line. Whatever you are thinking, do not think it." Kam Chek lowered his voice to a chilling whisper. "I do not want to kill you, Bo-leen. I will keep you alive at all costs. You will survive both marches, *ferang*, I shall see to it. You and your friend will be here for the rest of your lives. You will leave here only in death, with the worms and the maggots eating out your eyes. But your death is a long, long way from coming, Bo-leen. I assure you."

A terrible hunger to spill Kam Chek's blood seemed to swell Bolan's limbs with pressure. Damn, but he wanted to drive the blade of the knife he held into Kam Chek's stomach, rip out his guts with one long wrenching twist. It was a long time since he had experienced such an overpowering rage, such a burning desire for vengeance. A long time, yeah. Perhaps an eternity since the death of April Rose. What fevered his bloodlust even more at the moment was the mere sight of the traitor Davis. The ball-less rat just stood there beside Kam Chek, grinning in triumph, puffing on his cigarette.

"Get back to work, Bolan," Davis ordered.

Bolan didn't move.

Kam Chek drew his sword.

Bolan heard bolts cocking back, turned, saw the muzzles of two AK-47s pointed at his face.

Kam Chek chuckled, the samurai sword hanging low by his side. The sun's rays glinted off the gold of the hilt and the finely polished steel of the blade. "It will be very difficult for you to finish the harvest with only one arm, my friend," Kam Chek said. "That does not mean you cannot march tomorrow. If you have no legs and no arms, Bo-leen, you will still march. You will crawl the whole way, I assure you."

Bolan hesitated for another second, then he turned away from Kam Chek.

"It pays to be special, Bolan." Davis hurled the taunt at Bolan's back. The hatred that seemed to emanate from the bodies of other prisoners was palpable. "Right?"

Yeah, right, Bolan thought. You're real special, all right, guy.

Bolan would remember Davis.

When the time came.

No, he was not about to forget the King Rat.

Not until he was finished with the traitor. No. Not even the fires of hell were going to save the bastard from Bolan.

THE SCREAMS OF AGONY ENDED an hour after the prisoners broke for the night.

Inside the hut, Bolan, Grimaldi, and their seven fellow prisoners sat in angry silence. Each was lost in his own gloomy thoughts, perhaps wondering what had happened to Carver.

Ronny Brennan had been removed from the hut that morning. No one knew where the tortured druglord had been taken, or what had become of him. No one had asked. As far as Bolan was concerned, the punk had merely lain down in the bed of his choosing.

Struber finally broke the leaden hush. "Do you think he talked?"

"What if he did, man? So what?" Jones quietly growled.

"That's right," Bolan said, then looked at each man in turn. "We do it. Same plan. Same place. You'll know when."

"It's crazy," Struber protested. "We'll be massacred, for sure."

"It's even crazier to do nothing, Struber," Polanski shot back.

The soldiers and the ex-CIA man looked pointedly at Bolan.

Bolan nodded. "Get yourselves in the right state of mind. Harden up quick."

Struber let out a pent-up breath, shook his head. "I don't like it."

"Ain't nobody askin' you to like it, man," Jones said.

Silence. Plump flies and mosquitoes buzzed around the hut, dancing in the flickering torchlight.

Bolan and Grimaldi looked at each other. Bolan read the fear in Grimaldi's eyes, but the longer he held the pilot's stare, the more a grim resolve seemed to push away any shadow of doubt Grimaldi might have held about the breakout attempt. Grimaldi knew the score, and he believed. He and Bolan had been in plenty of doomsday situations together, had survived many campaigns together on the hellfire trail. Death had pressed its razor's edge more than once against their throats. But this time was different. This time they were not in the heat of a battle, with only their courage, skill and determination to defeat the enemy. This time they were not on the offensive, attacking the enemy. This time they were weakened, starved, beaten up. And their allies were a pack of miserable shackled creatures who had undergone years of punishment.

There was plenty to chew on, Bolan knew. Nobody wants to die. Never believe a son of a bitch who says he isn't afraid of death, he thought. Only an insane man, or a suicide, openly invites death. Okay, so maybe he'd invited death before. Hell, he thought he *had* invited death, countless times in scores of battle zones. But death, like anything else to the warrior, was something to be conquered.

So much still had to be done, Bolan knew. Too many battles still needed to be waged and won. Too many tabs needed squaring. But Bolan could not afford to look beyond the next few days. He had enough savages and soulless monsters on his hands already. And they needed to taste the cold edge of his sword.

"You think any of the guys from the other hut will spread the word?" Struber wanted to know.

"Shuddup," Ribitowitz snarled through clenched teeth. "You got a big mouth and a short memory, pal. If *you* end up in the black room, we're all finished for sure."

Struber spit, then lapsed into a brooding silence.

"It doesn't matter one way or another," Sellers chipped in. "We're on our own anyway." He looked at Bolan for confirmation, or perhaps denial. "Right?"

"We'll know soon."

"Ferangs!"

Kam Chek's voice shot through the hut, jolted the prisoners as if they'd been hit by an electrical charge.

The warlord stood in the doorway, a burlap sack in his hands. The bottom of the sack was dark with a crimson stain.

Bolan cursed to himself. One more score, he thought, one more score to settle up.

Scowling, but saying nothing, Kam Chek upended the sack.

Carver's head tumbled out of the sack, thudded on the dirt floor of the hut and rolled a few inches.

Struber vomited. A ripe stench began to spread through the hut like an invisible cloud. The prisoners ignored Struber.

Kam Chek tossed the sack on the floor, left the head lying at his feet. "Your friend has died a senseless and stupid death."

"You're a bloody fuckin' animal, Kam Chek," Polanski snarled. "Someday...I swear to God, someday...you'll pay."

Kam Chek appeared to be amused. "I shall remember what you have said, *ferang.*"

"You do that," Polanski said.

Bolan scrutinized Kam Chek's face. Judging by the warlord's initial outburst and by the look of disappointment in his eyes, Bolan guessed that Carver had gone to his death without breaking down and leaking the escape plan.

Kam Chek raked a cold gaze over the prisoners. "I suggest that you get a good night's sleep," he said. "We leave in four hours."

Kam Chek left the hut.

Polanski shut his eyes, squeezing the bridge of his nose with his thumb and forefinger. The big man's shoulders trembled. "The bastards...the fucking bastards...I'll kill them all...."

Sellers directed a strange, blank look at Bolan. "Carver was a good man. He was a friend to all of us."

Ribitowitz looked away from the severed head. "He didn't deserve this. Christ, he didn't deserve this."

A cold ball of fury lodged in his guts, Bolan looked at each of the faces around him. Every one was clouded with sorrow and anger. The men's rage, he knew, was directed at the savages beyond the walls of the hut. They didn't blame Bolan for Carver's death. They couldn't. It could have happened to any one of them.

And the guy had made the supreme sacrifice.

Now it was up to the rest of them to make sure Carver's death was not in vain.

Bolan read murder in the eyes that stared back at him.

The prisoners were committed. Now, more than ever.

18

An hour before dawn the prisoners were rounded up.

As Kam Chek shouted orders and cursed the slowness with which the prisoners assembled, more than sixty guards quickly fastened manacles around the wrists and the ankles of the men who would be force-marched to Bangkok. A lone klieg light bathed the scene.

Under the repeated scourge of the whips, the prisoners strapped the bales of raw heroin across the backs of dozens of horses, oxen and mules. Then the transport trucks were loaded to capacity. Finally, the heroin supply that was left over after the loading was piled in drums and barrels near the trail that led to Torquemandan's palace.

The three pigeons urged on the slave labor force. Each one of the rats carried a holstered sidearm, and threatened the other prisoners with death.

For Mack Bolan, the night seemed to have passed within the blink of an eye. It was time, he knew.

Time to face death.

Time to meet his destiny.

Time for judgment.

Time once again to win or lose.

In the Executioner's war, there was never a stalemate.

The column was formed. Under constant verbal harassment and whiplashing, the prisoners picked up the burlap sacks of pure poison. Bolan's pack was heavy. He guessed it weighed somewhere in the area of eighty to ninety pounds. He assessed the condition of the other prisoners. Some of the inmates were so weak already that they fell on their backs when struggling to get their arms through the straps of their packs. Bolan knew that many of these men were going to die; they would drop from sheer exhaustion. Others would be driven so hard, they would simply collapse, perhaps even cry out for death to take them.

It was going to be ugly. That much the Executioner knew.

As the guards used their AK-47s to prod him to his position at the very rear of the column, Bolan spotted Ronny Brennan. The druglord appeared dead on his feet. His empty gaze seemed to be focused on some point far ahead. The druglord, halfway up the column on the outer left side, his pack of heroin still at his feet, was now most definitely experiencing life on the other side of the wall. Bolan did not feel sorry for him.

Two guards converged on Brennan. One flayed him across the back, the other cursed at him, pummeled him about the head with his fists until Brennan bent and hefted the pack to his shoulders. Bolan thought he saw a tear break from the corner of Brennan's eye.

Grimaldi fell in beside Bolan.

Steely-eyed, Bolan looked at the pilot for a moment.

"Let's hang tough, Striker, huh?"

"The only way, Jack."

"Bo-leen! Look."

Bolan looked behind him, saw Kam Chek standing beside the rear transport truck. There, he held out Bolan's confiscated M-60, and smiled.

"Very nice weapon for a *ferang*, Bo-leen. These, also," he said, as the armament Bolan and Grimaldi had brought with them was passed among Kam Chek's cutthroats. The AutoMag. The mini-Uzi and Uzi SMG. The MM-1 and the two M-16s with the attached M-203s. Commando knives and garrotes.

It was all there, Bolan saw. Was the fool trying to tempt him?

One of the guards laughed as he took the M-60 from Kam Chek. The savage said something to Kam Chek in Thai.

The warlord looked at Bolan. "He says your weapons will do nice work later. Perhaps on you. Heh-heh."

Laugh now, bastard, Bolan thought, *you won't be laughing when I'm through with you.*

When the loading was finished, there was a half-hour wait. Bolan wondered what the hell the delay was all about. As he stood in line, the pack of heroin seemed to grow heavier by the moment, a lead weight rooting him to the spot.

Finally, the members of the Devil's Horn appeared along the trail. Ten scumbags, Bolan counted, including the chief cannibal, Torquemandan. They were all dressed in smart white three-piece suits. Not a rumple. Not a speck of dirt. Most of the slime didn't, or couldn't, look at the prisoners. Instead, they walked straight to the transport trucks, where they climbed into the cabs.

Bolan noticed a fat guy, whom he guessed must weigh more than three hundred pounds, take a seat in a jeep. A tall skinny guy followed the fat man into the jeep. Bolan suspected the skinny dude had a problem with his nerves, as he kept cracking the knuckles of both hands. Bolan hoped to shatter that guy's nerves for good.

Grimaldi was grimly watching the odd pair, too. "Who the hell are they supposed to be? Laurel and Hardy?"

No, Bolan thought, sick dogs—who need to be put to sleep.

A moment later Kam Chek approached Torquemandan and conferred with him about something. While they were still talking, Chaika Kan Khang, dressed in his green military blouse and slacks, walked to the head of the column. His medals rattled with his swaggering gait.

"Workers of the Imperial Revolutionary Army. Listen!" Khang clasped his hands behind his back, jutted out his chinless jaw. "Many of you have marched before. You know what is required of you. You know what must be done. For those of you marching for the first time, I will go over the rules. Listen carefully. You will only be told once.

"First, there is to be no talking among any of you for any reason. Even a word is punishable by death. Second, and most important, you will do exactly as you are told, when you are told. Disobedience is punishable by death. You must not at any time fall down. Exhaustion is punishable by death. You will not at any time relieve yourself until we break at night. Soiling yourself is punishable by death.

"There are those of you who are weak, we know this. The weak will die soon enough. There are those of you who are strong. You will survive. Under no circumstances are the strong to help or encourage the weak. This is punishable by death.

"Today, we will cover thirty-five miles. We will accept nothing under thirty-five miles, and if we must settle for less, ten of you will volunteer for a firing squad. Every day after today, we will cover no less than thirty miles. I hope that this is acceptable to you."

Bolan saw several pairs of shoulders sag, heard pent-up breath rasp the steamy air. Despair had already gripped several of the prisoners. Despair this early, he knew, meant certain death for those experiencing it. Thirty-five miles, he thought, was going to break the backs of the weaker men. A good day's march for a soldier was twenty miles, with food and water in the belly, and no more than a sixty-pound rucksack.

Khang stood in silence for several moments. He seemed to be studying the prisoners. Finally, as if to drive one more nail into the coffin, he said, "I wish you luck."

At last, the doors of vehicles slammed. A moment later, engines coughed, growled to life.

Kam Chek screamed for the prisoners to move out, as rays of golden light glowed in the sky to the east.

Whips cracked, scorched the legs and the buttocks of the prisoners.

A cry of pain rose from somewhere near the front of the column.

Mack Bolan choked down a groan of pain as he commanded his own wooden legs to move.

The death march began.

THE FIRST DAY OF THE MARCH quickly turned into a trial of endurance. The only way to defeat his suffering under the whip and carry the weight of the heroin pack, Bolan knew, was to will himself not to think about it.

After several miles of forced marching, with the frequent bite of the whip against his legs and Kam Chek shrieking insults at the prisoners, the effort of not thinking about the ordeal began to seem impossible.

One foot in front of the other. One yard, one mile at a time, Bolan told himself. He tried turning his thoughts to other people.

Like Hal Brognola. Where was he at this moment? What was he doing? Bolan felt a half smile tug at the corner of his lips. The big Fed was probably worrying right now about the two Stony Man warriors. Bolan pictured Brognola chewing his lower lip, maybe popping a couple of antacid tablets, chomping on a cigar. The Fed was a good man with a tough job.

Then Bolan's mind went back to better times long since gone. He thought about his childhood, the teenage years, the often painful time of growing that children experienced as they groped their way to adulthood. He stopped short, though, when his thoughts turned to the tragic loss of his family.

It was no good. He couldn't focus on any happy memories from the past for more than a few seconds, and frustration brought his cold rage surging to the surface.

His head was filled with the sound of Kam Chek's voice, with the savage's cruel words about his family's sudden, horrible end. All over again, Bolan felt the pain, a deep, clawing, clinging pain that knocked the breath right out of his lungs. No, though he would never forget, for now he must not remember. The past was gone forever. He had to stay in the present, or he was dead. He must feed the vengeance. And he must not forget for one second why he was here. And what he had to do.

After every half mile or so, Bolan would check on Grimaldi. The guy had been by his side for what now seemed like forever. He was holding on, but strain was already showing in his eyes. His stare seemed to swallow itself. Bolan loved the guy, the damn fool, he thought. Jack shouldn't be here. Bolan wished to God that Jack had gotten sick back in the States, had broken an arm or a leg and stayed home. But he knew Grimaldi too well. The ace pilot would have badgered, cajoled, pleaded with everybody within earshot to make the mission. He would have made himself such a beautiful, loyal pain in the ass to everybody....

Bolan turned his thoughts once again to the escape. He steeled his will back to vengeance, to the fight he so desperately wanted, to the destruction he so feverishly sought to wreak on the house of cards that was the Devil's Horn. As he marched he looked at the backs of the heads of the prisoners in front of him. These men had suffered too much, endured and survived more horror than any man had a right to be asked to bear. It was time to remove that weight once and for all. Forever.

The sun rose higher. By midmorning it cleared the jungle line. The temperature mounted, the heat was a fierce blaze, a sucking vortex. Swarms of flies and mosquitoes buzzed around the column. The insects picked at the blood and sweat that sheathed every face and body there; they resembled a rolling black blanket on the backs and legs of the pack animals. Chains rattled, a maddening din of tinkling metal. Engines rumbled in a sense-numbing drone. When the procession hit a dirt path that snaked through the forested hills, the lead trucks kicked up balls of boiling dust, and prisoners and guards alike became brown, dirt-caked mummies. The stench of sweat, blood and animal dung filled the air. Bolan quickly got used to the smell, indeed he focused on it to help clear his senses when fatigue began hardening to a cementlike heaviness in his limbs.

The guards, Bolan noted, changed shifts by the hour. Thirty AK-47-wielding cutthroats would march with the column while the relieved force would climb into the backs of the transport trucks. While resting, the guards ate bread and ham, drank greedily from their canteens, smoked cigarettes and laughed. They taunted the prisoners, dangling food and water before their hollow eyes like a carrot to a rabbit.

The whole enterprise was an abomination, Bolan thought. One perverse, goddamn twisting of life. A flaunting of godliness by devils who held the power of life and death.

For a brief moment, as a hot breeze punched a hole in the dust cloud and the column began moving down a steep slope between the foothills, Bolan spotted the other prisoners of his circle. Jones, Ribitowitz and Struber led the three-man-wide column. Karn and Tremain marched almost at the middle point, and Polanski and Sellers were four rows ahead of Bolan and Grimaldi.

Bolan made a quick assessment of the situation. There were five transport trucks, two armored personnel carriers and the jeep with the mounted .50-caliber machine gun. From the other prisoners, Bolan had learned that a relief force of Khang's mercenaries always waited for the column near the processing laboratory that was their destination. Tremain estimated this force at fifty guns. Another force of thirty cutthroats had been left behind at the fields to guard the leftover stock of heroin. But the heart of Torquemandan's mercenary army was here on the march, Bolan knew. He would have to cut out the heart first, then sever the head at the laboratory, and finally chop the legs off the body back at the field.

That was the plan of attack. There was only a slim chance, Bolan realized grimly, that the breakout attempt could be pulled off. He was counting on an initial moment of confusion and panic, on the part of both the guards and the prisoners who had not been informed of the plan to break out of bondage. Bolan knew that he, Grimaldi and the prisoners of their circle had to seize the initiative swiftly, and jolt the other prisoners into action by the sudden move.

"Bo-leen."

Turning his head, Bolan found that Kam Chek was directly behind him, in the same spot he'd held since they set out. But now there was another man beside Kam Chek. Bolan had seen him with the members of the Horn that morning. He was a short, stocky, dark-haired Asian who, for some reason, had shed his white jacket and silk shirt and had taken a whip from a guard. Bolan returned the Asian's hard stare. He read the guy as a savage.

"I must introduce you to Mr. Tuhban Mongkut," Kam Chek announced. He bowed his head slightly as he looked at the Asian. "He will be your companion for the duration of the trip. See that you accommodate Mr. Mongkut, *s'il vous plaît*. See that you show him the proper respect. He is a man of power and high place.''

I'll bet he is, Bolan thought. Mongkut's muscled torso, slick with sweat and coated with dust, looked like the forged plating of Roman armor. In his eyes was the look of a man eager to inflict pain, a man who had caused others great suffering through his own physical strength, a man who was proud of the fear he could instill in the hearts of weaker or defeated men. Bolan looked away from Mongkut, suddenly aware that he had a formidable adversary in this Asian of ''power and high place.''

The hours dragged by.

Several prisoners began to stumble from the line. When they dropped, they quickly climbed to their feet again as whips tore into their faces and arms.

By midafternoon, Bolan guessed that they had covered a little more than twenty miles. Raw spots had formed on both his arches from rubbing against the insides of his boots. The blisters were a minor discomfort compared to the burning ache that wrapped him from head to foot. Blisters would soon become the least of his worries, he suspected.

The prisoners had not eaten since shortly before setting out. Their pace began to drag noticeably.

As some of the prisoners began to succumb to exhaustion, Kam Chek, incensed, ran up and down the line. Screaming insults, he flayed the prisoners, and the guards followed his example.

Then, Bolan saw the inevitable happen.

One prisoner in the middle of the column cried out, then tumbled away from the right outside row. Another prisoner dropped to the trail a moment later.

Kam Chek shrieked for the column to halt.

Bolan and Grimaldi looked at each other, both showing anger despite their weariness.

And the horror began.

The transport trucks and the jeep squealed to a halt on worn brake shoes. Torquemandan opened the door of the truck he was riding in, and climbed out onto the step.

"What is it?" Torquemandan yelled back at Kam Chek.

"We have a loafer! A weakling!" Kam Chek shouted.

Torquemandan looked at the two fallen men with disgust. "Well, get rid of them. Hurry up."

Two guards with flamethrowers stepped forward.

The doomed prisoners lay motionless, dust settling over their outstretched bodies. One of them, an Asian, looked up at Kam Chek. There was pleading in his eyes. The other prisoner, a Caucasian, groaned, "I...can't move...can't...go on...."

"I won't stand by and watch this," Bolan snarled. He took a step forward, but froze as three guards swung AK-47s toward him and cocked the bolts on the Russian assault rifles. Turning, Bolan looked at Mongkut.

Mongkut spit on the ground, fingered his whip. He returned Bolan's hard-eyed gaze with defiance.

"No...no!" the white prisoner cried out as the guards dragged first him, then the other man, off the trail by their legs into a ditch.

Quickly, efficiently, the guards stripped the packs off the doomed men.

Kam Chek stood watching, clenched fists on his hips.

Tongues of orange fire roared out of the metal nozzles of the flamethrowers.

Screams ripped through the air. Flames lapped up the two prisoners. They thrashed in the ditch like fish out of water, their piercing shrieks of agony filling the air.

Seated in their jeep, the fat Rolly Woods and the skinny Charlie Wells soon turned away from the sight of the writhing human torches and faced front. Their faces were a pasty white.

Even after the men had burned to death, Bolan thought he could still hear their lingering howls. He shut his eyes, trembling with raw fury.

As the sickening-sweet stench of roasting flesh ripened the dust-choked air, one prisoner vomited. Another man fainted. Both prisoners were pulled away from the column and shot, point-blank, through the temples.

Finally there was silence.

Kam Chek stared at the human pyres for a long moment. He almost appeared mesmerized by the sight of shriveling, blackened flesh, by the crackle of the flames.

Then whips sizzled flesh, as the order was given to move on. Bolan's rage paralyzed him for a second. Thoughts of vengeance filled his mind.

Mongkut shoved Bolan in the back. "Move!"

As he walked past the burning bodies, Bolan looked Kam Chek dead in the eye. The Khmer Rouge bastard smiled back at him.

"There you see the penalty for weakness. Make sure that you are strong," Kam said.

Strong, yeah, Bolan thought.

He would show Kam Chek strong, all right.

With his own two hands he would show this monster strength. With the death grip that would crush Kam Chek's throat to bloody mush.

Behind the procession, twin spires of black smoke curled toward the sky.

19

By midmorning of the second day of the march, Kam Chek and his cutthroats had littered the trail behind the procession with bullet-riddled, burning corpses.

Bolan had counted fifteen prisoners who had so far been butchered for falling in exhaustion or despair. Kam Chek and his savages always slaughtered the prisoners without hesitation, without the least sign of remorse or doubt. Bolan knew that more prisoners would be murdered. But, at the moment, there was nothing he could do to save them. He felt utter, unshakable futility right then, and in his weary state he grimly wondered if such a feeling had ever killed a man. But the frustration, he realized, was only adding more explosive fury to the time bomb set to blow inside of him. In this case frustration was a saving grace.

Bolan chafed, though, impatient to reach the village at the midway point, which would be the site for the do-or-die breakout attempt. He doubted that he could stomach much more of Kam Chek's savagery and be forced simply to stand by and look on, shackled, helpless to strike back. His own physical strength was beginning to fail him, but the images of carnage on that trail of death stayed branded in Bolan's mind. He had watched men die cruelly, senselessly, for no other reason than to slake Kam Chek's thirst for blood. Rage kept Mack Bolan moving. Rage was his ultimate guiding force.

Earlier, Davis and the other two rats had helped to stoke the fire in Bolan's belly. The scum had executed several of their fellow prisoners with the same brutal glee with which Kam Chek and his savages carried out their butchery. Twice, Bolan had seen the traitors force other prisoners to step out of the line. Guards had kept AK-47s trained on the men selected by Davis. Under the threat of death, those prisoners were forced to execute their comrades, who had been selected by Davis's fellow rats, strangling the life out of them with rope. One of the executioners, his will broken, his physical endurance shattered, had dropped to his knees and wept bitterly. With one furious swipe of his samurai sword, Kam Chek had cut that man's head off, then he had kicked the severed head into the ditch. The packs that the dead men had hauled were removed from their bodies and tossed into one of the transport trucks.

By midafternoon, the march reached the village at the fifty-mile mark. As usual, the animals were fed first. Whenever there was an easily accessible stream or swamp, they were led there by prisoners and guards alike to drink their fill.

Finally, the prisoners were herded together in a clearing on the outer fringes of a rice paddy. Even while they were eating they were not allowed to remove their packs. Each was rationed to a bowl of rice, a piece of bread and a cup of water. They ate in silence, watching as Thai villagers carried from their huts offerings of meat, loaves of bread and sugarcane for Kam Chek and Kan Khang, the guards, and the white suits of the Devil's Horn.

Bolan looked at Mongkut. He had felt the Asian's stare boring into the back of his head for the past day and a half. At the moment, Mongkut had elected not to join Kam Chek, Khang and the others as they devoured the food they took from the villagers. Instead, Mongkut stood behind Bolan, watching him with eyes that didn't even appear to flicker. The man, Bolan knew, was going to be a problem when the time came.

Mongkut barked an order at two guards. He pointed at Bolan and Grimaldi, then strode off into the brush to relieve himself. The guards fired up cigarettes, seemed to ignore the prisoners as they drew on their smokes and talked to each other.

With dirt-begrimed fingers, Bolan pushed rice into his mouth. He was stiff, sore, and the blisters on his feet had burst, leaving behind burning, itching, raw flesh. He caught Tremain and Jones looking at him expectantly. No, it was too soon. It couldn't happen yet. Judging by the pace of the march so far—and he had no reason to think that it would change—he estimated they would reach the village at the midway point in the late evening the day after tomorrow. A little more time was still needed to wear down the guards, to make them long to end the march as quickly as possible, to work up their hunger to sate their lust in the halfway village. At this point, the guards still appeared alert, the piss-and-fire was a good twenty or thirty miles from being driven out of them. Yeah, Bolan knew that by then he, Grimaldi and the other prisoners would be even more beaten down by the march. But hope, vengeance and hate were their only, their very powerful, allies.

Tremain and Jones frowned as Bolan slowly shook his head.

Bolan looked down the ragged line of seated prisoners. He was searching for Brennan, not out of any concern for the druglord, but merely curious as to how the punk was holding up. Finally he spotted him, sitting slumped several yards away. Clearly, the former big shot from New York was not faring well. That haunted stare of disillusionment over Torquemandan's betrayal still lurked in Brennan's eyes. But Bolan detected something else in Brennan's expression also. Despair. The punk couldn't even touch his food. The Top Dog had given up, and Bolan didn't give him another day before he checked out for good. Bolan knew Brennan would never understand it all, not even as death was coming for him. Ronny Brennan had lived a lie. He had bought his life at the expense of the lives of others. In this instance, Bolan reflected, the punk had sold his soul to the Devil. Torquemandan. And now the Devil wanted the return on his investment of the borrowed time Brennan had bought.

Mongkut stepped from the brush. Bolan watched as the Asian snarled some angry words in his native tongue at the guards. He was chastising the guards, most likely, Bolan guessed, because they appeared to take the prisoners' captivity for granted.

Bolan hoped those guards were lax in their duties, just one more time.

As they finished eating their meager meal, some of the prisoners toppled over in exhaustion to catch a few moments' rest, even to sleep.

Bolan's own eyelids were drooping. He couldn't remember ever feeling so tired, so damn bone-beaten weary. There was a throbbing behind his ears, a fire burning in his brain. Fever? Malaria? He couldn't be sure. At least not yet.

A strange, peaceful warmth began to spread through his body, to envelop an ache that seemed centered right at the core of his being. His eyes closed. His head slumped forward. . . .

Bolan wasn't sure how long he'd been asleep when the electricity shot across his legs. Jolting awake, he heard Mongkut cursing him. Then the whip came down again, tore open another slash across Bolan's thighs.

The column was being ordered to move out of the village.

Bolan pulled himself out of his daze, shook off the grogginess, and clambered to his feet. Long shadows were stretching down from the hills to the west.

The sun was setting.

Another day in hell was almost over.

Or was it? Mack Bolan wondered, as the guards shoved the prisoners into formation.

Near the edge of the village, Bolan saw Kam Chek, Kan Khang and Torquemandan. They were arguing.

Bolan didn't care what they were bickering about. He cared about only one thing, something that transcended the physical pain and numbing weariness he felt.

He wanted to nurse that feeling until he exploded.

Vengeance.

Mack Bolan could think only about killing his tormentors. Nothing else seemed to matter anymore. Except, of course, survival.

TORQUEMANDAN LISTENED to the same song and dance from Khang and Kam Chek every year. Every year the two warlords insisted on the rest stops. They needed to replenish the troops' food and water, they argued. They desperately needed a rest, they claimed, or weariness would settle in, perhaps cause a dangerous lapse in concentration. But there was always more to it than that, Torquemandan knew.

What did they take him for anyway, he thought, a fool? It was the village women they wanted. Sex, plain and simple. In the end they always agreed that he was right, but their evasive reasoning always put him on the defensive. And when he was on the defensive in an argument his smooth tongue always failed him. And then he sank to their level, he thought, adopting the crude attitude of a barbarian, an unrefined, uncultured, bullheaded gangster.

He had a fortune in raw heroin to haul, process and distribute. And here they were, demanding he let them indulge their lust. But they didn't care about that; they thought it was his problem. He was sure he knew what they were thinking: the job would get done, so why not mix pleasure with business? They didn't exactly say this, hell no, he thought. They didn't have to say it, because he was perfectly able to read it in their patronizing tones, their feeble attempts at pleading their case with him.

Torquemandan always found the orgies during the rest breaks distasteful. But maybe it was good for morale. Happy troops, he forced himself to believe, were good troops.

Still, he was going to hold his ground on the issue. If he could get them to wait to spill their lust until they reached the next village, the procession would at least be halfway to its objective. And Torquemandan could claim half a victory.

Kam Chek was displeased. He spread his hands in an imploring gesture. "It is such a small matter, *Mon Général*. Surely a few hours will not matter. It will give the prisoners a chance to rest, my men a much-needed rest, also."

As if this cutthroat gook, Torquemandan thought, was actually worried about the prisoners. But if Kam Chek wasn't worried about them, then he should be. The prisoners were already dropping like flies, and this was going to cause a serious manpower shortage if the crap continued. But the bloodlust of Kam Chek and his soldiers seemed nowhere close to being satisfied. He wondered if the brutal warlord was making an extra effort just for Bolan's sake. Shit, the egos that he had to keep stroked, he thought.

Torquemandan looked at the prisoners as the guards whipped them into formation. He then glanced at the faces of Woods and Wells. Both men were chomping on chicken legs. The obese Woods ate like a man who hadn't seen a square meal in six months, devouring the chicken leg so furiously that the jeep shuddered slightly under his shifting weight. The sight disgusted Torquemandan.

What was worse, he was witnessing once more just how little stomach some of the members of the organization had for the cruelty inflicted on the prisoners so far. He had already allowed three distributors to fly ahead in his private plane to the laboratory. He recalled how the three had acted back at the palace, like petulant children, as if the march was something they had no desire to know about, as if death and suffering were beneath such accomplished men of the world. How the hell did those ball-less bastards, who belonged in an ivory tower, think the scag got to Bangkok in the first place? Well, he'd relented and let them fly ahead, and he was beginning to regret that decision, and even to resent the other members of the organization present. Was Mongkut the only one of them with any balls? he wondered. Maybe it was time to find out.

Maybe, he thought, these bigshot distributors of his here should walk the rest of the way. Maybe then they'd stop taking him for granted, and think hard about just where their prosperity came from. Because if he wanted to, he could take everything away from them, and leave them with nothing but blood on their hands. Their own hands.

This was the most important time of the year for the organization, and Torquemandan expected everyone to chip in and do his part. Or there would be hell to pay. The members there, sitting in the relative safety of their vehicles, were going in with the prisoners, all right, all the goddamn way to the processing compound. They would just have to wait for two or three weeks if necessary, until the heroin was processed, cut and distributed. And their bank accounts had better be plenty fat, he thought. He had told them all months ago that this was going to be the biggest harvest to date. He had told them to be ready to fork over massive amounts of cold, hard cash. Mountains of the green stuff.

"Perhaps," Kan Khang said to Torquemandan, "you are correct, *Mon Général*. We will wait until we reach the next village. By then, all of us will surely need a rest. And, there are many more women there than in this . . . pigsty." He looked around contemptuously at the dozen thatch-roofed huts as an ox lumbered down the dirt street. At the far end of the village a group of half-naked children were huddled with their parents. The villagers were watching the exchange between the three men with obvious fear.

Kam Chek threw up his hands. "Ah, very well. Does that meet your approval, *Mon Général*?"

No, it damn well didn't meet his approval, Torquemandan thought. But what the hell could he do? Kam Chek, Kan Khang and his men were nothing but Khmer Rouge and Pathet Lao riffraff, cutthroats who would probably just as soon turn on the master as the slave. And the *Mon Général* shit was starting to get on Torquemandan's nerves a little. He would indulge them because he saw no choice. He didn't need a mutiny, after all. Besides, he liked to sample the flesh of the Thai village women himself. He wondered why his warlords didn't point out his hypocrisy. But, then, he would have sworn he saw accusation in their stares.

Still, he held the upper hand, even in the silence of cynicism. For he was well aware of their own hypocrisy, and Kam Chek and Kan Khang were smart enough to know when to keep their mouths shut. During the course of the year, every village on the Thai peninsula was visited by the two warlords and their mercenary brigands. Sometimes Kam Chek would be gone for two months at a stretch, roaming the countryside at will, raping, pillaging, capturing peasants and bringing them back to work the poppy fields. No, Torquemandan thought, those two weren't fooling anybody.

He sighed. "Yes, very well, the next village. But the rest stop must not be as long as it usually is, understand?"

Both Kam Chek and Kan Khang nodded in agreement.

Torquemandan dismissed them both, then walked back over to his truck. He was anxious to get this year's march over with as quickly, as painlessly as possible. For some reason, he was feeling the strain of keeping the whole damn thing going, making sure his mercenaries towed the line.

He hoped he wouldn't end up regretting his decision to allow his cutthroats to indulge themselves at the next rest break. If there was any shit, any shit at all, he told himself, heads would roll.

And the black room would be filled to capacity.

Indeed, his torture chamber wouldn't be vacant for a long, long time.

DURING THE MORNING of the third day of the march, two more prisoners collapsed, unable to get up. One of the fallen men was Ronny Brennan.

From his position at the rear of the column, Bolan saw the New York drug czar meet his doom. Ronny Brennan died exactly as he had lived. Like a maggot.

Immediately Kam Chek alerted Torquemandan, who took the warlord's Tokarev pistol and walked right up to Brennan.

Brennan looked up at his lord and master and raised his pulped hand as Torquemandan pointed the pistol at his face. Brennan was delirious, but when he realized he was about to die, terror seemed to surge renewed life into his punished body.

"N-no...please, Mr. Torquemandan...you can't... N-o-o...I don't want to die!" Brennan cried out.

Kam Chek snickered.

Torquemandan squeezed the trigger of the Tokarev, drilled a third eye through Brennan's forehead with the 9 mm slug. Then Torquemandan thrust the pistol back at Kam Chek.

Brennan was left where he lay.

Kam Chek spit on the dead pusher's body, kicked it off the trail.

As the column moved out, most of the men limping, sagging, they reminded Bolan of a great wounded beast hobbling off to its cave to die.

He turned his head to check on Grimaldi. Bolan was worried about the ace pilot.

Grimaldi's jaw was slack, his mouthline a shriveled, sun-cracked slit. His face was a mask of crusted blood and dried dust, and his eyelids drooped over bloodshot orbs. He limped along, but as he turned to look at Bolan, he lost his balance and pitched to the ground.

Bolan stopped, stooped over Grimaldi. He was disregarding Khang's order of punishment by death for helping a fallen prisoner. But yeah, he thought, maybe the rat, Davis, was right after all. He was special there. Special only as long as he was alive and able to suffer.

"Pick him up!" Mongkut shrieked. He lashed Bolan across the back of the head with his whip.

The disturbance brought Kam Chek and three guards running to the rear of the column.

"What is this, Bo-leen?" Kam Chek screamed. "He stands and walks now or I will have him shot!"

"I'm all right, Striker," Grimaldi groaned.

Kam Chek unleathered his Tokarev.

Bolan hung Grimaldi's arm around his shoulder, tugged his friend to his feet. Bolan's eyes were like two chips of granite as he looked at Kam Chek.

"You use it on him, asshole, you might as well keep pulling the trigger. It'll take more than a handful of those nine-millimeters to keep me from ripping your throat out first."

Kam Chek was stunned that Bolan would defy him. For a second, he even seemed uncertain what to do, and while he hesitated the moment of danger passed for Bolan. Kam Chek backed off, the muzzle of his Tokarev wavering from its target acquisition on his chest.

But Kam Chek had to save face. He laughed. "No, no, Bo-leen. You will not force my hand. No, no, no. You and your friend are weakening, Bo-leen. You are perhaps wishing for death at this point, *oui*. You will not get it. Move!" he barked.

Mongkut flayed the legs of Bolan and Grimaldi, his whip scorching air and flesh like the crackle of electricity. "You heard him, you white pigs. Move!"

Kam Chek holstered the Tokarev but draped his hand over the hilt of his sword. "He walks by himself, Bo-leen . . . or he doesn't walk at all."

But Grimaldi was already pulling his arm away from Bolan. He wobbled for a moment, then began trudging ahead. "What's all the fuss about anyway?"

Bolan ignored Grimaldi's attempt at humor. He could tell the guy was in a bad way. Starving. Dehydrated. Perhaps sick with malaria. Perhaps bleeding internally from his injuries. No, there was nothing to laugh about. But Bolan couldn't help but admire the guy's guts.

Still, Grimaldi, Bolan feared, was on the verge of collapsing.

Never to get up again.

Tremain looked back at Bolan. The Executioner looked the ex-CIA agent in the eye.

Bolan hoped Tremain read his stare. Tomorrow was the time, Mack Bolan thought. Tomorrow would bring either freedom or death.

Hang in there, Jack, Bolan thought. One more day.

One more lousy goddamn day in hell. Another handful of endless miles.

Bolan sensed that the strain of the forced march was at last eroding the morale and the physical hardiness of Kam Chek and his butchers. Fast.

Bolan saw Tremain nod, then face front.

A sign.

Tomorrow, yeah. If only they could hold out that long.

20

Bolan's mind was made up. It was time to act. Time to
live, or time to die. He had long since reached a point
where it took all his willpower to avoid acting prema-
turely against the barbarism of Kam Chek and Kan
Khang. Up to the present, the warlords had held all the
right cards. Now their own cannibalism was about to
deal them a losing hand.

The column of prisoners had reached a plain that
was set inside a hill-ringed valley. The procession
halted just outside the village, which comprised between thirty and forty large thatch-roofed huts, *yakas*
built from grass and bamboo. Sprawling rice paddies
and maize fields surrounded the huts. A dragon-bone
pump, *rabat*, jutted against the thickening gray veil of
dusk to the far north of the village. Hogs and oxen
waddled down the village's intersecting streets, which
quickly became congested with men, women and
children walking away from their huts to greet the
mercenary army.

Khang's army, right, Bolan thought, as Mongkut
called for the column to halt. Pillagers. Rapists.
Thieves. The villagers didn't exactly appear eager to
receive these twentieth-century Huns with open arms,
Bolan noticed. Children pressed their bodies against
their mother's skirts. Fear, anger shadowed the faces

of the Thai men. From somewhere in that tightly
packed mob, a baby cried.

Right away, the transport trucks, jeeps and animals
were separated from the prisoners. The vehicles were
lined up at the end of a long trail. The trail paralleled
a murky stream, which tumbled down from the forested mountainside and gurgled its course past the
village, flowing south.

Quickly corraled, the animals were fed and watered
by the prisoners.

Kam Chek, Kan Khang and more than half of their
brigands, however, didn't have time for such triviali-
ties, Bolan noted. The low laughter of the barbarians, as they lumbered into the village, carried easily to
Bolan's ears.

Bolan felt the adrenaline rush, a fire racing through
his veins, burning away, it seemed, every trace of exhaustion and pain. With grim determination he steeled
himself. He was ready.

Bolan sat down next to Grimaldi, after accepting his
pitifully meager ration of food and water from a
guard. As chance would have it, Bolan saw that this
particular guard toted Bolan's AutoMag. Raking his
gaze over the encampment, Bolan counted the enemy
numbers. They were thirty strong. More than half the
enemy force, including Torquemandan, the Devil's
Horn members and the camp pigeons, had gone into
the heart of the village.

Meanwhile, Kam Chek, Kan Khang and the other
mercenaries wasted no time taking the women they
wanted. Within seconds, the streets were clear, except
for the sentries stationed in front of the huts where
orgies were taking place, to ward off any attempt by
the village men to save their women from ravishment.

Several of the village men tried pleading with the guards, but the guards merely laughed in their faces and pushed them away.

The guards who had been left on the outskirts of the village to watch the prisoners seemed disappointed, resentful at having been made to wait their turn to expend their damned-up lust. Tough luck, Bolan thought. And their luck was going to get a whole lot tougher.

Bolan finished his scanty meal as, one more time, he went over in his mind the details of the breakout. Thirty AK-47s, his AutoMag and the seized M-16s and Uzi subguns against one hundred men. Though they were better nourished and rested than their captives, the march had been no picnic for the guards. Several of them had now relaxed their vigilance and were sitting propped against the trunks of areca palm trees. They smoked and ate, but kept to themselves, seeming to ignore the prisoners completely.

Only Mongkut was still very much on the alert, but even he, Bolan knew, would sooner or later have to take a break to eat or to relieve himself.

Finally, he did so. The principal whipmaster for the march called over two guards and snapped orders at them. Then Mongkut walked away, disappearing into the gloom of the jungle. The guards waited until Mongkut was out of sight before firing up cigarettes. Bolan spotted the keys to the manacles hanging from the belts of those sentries. One of the sentries had Grimaldi's M-16 slung around his shoulder.

Bolan looked at Grimaldi, saw the grim set of his expression, hard as stone. Bolan nodded to the pilot, then caught the eye of Tremain and Jones and gave them the signal. The black soldier and the ex-CIA agent turned, looked down the line, nodded at the other prisoners of their circle.

Bolan could feel several dozen pairs of eyes riveted on him. Those who were staring fixedly at him were with him now. At least, he hoped so. Somehow, the word had gotten to those men. Perhaps only one word had reached them. Escape. Perhaps, that was all they had learned, all they needed to hear. Perhaps.

If the guards looked their way now...

But they did not.

Silently, Bolan and the other eight prisoners who were briefed on the plans for that deadly moment, slipped out of the heroin packs they had carried so many miles.

Leaping to his feet, Bolan made his move. The two guards were less than five feet away, and had foolishly turned their backs on him, concerned more about when Mongkut would return than about sentry duty. Some guys just have to learn the hard way, Bolan thought. He twisted, swinging his chained hands and arms behind him.

Carelessness brought the sentries to their last seconds on earth.

Rage powered Bolan's muscles. He swung his arms with the same pitiless whipping motion he had endured at the end of the guards' bullhide leather. Alerted by the rattle of chains, the guard on Bolan's right began to turn. His look of naked terror and shock became his death mask. Bolan dropped that cutthroat, his chains driving off the side of the guerrilla's skull. Bone cracked like boot-crushed Styrofoam. At the same moment as Bolan's attack, Grimaldi, gnashing his teeth, whipped his chains down over his head, shattering the second sentry's skull and lancing bone splinters into brain.

Blood and muck sprayed the faces of Bolan and Grimaldi, but they didn't even flinch under the gory shower. They could not afford to stop now for anything or anyone. Moving in the wink of an eye, they snatched the keys off the belts of the guards as soon as the dead men slumped to the trail. Like lightning, they inserted the keys, twisted the locks. They broke free of their bonds. There wasn't a second to waste now, Bolan saw, as the trail boiled up with shadows of death.

Tremain and Jones jumped the guards nearest them, caving in their skulls with swinging chain links.

Panic broke out in one wave of lightning frenzy.

At the front of the column, the guards shouted, opened up with AK-47s. A guard leaped into the jeep, and a .50-caliber machine gun roared as he cut loose with the big maneater. But the sudden chaos had already jolted the other prisoners into action.

Within a split second, though, there were casualties among the prisoners. And death.

Struber and Sellers collided with each other as slugs chewed up their chests, blood gushing away like mini-geysers from the ragged holes in their torsos, front and back. They howled in pain, then died.

The pack animals, panicked by gunfire, screamed and thrashed into one another. The skittish horses broke away first, whinnying. As a stampede broke out, the heroin sacks slipped from the backs and flanks of the terrified animals. The jellylike uncut opium burst from packs trampled by hooves.

Bolan stripped his AutoMag off the dead guard who had been sporting it, and stuffed spare clips for the Uzi SMG into his belt. Grimaldi seized his M-16 and some ammo from another guard. Eyes wild, Bolan searched the edge of the jungle to see if Mongkut was returning. There was no sign of the bastard yet. But Mongkut would show, Bolan knew, and the Executioner would be ready for the Asian whipmaster.

Bolan and Grimaldi turned grim attention back toward the prisoners and guards. As Bolan had hoped, even the prisoners who had not been in on the escape plan bolted into action against the guards as one unified body, intent on murder, committed to evening up some very lopsided scores. Outnumbered more than three to one, the mercenaries were overwhelmed by the prisoners within seconds. Even though the momentary stutter of AK-47s mowed down a dozen of the chained men, the captives were not going to be denied their vengeance, or their chance for freedom. One massive wall of human fury was unleashed, a rolling thunderhead of fists, feet and swinging chains as the inmate horde descended on the stunned guards.

Still, the hail of .50 caliber and 7.62 mm lead scythed through the hearts of many prisoners. Men screamed, spun, dropped where they stood.

Swiftly, Bolan and Grimaldi moved along the outside flank of the swirling cloud of flesh. Together, they triggered their weapons, Bolan's Uzi and Grimaldi's M-16 roaring, stitching those guards who had managed to hold their ground and were slaughtering prisoners with long sweeping bursts.

Both night warriors then swung their aim toward the jeep. A millisecond later, the cutthroat in the jeep behind the .50 caliber sailed away into the air, his jaw and half his face and skull following the flight of his body in an explosion of bone, blood and gristle. The retaliation of the .50 caliber was thwarted for the time being.

Tremain had got hold of an AK-47, which he swung like a baseball bat. The butt splintered a guard's jaw, the impact lifting the limp man off his feet.

"Take cover!" Bolan shouted at the others, as he angled toward the transport trucks.

But his order went unheard at that moment. The breakout was turning into a tumultuous venting of murderous rage, of vengeance and hatred suppressed for agonizing eternities. Groups of prisoners pummeled their captors senseless. Screams of terror lanced the air. Bones snapped and cracked like dry twigs, and there were unearthly sounding belches, as boots piledrived into guts and vomit spewed violently from gaping mouths.

Reaching cover behind a transport truck, Bolan looked back.

Guards who had been knocked to the ground and disarmed attempted to crawl away from the human caldron of wrath. Chains pelted their bodies. Boots drilled into their asses. Their cries for mercy were ignored by their former captives, indeed their very pleading seemed to further incense those they had enslaved and brutalized for so long. Not all the prisoners, however, joined in the fight for freedom. Some, after working feverishly to unlock their chains and free themselves, charged off into the jungle and vanished. At the end of the opening onslaught, Bolan counted up a fighting force of sixty, not one hundred, men, and only half of them brandished weapons.

A split second later, Kam Chek's barbarians in the village made the hellzone even hotter. Alerted by the furor, Khang and Kam Chek poked their heads out the doorway of a large hut at the far north end of the village street. From there they shrieked orders to their brigands. Then they and their mercenaries tugged on pants and shirts, and scrambled into position. Some flung themselves into doorways, others dropped into prone position beneath the raised foundations of *yakas*. The muzzle-flashes of AK-47s stabbed through the twilight gloom.

Puffs of dirt coughed up around the transport trucks. Lead hornets screamed off the armored hulls and drilled into the trail as the prisoners who had chosen to stay and fight scurried for cover behind the line of vehicles.

The pack animals continued to scream, crushed one another with deadweight as slugs raked their bodies and sliced off chunks of bloody hide.

Grimaldi jumped into the back of a truck. He rummaged around for a moment, then, brandishing the MM-1, he called, "Striker!" Bolan caught the multiround projectile launcher that Grimaldi threw to him.

"What's next, Sergeant?" Larry Jones growled. He was crouched beside Bolan. Above their heads, lead-jacketed steel whined off the metal of the truck.

The escape attempt had got off to a good start, but was not going according to plan. Bolan had hoped the initial shock of the prisoner uprising would bring the rest of Kam Chek's cutthroats running from the village. It hadn't worked that way. Instead, the mercenaries were turning the village into a stronghold. Bolan feared the worst.

Moments later, he discovered just how the warlords intended to turn the tables back in their favor.

"Hold your fire! Hold your fire!" Kam Chek shrieked.

All weapons ceased firing. The final chatter of AK-47s rang out in a hollow echo.

Tremain and the surviving prisoners of Bolan's circle gathered around him. They waited, listened. Dust swept over them in a thick, choking brown sheet.

"We pulled it off," Harry Karn said in a tremulous voice. "By God, we did it!"

"We ain't done nothin' yet, man," Jones rasped.

Bolan knew the black soldier was right about that. The Executioner had a bad gut feeling. They had gambled. And won? So far. But what next?

"Bo-leen!"

Bolan peered over the hood of the transport truck. Near the far end of the village Kam Chek stepped from a doorway. The warlord dragged a small boy beside him, fisting a handful of the child's hair.

Bolan cursed.

Kam Chek stopped in the center of the village. "Bo-leen, you listen to me. If you care about saving innocent lives, you had better throw down your weapons. Now!"

"Shit!" Jones snarled, the sinews in his hands rippling, the veins in his neck prominent, as he gripped his AK-47 tightly. He looked as if he wanted to break the weapon in two with his bare hands.

Grimaldi hopped out of the bed of the transport truck, hit the ground, and wheeled behind the vehicle.

Bolan thought fast. This was a standoff. The bastards held the entire village hostage. But Bolan had some bargaining power of his own. He held their precious fortune in heroin. It was all he had to deal with in exchange for innocent lives. He hoped it would be enough.

"Kam Chek!" Bolan called out. "If you people want your heroin back, you'll let every man, woman and child there go free. Unharmed. You kill them, we'll come right in. And you won't die easy, *mon ami*. I promise you that."

Kam Chek appeared to think about the situation for a moment. His hostage pulled at his hands, struggling to break free, crying out in pain. Kam Chek shook the boy as if he were a wet rag. "Shut up! Stand still!" he hissed.

"Nobody gets to these trucks, Kam Chek, unless they get by us!" Bolan went on. "You'll save yourself a lot of trouble, and a lot of lives. Like the lives of your men, Kam Chek. Let those people go."

Bolan had no intention of turning the heroin over to the Devil's Horn again. Likewise, he knew that Torquemandan and his warlords would not just let him and the other prisoners walk away from this engagement. The Devil's Horn might let the villagers walk away. But Bolan already knew that the whole bloody affair was building toward an even gorier slaughter. Still, it was necessary to move one step at a time. He was gambling that the Devil's Horn would relent at this point. It was a question of who could outbluff whom.

Dragging his hostage, Kam Chek headed back to the hut at the end of the village for a conference with Torquemandan. He vanished through the doorway to the hut.

Tension mounted among the escapees. Karn voiced the anxiety that gripped everyone there. "He's not going to deal, you know that? They'll kill everybody there, then attack us."

"We have to wait and see, soldier," Bolan answered. "We rolled the dice, and this is what we came up with. You watch—Torquemandan's greed will win out. He'll have to deal."

"I hope you're right, man," Jones breathed.

So do I, Bolan thought. Too many innocent lives have been snuffed out already.

"And if he doesn't deal?" Polanski wanted to know.

"Then we try something else," Bolan answered. "Try a little harder approach."

Kam Chek reappeared, walked back to the center of the village. He still grasped the boy by the hair.

"Bo-leen. It seems you have overestimated your position. We can afford to wait and hold you off, if necessary. When we do not show at our destination, the relief force stationed at the laboratories will come in search of us. Your position is hopeless. We will not deal. The best you can do for yourself and your comrades is to surrender without delay. You will be treated mercifully, I assure you."

Bolan ignored the guffaws and the snickering. An iceball of fury lodged in his stomach. Torquemandan had called his bluff. But Bolan wasn't about to throw in the towel. Not yet. Not ever.

"I suggest you reconsider, Kam Chek," he called. "I've got sixty men here. We'll make an accounting of ourselves, bet on it, friend. I'm pulling out with the heroin, but I'll be nearby. When you change your mind, just stand there and shout. My offer, and my threat, still stand. You start killing villagers, I'll stomp every last ounce of the poison in these trucks straight into the mud. And you'll find out damn quick that the world isn't big enough to hide you and your comrades. Have I got a *oui* on that, *mon ami*?"

"You are a very stubborn, but foolish *ferang*, Boleen," Kam Chek said with a smile. Then, without warning, he pulled the Tokarev pistol from its holster.

"Oh, God, no," Grimaldi rasped through gritted teeth.

Kam Chek leveled the muzzle of the Tokarev against the boy's temple. The child stood paralyzed for a split second, then screamed as Kam Chek squeezed the trigger. Blood sprayed away from the child's shattered head. Kam Chek threw the little body to the ground.

A woman wailed in anguish. A moment later, she ran from a hut, stumbled down the street with an awkward swinging gait. Horror was written on her face.

Bolan had seen enough. His guts knotted up with hatred, he lifted the Uzi over the hood of the truck. He drew target acquisition on Kam Chek's face, and his finger tightened around the trigger.

"Mack, no!" Grimaldi implored. "They'll kill everybody."

Bolan steadied the tremor in his arms. He looked Kam Chek dead in the eye. The bastard just stood there, clenched fists on his hips, ignoring the bloodstained body of the child he'd just murdered in cold blood. The woman draped herself over the small corpse. Her racking sobs chilled the silence.

Bolan so badly wanted to squeeze the Uzi's trigger that it was all he could do not to erase Kam Chek's grinning visage, turn that face into crimson mush. But

Bolan knew Jack was right. If Kam Chek died, the mercenaries would most likely massacre the villagers.

You win, you soulless bastard, Bolan thought. For now.

Bolan let the Uzi fall to his side.

Kam Chek chuckled.

A terrible hatred threatened to overpower Mack Bolan, a black, icy feeling that ate at his guts.

The woman weeping for her child echoed through Bolan's head. The cry of pure misery fed his hatred for Kam Chek and for everyone connected with the Devil's Horn.

21

"What are they doing now?"

Torquemandan cringed, then despised himself for doing so. His voice sounded weak and scratchy to him, and he could have sworn he detected a note of panic in his question. But why the hell shouldn't he panic at a time like this, anyway? he asked himself.

Viciously, silently, he cursed himself for allowing his mercenary cutthroats to dictate the routine for the march. Now, a fortune in heroin was about to go straight down the toilet, and the only thing he could do about it was peer out a hole in this tumbledown hut and feel like some rotten, frightened street punk who's about to get his ass beat. Worse, he felt as if he was hiding, like some rat in a hole. "Hole" was fucking well right, he thought. This village was nothing but a hole. But just who was dug in at the moment, quaking in fear? he asked himself in disgust.

He turned and looked at the rats who had gotten them all buried in this hole in the first place. As he looked at Kan Khang, Kam Chek, and the nine members of his organization, all huddled down inside the front wall, watching their wealth roll away right before their eyes, Torquemandan didn't know whether to feel rage, disgust or contempt. Perhaps what he should do was grab the gun off that punk, Davis, and start blowing heads off. But he knew he couldn't do that. He needed these jerks. He needed them to seize the scag and take back the night.

Then the sound of an engine growling to life drew Torquemandan's attention back to the street.

Three transport trucks were turning away from the village and starting to roll across the rice paddy. He saw eight, maybe a dozen shadows move around in the moonlight, pitch pack after pack of heroin into the remaining two transport trucks. Then the shadows were recognizable as men as they leaped into the jeep. Damn it! They were taking everything, he realized with horror. Everything but the armored personnel carriers. Just leave me something with wheels, you sons of bitches, Torquemandan said to himself. His mind was working furiously. If he couldn't win here, he decided, he'd better cut his losses, get back to the palace, scrape together all the raw heroin in reserve there and move his business elsewhere.

"Khang, why aren't your soldiers doing something, dammit?" Torquemandan glowered at Khang. For a moment, he thought a smile flickered over Khang's lips, but in the wavering torchlight it was hard to tell.

"What would you have us do, *Mon Général*?"

Torquemandan had to admit he didn't know what his next move should be. He had thought Bolan would cave in when his bluff was called. But the guy just blew the smoke back in their faces. Bolan the hardass. The bastard.

They had just three options. Take flight, fight or wait for the reinforcements to show up. But Torquemandan knew that wait could take days. Days that were numbered. He made the only decision possible.

"Kam Chek, get your ass in gear," Torquemandan growled. "Here's where you finally earn your keep." Torquemandan paused, more out of sudden fear than anything else. Kam Chek was fingering the hilt of his sword. And Kam Chek, he could tell, most definitely did not like to be talked to in the tone of voice he'd just used. Too bad, Torquemandan decided.

"As you wish," Kam Chek said, his words clipped, his voice a low growl, like that of a trained attack dog about to bite off a stranger's hand. "How shall we attack this problem, *Mon Général*?"

That's better, Torquemandan thought. Respect. He still commanded their respect. "Round up your men, whatever the hell you've got left. Half of them stay here to guard the hostages. The other half go with you."

"Are you suggesting we hunt down Bo-leen and the prisoners, *Mon Général*?" Kam Chek asked silkily.

Torquemandan clenched his jaw. "I'm not *suggesting* anything, Kam Chek," he snapped. "It's the only option we've got. With millions of dollars out there in the hands of some maniac, I'm not about to sit here and do nothing."

Khang spoke up, his eyes narrowed. "Are you not forgetting, *Mon Général*, that perhaps as many as one hundred prisoners are on the loose in the jungle around us? Worse still, it is dark. In such conditions, the defender has the advantage. He can wait in the deepest, darkest shadows of the jungle for the prey to invade his territory."

"I thought you people were supposed to be the world's greatest guerrilla fighters, Khang. I thought this bush fighting was your specialty, huh?"

Neither Khang nor Kam Chek liked his implication, Torquemandan saw. They went as stiff as bamboo, as silent as death. He was questioning their bravery, and he'd struck a nerve.

Finally Khang jerked a nod at Kam Chek. "Go."

Now we're getting somewhere, Torquemandan thought. Now there's going to be action. And results.

Before the Devil's Horn leader could say anything further to Khang, a tremendous explosion erupted from somewhere with a sound like rolling thunder.

As he looked out to the street again, Torquemandan saw one of the two armored personnel carriers mushroom into a fireball, flaming wreckage riding the crest of a searing wave. Damn! he thought. It was Bolan. The hardass had just blown up one of the only two vehicles Torquemandan could use to escape if Kam Chek failed to bring back the bastard's head.

Torquemandan and the other members of the Devil's Horn in that hut listened to the night, but they heard only the crackle of fire.

Turning his gaze away from the fiery debris, Torquemandan stared at the hulking silhouette of the lone transport truck. Was it still sitting there unharmed because the hardass didn't want to waste any more high-explosive rounds? he wondered. Or was the vehicle meant to serve some other purpose?

Like bait.

MACK BOLAN INTENDED to be the one who took back the night.

By force. By fire and blood. By death.

Driving the jeep, Bolan had led the other vehicles far across the plain. Now he braked the rig, killed the engine, signaled for the rest of the column to halt.

They were a little more than four hundred yards south of the village. In the distance, the flames of the armored troop carrier were licking the night. Destroying the troop carrier with the MM-1 had been meant to serve as his personal message of doom for the barbarians—unless they gave in to his demands to free their hostages. And even if the enemy relented, Bolan still intended to kill them all. He had no choice but to kill them all.

The other APC still sat, shining dully beneath the white fingers of light filtering down over the village from a full moon. A rat trap, damn right, Bolan thought. He was out of effective range with the MM-1, but he was about to change that. Very soon.

The strike force under Bolan's command assembled along the foothills. He had already briefed them; they knew what must be done.

Quickly, Bolan, Grimaldi and the others hauled several drums of gas from a truck. Uncapping the drums, they sloshed the gasoline beneath all the vehicles. Two flamethrowers had been discovered in a truck bed, and Bolan intended to use their fire to erase the poison of the uncut heroin from the face of the earth. Only the jeep and the supply truck, laden with food and fresh water, would be spared.

Toting AK-47s and commando knives that they had stripped off the dead, Bolan's grim-faced soldiers appeared eager to carry the sword to Kam Chek and his cutthroats.

"Everyone knows what to do, right?" Bolan asked.

Jones cocked a lopsided grin. "I think we've done this bit before, Sergeant," he told the Executioner.

"Yeah, I suppose you have," Bolan answered. Each of the surviving prisoners from Bolan's hut would lead a group of men through the jungle. They would circle the village, trying to determine exactly where hostages were being held. Then they would move in, delivering swift and silent death by knife or with their bare hands. If they took the mercenaries by surprise, Bolan hoped the cutthroats would turn their attention away from the hostages when they found themselves embroiled in a life-or-death struggle.

It was a hope, yeah, not a certainty. But Bolan knew that the villagers could be saved. Must be saved. Bolan swore not another innocent life would be taken by the savages. Too many gentle souls had already perished. Memories of the senseless violence and cold-blooded murder Bolan had witnessed during the past several days would leave a bitter taste in his mouth for a long time to come.

As planned, Karn had stayed behind with those prisoners who had not taken arms during the breakout. If the situation turned desperate and Bolan was faced with another stalemate, Karn had orders to torch the trucks loaded to overflowing with the heroin. The panic and horror Torquemandan, his partners and their mercenaries would feel as they saw their treasure vaporized would surely break their backs. Bolan intended to strike decisively, with deadly lightning force, during the seconds of paralysis that the avaricious vultures would experience as their dreams went up in smoke.

For some reason, Bolan noted, Bruno Polanski had opted to strap on the second flamethrower. He caught Polanski's eye, and Bruno offered an explanation.

"We didn't have enough weapons to go around, Sergeant," the big Polanski said. "The way I see it, you'll need every gun you can muster here. Besides," he said, the ghost of a grin on his lips, "payback's gonna be hell for those bastards. An eye for an eye, as far as I'm concerned."

As Bolan nodded, he heard the faint rattle of brush. Looking past the assembled strike force, Bolan saw three figures step off the trail. They were the two Thais and the Montagnard, Jhade. They had volunteered to stay behind at the village for a while so that they could alert Bolan if they noticed any new developments there. From the recon men's taut facial expressions, Bolan could tell something had happened.

"Kam Chek has left the village," Jhade announced. "We counted sixteen men with him. They went behind the village, then moved on up the hills."

Bolan digested the intel. Apparently Torquemandan had ordered that the fight be taken to their adversaries. Good, Bolan thought. They would meet those human vipers head-on.

"I know these hills," one of the Thais said. "I have lived here all my life—before Kam Chek captured me and killed my family." His voice was bitter. "They will take the main trail that runs like a backbone through the hills. I am sure of it. There are two other trails that lead back toward the village. The trails join at a clearing, about halfway back."

Bolan unslung his Uzi SMG. The AutoMag was hooked inside his belt, opposite his commando knife. "All right," he announced, "let's go greet Kam Chek."

"And give him a real warm welcome," Polanski muttered.

Swiftly, silently, Bolan led his thirty-man vengeance force into the jungle. Within moments, they were gone, melted into a maw of blackness.

Gone to seize back the night.

KAM CHEK FIGURED Torquemandan was using him
for a patsy. Very well then, he decided, it was time for
a change anyway. Time to strike down the *ferang*.
Kam Chek was not a man to be taken lightly. When
this was over, he would kill the *ferang*. But Torquemandan would not be allowed to die easily, or quickly.
No. Kam Chek vowed to disembowel the CIA renegade with his sword. Torquemandan would watch his
own guts spill from his belly in a torrent of blood. And
Kam Chek would look him in the eye, and laugh. He
would dance all over the dead *ferang*, then spit on his
rotten carcass. Then he would take whatever raw heroin was left and distribute it himself. He knew he had
to include Khang in the power play, but that was fine
with him. Khang was of his own blood, he owed a
certain amount of loyalty to his fellow warlord. For
years Khang had struggled alongside Kam Chek
against the Americans and the hated Montagnards
before the long-awaited victory by the North Vietnamese.

But he had to finish this business with Bo-leen first.

The Tokarev in one hand, his samurai sword in the
other, the sadistic warlord followed his soldiers down
the trail. They were moving too fast, making unnecessary noise as they trampled brush, snapped twigs.
They were scared, he guessed, and he cursed silently.

Then he sensed some presence in the jungle, some
movement that only years of brutal experience in bush
fighting could detect. He decided he'd better fall back,
and swiftly crouched behind a tree.

His instinct soon proved to be correct.

He saw shadows ahead slide behind several of his men, saw the flash of steel as it reflected the shafts of moonlight that broke through the jungle canopy. He heard the brief cries of fear and pain. Autofire shattered the silence as his men panicked and raked the brush with long bursts from their AK-47s. Then he saw muzzle-flashes spearing the darkness on both sides of his troops. One by one, his men reeled to the side of the trail as the lethal fire pinched them in from the flanks. Their death screams hung in the air around Kam Chek, echoing their agony.

Kam Chek realized he could not stay where he was. He would be massacred next.

He turned, angling off the trail into the deep jungle. He cursed Torquemandan, more determined than ever now to skewer the cowardly *ferang* for sending him and his men to their deaths.

Then, before Kam Chek's eyes, the night exploded.

An orange stream of fire blazed from the darkness, scorched straight toward his face.

"No-o-o-o!" Kam Chek shrieked. The dragon's tongue of flames washed over him.

MACK BOLAN STEPPED out of the darkness. His tall figure was a dark gray silhouette in the moonlight. Then he was illuminated by a fiery glow, his face so battered it resembled a grim mask as he cautiously approached the human torch that was Kam Chek.

The Executioner watched Kam Chek burn. The stench of frying flesh was almost overpowering. Justice was being meted out in this most horrible of deaths. The images of the men Kam Chek had butchered without a qualm were seared into Bolan's mind. Kam Chek was getting exactly what he deserved.

Out of the corner of his eye, Bolan saw the men of his strike force move cautiously from the brush. They had won this victory over their longtime tormentor. They, too, watched in silence as Kam Chek thrashed on the ground, trying to smother the flames that engulfed him. They savored the moment.

Shrieking like a banshee, Kam Chek slapped at his face and head. Then he noticed the onlookers. He bolted to his feet, attempted to run away from the men he had punished so unmercifully for so long, as if their witnessing his agony was the final disgrace.

Bolan swept up the samurai sword, which had fallen to the trail. Fisting the sword in a two-handed grip, he took three long strides toward the burning demon. With a mighty swipe of the blade, fueled by disgust, rage and black vengeance, the Executioner severed Kam Chek's head from his shoulders. The head thudded to the ground, rolled several feet, then came to rest in front of Bolan, a ball of fire. The rest of Kam Chek's body convulsed in death throes, then toppled to the ground, ramrod stiff, crushing a clump of jungle plants.

Bolan let the sword fall from his hands.

Bruno Polanski stepped from the brush beside the blazing lump of flesh. The nozzle of the flamethrower gleamed silver, catching flickers of the fire.

The head and body of Kam Chek shriveled up, were reduced in minutes to ashes and blackened bone fragments.

Grim-faced, the Executioner turned away, and silently led the shadowy procession of avengers through the jungle toward the village.

22

In the village, Torquemandan heard the terrible shrieks of a man in agony. Under other circumstances, he would have relished the sound of that scream. But a chill went down his spine. He recognized the voice, even as it cried out in pain. Kam Chek. Something had happened to Kam Chek. And he feared the worst.

Bolan would be coming for him next. It was time for him to leave Khang and the others to whatever fate they might suffer. He did not care if they lived or died.

Concerned only with returning to his palace and salvaging what was left from the ruins of his empire, Torquemandan made sure that Khang's back was turned to him, that the other members of the Devil's Horn, in their moment of terror, were ignoring him now. As the warlord and the white suits looked out into the street, Torquemandan slipped through the back doorway of the hut. His heart thumping in his ears, he darted into the gloom between the areca palms. Almost at once he angled away from the village, moving along the western fringes behind the huts. Each minute seemed to crawl by as his every thought turned to flight. His sights set on the only remaining troop carrier, he ran in a crouch toward the vehicle. When he reached his objective, he quietly opened the transport truck's door, started to climb into the cab.

Then he felt cold iron pressing against his spine. He froze.

"Were you going somewhere, *Mon Général*? Perhaps back to the palace?" The voice was Khang's. There was anger in that voice, the sound of a man betrayed, a man who was quite prepared to commit murder.

The passenger door opened and Davis hopped up into the cab. The Colt .45 in his steady hand was an inch from Torquemandan's face.

"Get in, *Mon Général*," Khang ordered, jabbing the muzzle of his Tokarev against Torquemandan's spine. "We will all go together. We will all benefit from this terrible tragedy, *oui*?"

Torquemandan hesitated and looked at Davis. The fucking punk! he thought. He actually has the balls to smile at me!

Torquemandan considered spinning around, knocking the gun out of Khang's hand, then making a desperate lunge at Davis. But he would be dead, he knew, before Khang hit the ground.

As Torquemandan's mind raced in a desperate search for a way out of his predicament, autofire suddenly ripped the night. Shadows stormed into the north end of the village. Then Torquemandan saw figures in white suits spill from the doorway of the largest hut in the village.

The suits were no longer white.

They were stained red with blood.

"Move! Now!" Khang snapped, and shoved Torquemandan into the cab.

CROUCHING BEHIND THE CORNER of a hut, Bolan hosed down three of Khang's mercenaries with a burst from his Uzi. From across the street, Grimaldi fired on the enemy, his M-16 stuttering out lethal rounds, clipping four of the savages as they attempted to flee the killzone.

Then Bolan and Grimaldi saw the reason for the hasty, pell-mell retreat of their opponents.

The troop carrier lurched into gear, its engine rumbling to life as it rolled down the trail. The armored carrier bucked into second gear, angling away from Bolan's line of lethal tracking fire. The driver was safe for the moment, but not for long, Bolan thought. He wanted to keep those rats from escaping any way he could. He triggered the Uzi in a sweeping ground-level burst that blew out the front and back tires on the driver's side, popping rubber into limp tread. But it was not enough. The truck lumbered through a series of ruts, careening toward a line of trees, but then the driver straightened out the rig, throwing the front end off its collision course at the last possible second.

The troop carrier disappeared down the trail.

Bolan cursed.

"Mack!"

Alerted by Grimaldi's anxious voice, Bolan saw three mercenaries racing for a hut in the very center of the village. He read desperation in the enemy's breakneck speed to reach that hut. The hostages. The enemy's trump card.

Bolan broke from cover as the men of his strike force poured into the street from all points on the compass. Several of the remaining mercenaries pleaded with the freed prisoners to spare their lives.

Their plea was denied. They were shot where they stood, their hands above their heads.

Flinging aside the Uzi and drawing the AutoMag, Bolan closed on the targeted hut. He bounded up the bamboo stoop as the last mercenary through the doorway whirled to face him. Bolan cannoned a .44 round that tunneled a gaping hole in that barbarian's chest, flinging him back through the doorway.

Screams of pure terror ripped from inside the hut. Women's and children's screams.

Bolan acted with blinding speed. Surging through the doorway, he locked deathsights on the two mercenaries who were making a final bid to save themselves, again at the expense of innocent lives.

Through the wavering sheen of torchlight, Bolan saw the frightened tearstained faces of the hostages. Their brown, half-naked bodies packed together, they were kneeling in the middle of the hut, as if praying for deliverance.

Bolan answered those prayers, squeezed Big Thunder's trigger twice.

Two deafening peals.

Two heads exploding in black eruptions of bone, blood and brains.

Two corpses blasting through the flimsy grass walls, catapulting into the darkness beyond.

Bolan checked the villagers. No one appeared injured, just shaken badly by the time bomb of death that had detonated before them. A second later, as the killing shots gave way to total silence, Bolan read the relief, the gratitude in the eyes of the Thai people.

During his campaigns in the killing fields of Southeast Asia, Bolan had learned a smattering of Vietnamese, Lao, Burmese and Thai.

In Thai, Bolan told the hostages that their suffering was over. Kam Chek and his soldiers were dead. They had nothing to fear anymore, and could get on with their lives.

Bolan moved back out into the street, where Grimaldi quickly informed him that there was no sign of Torquemandan or Khang in the village. Some of the savages were still at large.

The free men of Bolan's strike force gathered around the Stony Man warriors.

Bolan looked at Tremain. He noted the weariness in the ex-CIA agent's eyes. These men had won their war, they had broken out of the bonds of their captivity. Bolan had shown them the way, and he read the appreciation, the respect on every face before him. They were ready to leave behind the hell they had endured for so many years. Ready, yeah, to pick up the pieces and begin a new life.

But for Bolan, the war was not yet over. Not by a long shot.

"Tremain," Bolan said, "Grimaldi and I are going after Torquemandan and Khang, but the battle's over for you and these men. We still don't know whether that relief force is on its way. I figure if we burn down Torquemandan's house it may just break the backs of whoever's left over. That transport truck should get you and the others to Bangkok okay. Can you take it from here?"

Tremain nodded, his eyes sparking with a look of renewed determination. He offered his hand to Bolan, and Bolan shook it.

"Any chance we might get together for a brew back in the States, Sergeant?" Bruno Polanski smiled.

"There's always that chance," Bolan answered, then quickly turned, put that group of brave soldiers behind him. "Maybe...someday," he mumbled to himself. Though it didn't seem likely. Then, for a second, he entertained the thought of seeing those men again. They were survivors, but they were more than that. They were soldiers who had fought the good fight, and the world needed more men like that. Courageous men who had endured, and whose actions would live on as an example for others to follow.

Then, with Grimaldi at his heels, Bolan began to run across the plain, heading back to the jeep.

The night was still alive with savages.

BOLAN RELEASED A TONGUE of fire from the flamethrower. The pools of gas beneath the transport trucks loaded with heroin ignited in a roaring blaze. Karn and the other free men watched from distant safety, clustered around the supply truck, while Grimaldi emptied a jerry can into the jeep's fuel tank, getting it ready for the final huntdown.

A series of explosions lifted the burning trucks off their wheels, as hunks of metal ripped away from the fiery mass. Bolan turned away from the raging wall of fire, satisfied that the cleaning inferno would do its purifying work on the poison it was consuming. The Executioner's sweat-slick face glowed in the dancing firelight.

Bolan looked toward the group of freed men crowded around the supply truck. He started to walk toward them with some final words of encouragement and farewell. But he never got there. Suddenly, he saw Grimaldi yanked back toward the side of the jeep as a dark figure sprang up from behind the .50 caliber machine gun. There was a flash of white teeth bared in a feral snarl, then Grimaldi was fighting for his life, pinned against the side of the jeep as the whip tightened a binding hold around his neck.

For an instant, Bolan considered grabbing the flamethrower pack, then rejected the idea because of its cumbersome weight. He drew the AutoMag. As he was directly behind Grimaldi's attacker, he took several steps to the side, angling for a clear killing shot.

Then, in the radiant sheen of firelight, Bolan recognized the attacker. Mongkut.

Desperately, Grimaldi clawed at Mongkut's face, groping for his eyes.

Bolan steadied his aim with a two-handed grip. The AutoMag bucked, roaring out a 240-grain slug. The .44 thunderscreamer muzzled a true line at 1640 fps, with muzzle energy of 1455 pounds. Big Thunder's flesh shredder decapitated Mongkut, the impact flipping the corpse over Grimaldi's head.

Bolan ran to Grimaldi, and found he had delivered the headbursting shot not a second too soon. As Grimaldi struggled to stand up, Bolan helped him. Bracing himself against the side of the jeep, Grimaldi gagged for several moments before the color began returning to his face.

"Dammit, Striker," Grimaldi said, coughing, "how about a little vacation after this? All work and no play makes Jack a dull boy, y'know?"

Bolan grinned, but the expression vanished as soon as it touched his lips. A little R and R sounded good, but not yet. Not until they had toppled the walls of Torquemandan's kingdom for good. Forever.

"You got it, Jack," Bolan told Grimaldi, helping him into the jeep. "Can you go one more round, guy?"

Grimaldi sucked in several deep breaths as he climbed in beside Bolan.

"Let's take it in, Striker. All the way for the knockout punch."

That was exactly what Bolan wanted to hear.

No. Strike that. Exactly what he expected to hear.

BOLAN GUIDED THE JEEP down the trail, the same trail that was stained with the blood of all the men who had died there. So needlessly. So damn senselessly. With vengeance driving him on, Bolan was determined to catch Torquemandan and hold him accountable: for his greed, for his savagery, for the unforgivable atrocities he had committed or had had others commit for him. Any way you sliced it, Torquemandan was still a cannibal.

It took a little more than an hour of hard riding over the rugged, winding trail, but Bolan finally caught up with the armored troop carrier. With two of its wheels shot to hell, the driver of that getaway vehicle had to struggle to keep the rig on a straight and steady course.

Bolan sent the jeep surging ahead in high gear. "Get ready, Jack!"

Manning the .50 caliber machine gun, Grimaldi swung the long muzzle up and straight ahead, gently moving the maneater on its tripod mount and into target acquisition on the troop carrier.

Bolan hit the high beams. The twin lines of light widened, sweeping over the rear of the troop carrier. First, he cut the gap to within forty yards, then bearing down hard, he closed the distance another twenty feet.

Bolan and Grimaldi waited.

Then the trail wound to the left, presenting the driver's side of the APC to Grimaldi for a clear line of fire.

Grimaldi cut loose with the machine gun. Shell casings whirled around his bruised, swollen face. Smoke and flame poured out the muzzle as the maneater pounded out its furious, deadly payload.

Bolan twisted the wheel, following the bend in the trail. The jeep bounced in and out of a rut, causing Grimaldi to lose his balance for a second, and to release the machine gun's trigger reflexively.

Quickly the pilot resumed his hellish spraying of the troop carrier.

The jeep's high beams washed over the cab of the troop carrier as its front windshield exploded in a shower of glass. Slugs ricocheted like angry buzzing hornets off armor plating.

Then the troop carrier slewed off the trail. A second later, metal rended as the nose end of the armored truck bulled through a stand of teak trees. Bits of brush and battered tree bark shot away from the rampaging rig as it hit a hump in the jungle floor and flipped onto its side.

Bolan braked the jeep. He left the engine running and the lights on. They bathed the crumpled hulk in glaring white.

Grimaldi leaped out of the jeep, an M-16 in his hands.

With Big Thunder filling his fist, Bolan ran toward the capsized wreck. It was time to finish off the vile quarry.

The driver's door opened, sticking up into the air. Bolan hit a combat crouch.

Khang burst through the opening, swearing, frantically squeezing off rounds with his Tokarev.

Two slugs whined off the trail, blazing wide of Bolan and Grimaldi. Khang's last desperate stand was about to come to an end and Bolan's AutoMag roared at the same time that Grimaldi's M-16 stammered out a 3-round killing charge. The combined leadpower blasted open Khang's chest, lifting him out of the doorway with muzzle punch that sent him somersaulting jerkily over the roof.

Cautiously, listening for any signs of life inside the cab, Bolan moved up on the troop carrier with Grimaldi right behind him.

"Don't shoot! Please! It's finished!"

Bolan recognized the voice. Davis. The King Rat.

"He's dead! Torquemandan's dead! It's over! I surrender!"

A second later, two trembling hands, then Davis's head, poked up through the open doorway. Fresh rage surged through Bolan at the sight of the rodent.

"Cover me, Jack," Bolan said. He slipped the AutoMag inside his belt. With Davis still frozen in his position of surrender in the doorway, Bolan hooked his hands over the metal lip above the front fender. Stifling a groan of pain as his injuries made themselves felt, Bolan hauled himself up onto the fender.

He looked past the dangling shards of glass into the cab of the APC. There was no sign of Torquemandan.

"He's on the floor," Davis blurted. "He broke his neck, I think."

Bolan stepped off the fender, straddled the doorway. Davis looked up at him, shaking with fear. The Executioner drove the heel of his boot hard, stomping on that face. There was a sickening crunch of bone and cartilage as Bolan pulped Davis's nose.

Howling in pain, both hands clutching at his face, Davis tumbled back into the cab.

With one hand grasping the frame of the doorway, Bolan bent and pulled the AutoMag out of his belt. Then he looked into the cab.

There he found Torquemandan. The head cannibal's empty stare looked up at Bolan. Torquemandan's head lolled at an impossible angle to his body. A broken neck, just as the King Rat had said.

Davis was crumpled up in a heap of misery against the passenger door. He showed Bolan his palms. "P-please. It's all over! Can't you see?"

Bolan sighted down the AutoMag. "I can see just fine."

"No-o-o-o! You can't! They forced me! They made me kill those men! You saw them do it! No-o-o-o!"

The Executioner pulled the trigger. Big Thunder bucked once.

And Davis died. Just as he had lived. Like shit.

Now there was just one more thing to do.

One last house on this trail of horror that needed torching.

EPILOGUE

By midafternoon the next day Bolan and Grimaldi reached the harvested poppy fields. The sentries who had been assigned to guard the reserve supply of raw heroin were greeted by swift and merciless execution. As Grimaldi steered the jeep toward the poppy fields, Bolan opened up with the .50-caliber maneater. About a dozen mercenaries attempted to flee across the barren poppy fields, but their race to outrun Bolan's tracking hellfire was in vain. The Executioner shredded the remaining troops with two HE rounds from the MM-1.

Then Bolan and Grimaldi set about their final task.

The cleansing flame.

It took the better part of two hours, but Bolan and Grimaldi torched the barren fields, the reserve heroin, the prison and, finally, Torquemandan's palace. With flamethrower and whatever gasoline they could scrounge up from the fuel depot and ignite, they turned the valley into an inferno.

Scorched earth.

Topping the crest of the hill that had been the site of their capture, Bolan and Grimaldi stood side by side. Silently, they watched the fire blaze across the acres where poppies had flowered and yielded a harvest of death.

Bolan was tired. A bone-numbing ache threatened to knock him off his feet. He knew Grimaldi was just hanging in there now, too. The pilot was a walking skeleton, who would carry the scars of this grim campaign for the rest of his life. And so would the Executioner.

Bolan watched as individual conflagrations in the fields mounted and merged into a wall of raging flames.

Flames that ate into soil that had soaked up so much blood.

How many had died over the years, here in this hell? Mack Bolan wondered.

He would never know.

He was not even sure he wanted to know.

Sure, once again, they had lopped off a few tentacles of the Hydra.

But another Torquemandan, another Kam Chek, another Kan Khang, Bolan knew, would rise up to replace the dethroned savages.

And there were plenty of Ronny Brennans, too.

Too goddamn many.

Bolan saw the black thunderheads sweeping across the sky from the west. The flames would die out soon enough, but the storm would douse the fire mountain completely, keep it from spreading beyond this valley.

Bolan turned and looked at Grimaldi.

They had both lived through hell. Again. They had survived.

Bolan read in Grimaldi's punished gaze the same thing he was thinking. He was sure of it. He had known the guy too long not to be able to finger the afterthoughts on a campaign like this.

There would be other killing fields. Bet on it.

"Let's go home, Jack," the Executioner said, as the fire roared toward the darkening sky.

"I'm with you, Striker," came the weary reply.

Available soon!

DON PENDLETON's

MACK BOLAN

TROPIC HEAT

The probing tentacles of the drug network have crept far
enough into the streets of America. The only solution is
to cut the cancer out at the source. The only man equal
to the task is Mack Bolan!

SB-9

TAKE 'EM NOW

FOLDING SUNGLASSES FROM GOLD EAGLE

Mean up your act with these tough, street-smart shades. Practical, too, because they fold 3 times into a handy, zip-up polyurethane pouch that fits neatly into your pocket. Rugged metal frame. Scratch-resistant acrylic lenses. Best of all, they can be yours for only $6.99.

MAIL YOUR ORDER TODAY.

Send your name, address, and zip code, along with a check or money order for just $6.99 + .75¢ for postage and handling (for a total of $7.74) payable to Gold Eagle Reader Service. (New York and Iowa residents please add applicable sales tax.)

Remove from pouch...

unfold once...

unfold twice...

and they're ready to wear.

GOLD EAGLE

Gold Eagle Reader Service
901 Fuhrmann Blvd.
P.O. Box 1396
Buffalo, N.Y. 14240-1396

GES-1A

Offer not available in Canada.